MIKA LANDED HEAVILY, as yet unused to the peculiar anatomy of the griffon. He stalked forward on his heavy hind legs, his taloned forelimbs held at the ready, moving toward the delicious scent.

Inside the barn, he sensed the quickening of nervous hearts and heard a flurry of hoofbeats as the captives within paced frantically in their stalls, sensing the nearness of danger.

His demon hand, now a demon claw, tore into the doors held shut by an immense bar and wrenched them open. The doors swung wide, and Mika was nearly overcome with the heady scent of horseflesh.

Ignoring the lowing cows and the hysterical hens, the griffon strode directly toward the corner stall, which held an immense white stallion, surely the farmer's pride.

The stallion fought for air, fought to breathe, fought to hold its head erect. It lashed out with powerful hind legs as the griffon forced it to the ground.

The griffon consumed the horse on the mound of a tall, barren hill where it was able to see in all directions. Never had a meal satisfied Mika more. Beak and talons ripped into the flesh of the stallion, reducing the beautiful creature to a tiny pile of scraps, hooves, mane, tail, and other inedible bits. Then the griffon rose, heavily, into the night sky.

Book 6

THE NAME OF THE GAME

by Rose Estes

A journey to a land of wizards, kings, and magical gems

Cover art by Clyde Caldwell
Interior art by John and Laura Lakey

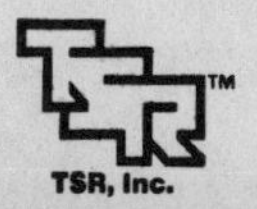

GREYHAWK® ADVENTURES

Book 6

THE NAME OF THE GAME

Distributed to the book trade in the United States by Random House, Inc., and in Canada by Random House of Canada, Ltd.

Distributed in the United Kingdom by TSR UK Ltd.

Distributed to the toy and hobby trade by regional distributors.

First Printing, June, 1988
Printed in the United States of America.
Library of Congress Catalog Card Number: 88-50062

9 8 7 6 5 4 3 2 1

ISBN: 0-88038-614-2

TSR, Inc.
P.O. Box 756
Lake Geneva, WI
53147 U.S.A.

TSR UK Ltd.
The Mill, Rathmore Road
Cambridge CB1 4AD
United Kingdom

This book is for Barb Erwin and Sheila,
Kathy Lynch, Doug and Sharon Blume,
Dan Eamon, and Kyle Maher, the
best friends a Wolf Nomad or an author could ask for.

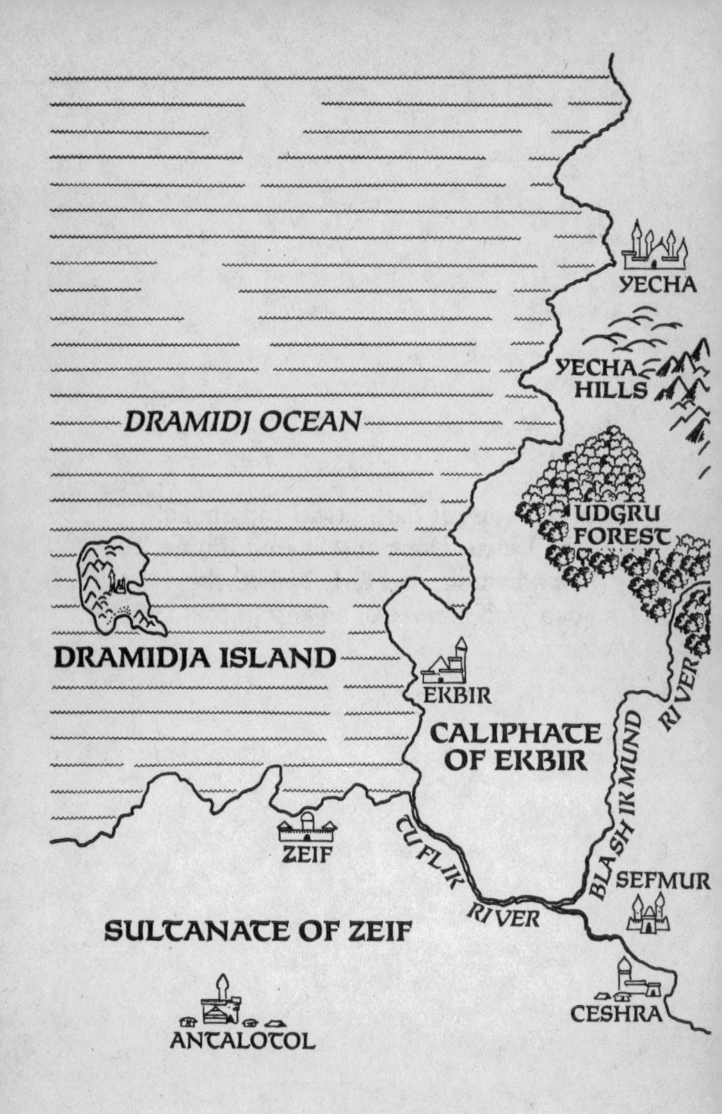
YECHA
YECHA HILLS
DRAMIDJ OCEAN
UDGRU FOREST
DRAMIDJA ISLAND
EKBIR
RIVER
CALIPHATE OF EKBIR
BLASH IRMUND
TUFLIK
RIVER
ZEIF
SEFMUR
SULTANATE OF ZEIF
CESHRA
ANTALOTOL
PLAINS OF THE PAYNIMS

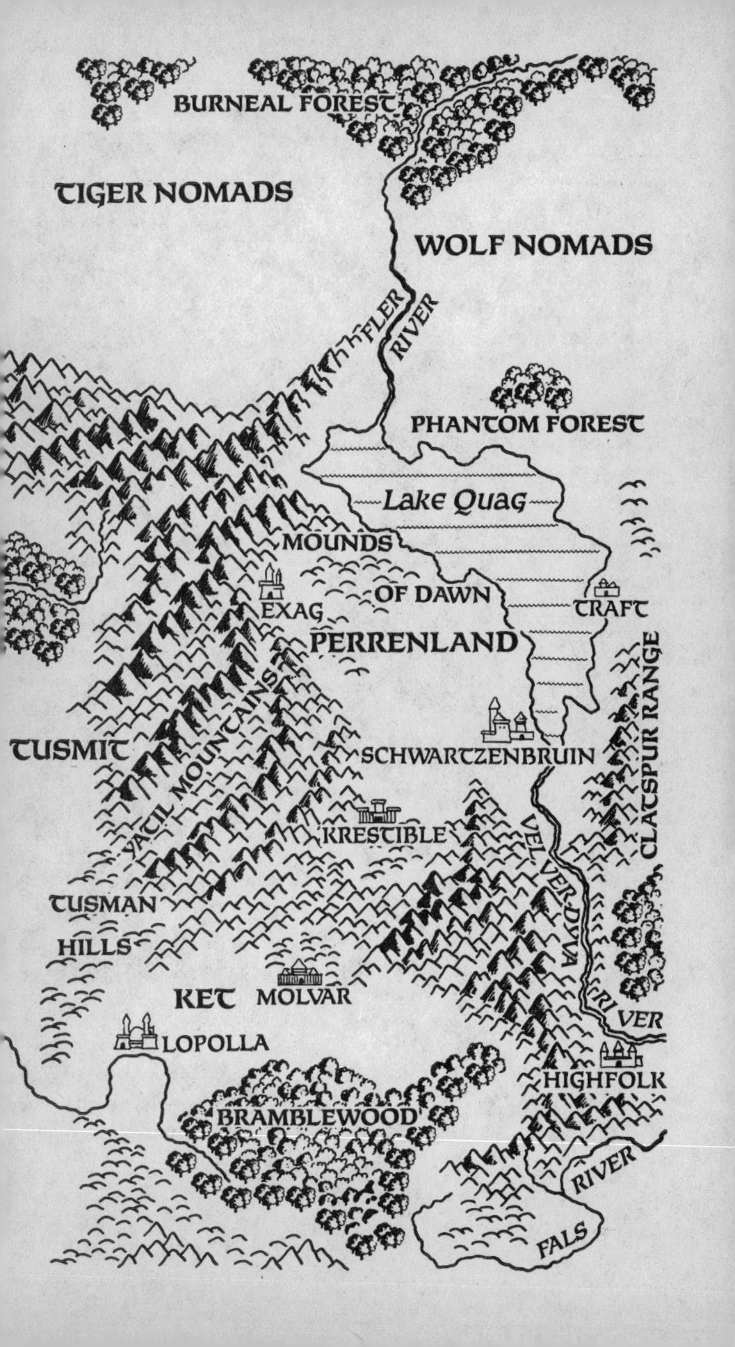
BURNEAL FOREST
TIGER NOMADS
WOLF NOMADS
FLER RIVER
PHANTOM FOREST
Lake Quag
MOUNDS
OF DAWN
EXAG
CRAFT
PERRENLAND
YATIL MOUNTAINS
TUSMIT
SCHWARTZENBRUIN
CLATSPUR RANGE
KRESTIBLE
VELVERDYVA
RIVER
TUSMAN
HILLS
KET
MOLVAR
LOPOLLA
HIGHFOLK
BRAMBLEWOOD
FALS
RIVER

LINEA WAS BORED. To be more precise, Linea Tsurin, Hettentochter of Dorbin the Grand Hettman of Southern Perrenland, recently deposed, was bored.

Linea rested her lovely elbows on the cold, hard stone of her window, propped her beautiful chin on her shapely hands, and sighed. Her delicately curved, coral lips formed a precious pout, which was completely wasted, for there was no one to hear her complaint or rush to offer her comfort. Linea sighed again, so thoroughly bored and depressed she actually forgot that she was alone.

How beastly of her father to get deposed from his very own throne. And all because of that stupid game. Why hadn't he stopped to think what the loss of the kingdom would mean to her before he wagered everything on a toss of the knucklebones?

Somewhere in the back of her somewhat underused mind, Linea knew that her father could scarcely be enjoying the ignominy of his downfall, but she chose not to think of her father's discomfort, being much too preoccupied with her own. After all, she had a reputation to uphold, that of the best-dressed, most beautiful girl in the entire Canton. And how was she to do that without the unlimited supply of grushniks that her father had always provided? Really, it was just too irritating! If only her father hadn't played that stupid game. . . .

Linea spent the rest of the morning wandering forlornly from one empty room of her chambers to the next, still wearing her silk nightdress and robe, her long, curly, blonde hair unbrushed, wondering what she was going to do.

There had been no anxious rush to her side when first she awakened, no solicitous murmurings asking how she had slept, no warm, scented cloth to delicately wipe away the sands of sleep, no bevy of handmaidens waiting to clothe her in her newest gown and dress her tangled hair.

The only exception had been a faint scratching at the door and a low whimper, almost as though a wounded animal were crouching outside. Linea ignored the sound until it persisted, then she sighed and opened the door slightly, allowing the creature to creep within, where it shivered nervously and cringed at her feet.

Linea looked down at the thing with a curious mixture of contempt and fondness, wondering why the gods had seen fit to leave her Womble when they had removed everything else from her life. A serving maid would have been far more useful. Womble could do nothing more useful than adore her.

Womble was an aurumvorax, an eight-legged,

badger-catlike creature from some distant land, acquired by her father on one of his adventures as a young man. Womble had been a tiny, hairless male kitten then. At first Linea's father had spent much time with him, teaching him how to behave among humans, intrigued with the way he startled people with his sharp, copper-colored, serrated teeth and eight sets of razor-sharp claws.

He was a metal-eater, and when he was in his young, formative state, the hettman had kept him supplied with a steady diet of meat and gold. The meat strengthened his body while the gold strengthened his bones, teeth, claws and his luxurious golden pelt. As he grew older and reached his full length—man's length from head to the tip of his tail yet no more than knee-high—the hettman had weaned him to a diet of copper and lesser metals. But Womble, as the creature was called, never lost his fondness for precious metals—gold, silver and platinum—and stole and devoured them whenever the opportunity arose.

People did well to be alarmed in Womble's presence, for the aurumvorax was extremely dangerous, with lightning-swift mood swings and reflexes, occasionally taking the life of one unfortunate enough to come into his reach, but more often satisfying himself with belt and shoe buckles, keys, and odd bits of jewelry. Beware the body parts that got in his way. But though Womble yearned for the home he barely remembered, he remained fiercely loyal to the hettman.

Then the hettman had married and become the dorbin, and his freedom had dwindled, leaving less and less time to devote to the aurumvorax. Worse, the dorbin's wife had not liked Womble, claiming that the creature smelled bad, ate all the metal objects he could steal, and left a layer of fur floating in the air that clung persistently to her clothes.

The hettenfrau would have banished the creature had it not adored the newborn Linea and spent hours and hours beside her cradle, making her laugh with its antics and rocking her back and forth when she cried. Serving wenches could have performed the same duty, but Womble's obvious devotion and willingness to take on the chore meant that the serving women could devote their time to the hettenfrau and keep her clothes fur-free, an arrangement that she soon came to appreciate. She might well have outgrown her dislike for Womble or even learned to love her infant daughter, but unfortunately she developed lead poisoning from the metals in her make-up. So vain was she that even though her illness was diagnosed, she could not bear the thought of being seen bare-faced and soon succumbed. She made a lovely corpse.

The hettman found himself busier than ever, and Linea was left to her nurses and to Womble.

Nor had Womble's devotion waned over the years. He had played gently with the infant, gamboled with the girl and worshiped the beautiful young woman that she had become, paying her the highest honor of his kind by not eating any metal objects that belonged to her, no matter how delectable.

But as she grew older, Linea became more and more aware of things that had not mattered in her youth. Now she saw Womble as he must appear to others—the shambling eight-legged gait, his annoying habit of eating the silverware, and, worst of all, the ever-present cloud of floating hair. She grew embarrassed to be seen with him, despite the devotion that shone in his silver eyes. More and more often she had no time for him, preferring to spend it in the company of others.

Hurt by her abandonment, Womble had retreated to a small, damp cave he had dug beneath the roots of a large tree at the edge of the stinking, stagnant moat. There he nursed his inner pain and brooded over his lost home, but returning home was not possible; it was far away and far beyond his limited abilities.

Then the unthinkable occurred. The dorbin toppled from power, and once again Womble's beloved Linea needed him.

Linea sighed and threw her shapely arms around Womble's thick neck as hot tears spilled down her delicately tinted cheeks. "Oh, Womble, whatever am I going to do?" she sobbed bitterly, drawing comfort from Womble's rumbling purrs as he rubbed his broad head against hers.

Linea was no fool. She had known that things would change now that her father had lost his throne, but she was unprepared for the enormity of the change as it affected her. She had been served from the very moment of her birth and, in truth, Linea had absolutely no idea *how* one went about caring for one's self. Everything, every single thing that needed doing, had always been done for her by others.

Never once had she folded back the silk covers as she stepped from her featherbed. Never had she buttered her own toast or cut her eggs. Never had she laced her own bodice or tied her shoes. Her every thought, her every desire, had always been anticipated by the many women whose lives depended on serving their mistress to the utmost of their ability.

Linea wandered through her empty chambers with Womble at her heels, wondering what to do. Even if she had known how to dress herself, there were no new dresses for her to choose from, and of course it was unthinkable that she might actually wear a dress that she had worn before.

By mid-morning, Linea was in pain, real pain. She was amazed to learn how much pain hurt! Sharp pangs pierced her belly and, not recognizing them for hunger, she wondered if she were dying. It would serve her father right if she did die!

An especially sharp pain wrapped itself around her tummy, and, doubly wracked by the thought of dying and the lack of anything new to wear, Linea began to cry. At first her tears were delicate and fragile as befitted one of her exalted rank; they trickled slowly down her rounded cheeks in perfectly formed crystalline drops and curved around her trembling lips. Then, as no one other than Womble rushed to comfort her and she realized that it was actually possible that she might *really* die, just like common people, her tears poured down her face, increasing both in size and intensity. Soon, her willowy body was racked by great, gulping sobs, and she bawled and wailed as though her heart would truly break. Faced with such intense grief, grief that he had no way of easing, Womble was helpless and soon lapsed into a torrent of tears of his own.

Those same sobs were music to the ears of the two men who crouched outside Linea's door. Turning to face each other, they shook hands exuberantly and pounded each other on the back, their faces wreathed in broad smiles.

"I told you it would work," the large, pear-shaped man said to his smaller companion.

"Indeed," said the other as he stroked his long, white beard. "Now, perhaps, she will be more malleable."

"Bear in mind that we are not speaking of some common lass; this is the hettentochter. We may have contrived the downfall of her father, but she will not be removed so easily, nor die as conveniently as her mother. I do not have to remind you that women are not allowed to play The Game, so that method is out. Nor can we simply, uh, 'remove' her. Her presence is too well known, and she is beloved by the people, fools that they are. Yet she stands between us and all that we desire: true control over the canton. The only way to be rid of her is to marry her off to someone whom we can control. And not just anyone will do, he must be a prince as well as willing."

"But, but . . . Franz, dear friend, how are we to do that?" asked the smaller man. "Well known and beloved she well may be, but everyone, may I remind you, simply *everyone*—much less available princes within a radius of one hundred leagues—knows about the Hettentochter Linea. Her incredible beauty is surpassed only by her incredibly spoiled nature. No one in his right mind would choose to marry her on purpose."

"Well then, Seldom, we shall have to make it our business to find ourselves a prince who knows nothing of her nature and is not in his right mind. Someone who will both marry the Hettentochter Linea and bend to our will. Then we will see to it that both of them meet with an 'unfortunate accident.' The royal line will be broken. There will be no heirs left to inherit, and the throne will thus default and pass into my hands. I will be His Royal Gravity, Franz Travail, Dorbin of the Canton of Krestlav and Grand Voorman of all of Perrenland!"

"And me, Franz, don't forget me," said Seldom as he twisted the ends of his beard between nervous fingers. "Don't forget that I am to be prime minister— you promised!"

"Of course, Seldom, of course. You know that I would never forget a friend," Franz said smoothly, his pale blue eyes twinkling behind thick, round spectacles. And it would have taken keener eyes than Seldom's to note the iciness that lurked behind the twinkle.

"Come, my friend," he said, clapping the smaller man on the back. "We cannot allow our precious hettentochter to redden her lovely eyes. Let us hurry to her and assure her that with us at her side, all will be well."

MIKA OPENED ONE EYE SLOWLY and saw a sea of deep burgundy stretching away to the far edge of the horizon. He blinked once, twice, and brought the sun—or was it the moon?—into focus, eliminating its two shimmering companions until there was but one golden orb dancing on the dark red surface. The world restored to its proper order, he concentrated on opening the other eye. That, however, proved infinitely more difficult.

Shakily, Mika brought his hand to his face and explored his features with trembling fingers. He heaved a sigh of relief as he discovered that no dread accident had befallen him as he slept. The eye was merely gummed together.

Using both arms, he pushed himself up off the table and out of the pool of spilled wine. He acquired full vision as well as a thumping, throbbing, pounding headache.

"What happened? Where are we? Did I have fun?" he groaned through gritted teeth. But TamTur the wolf was sprawled beneath the table in a wine spill of his own, and he merely whined in response to Mika's words, covering his muzzle with a trembling paw.

"All this fun could kill a man," muttered Mika, rising unsteadily from the chair and feeling each and every one of his bones and muscles voice their protest.

Propping himself up against one of the grimy walls, he looked about him, seeing the dark, smoky room filled with tables and other slumped figures, snoring and twitching in alcoholic slumbers. Slowly, memory returned to him.

It had been a night like many others in the recent past, filled with too much alcohol and too little purpose and too many cheap women who looked better the more one drank. For a heartbeat he thought of the clean, windswept forests of home, of the brisk, fresh air that swept down from the lands of black ice to the north, and he was overwhelmed by a sense of longing. Shame was present as well, for there was no honor, no purpose, in the dissolute life he was leading. Where were the stern ideals of the Wolf Nomads? Where was his pride? How had he come to sink to this level, living only for wine and women, and, more to the point, what was he going to do about it?

Mika put a hand to his throbbing temples and tried to focus on the problem, but it hurt to think, and already he was losing sight of the question. Promising himself that he would think about it soon, he staggered toward the barmaid, in search of relief for the tremendous thirst that was demanding his full attention.

He had nearly reached the woman, a bawdy lass whose cheerful, accommodating ways drew attention away from the fact that her skin had more wrinkles than an ancient map, when the door flew open and crashed against the far wall. Bright sunlight poured in through the opening, and the room echoed with the thumping of heavily shod boots.

A chorus of groans erupted from those poor souls still collapsed around the room as they tried to shield their eyes and ears against the unwelcome intrusion. A few less-inebriated ones tried to scramble to their feet. One had nearly reached the back door when it, too, crashed open, and another group of men entered and seized the follow before he could make good his escape.

Mika watched as the newcomers, large, burly men outfitted in heavy, mailed leather, seized the unfortunate, unsuspecting men immersed in their peaceful alcoholic dreams and dragged them into an upright position.

Mika's mind raced, and his hand reached for the hilt of his sword as one of the soldiers turned toward him. Taking note of Mika's action, the man stopped and the two studied each other carefully, each taking the other's measure.

Mika saw a man, shorter than he, but broad and heavily muscled. The man's head had been shaved clean, and his scalp gleamed as through it had been oiled. His brows were thick, dark bars above glittering black eyes, and his nose had been broken and reset carefully more than once. His leather armor was no different from that of any other man in the room, and he wore no badge of rank, yet it was obvious that this was a man long-used to command. The man grasped a short sword of his own, and from the set of his immense shoulders and the plant of his muscular legs, it was apparent that he was no novice to warfare.

Staring out of those same dark, glittering eyes, Houck, the captain of the guards, saw a man taller than he but broad in the shoulders and lean as the wolf who snarled at his side. His skin was bronzed from a lifetime of living out of doors, his eyes a curious shade of gray tinged with red from too much alcohol and too little fresh air. His nose was high bridged, beaked like that of a bird of prey, and his mouth was a tight line of anticipation.

The captain took note of the long, dark hair bound up in an elaborate braid that began at the peak of the man's forehead only to double back on itself at the nape of the neck. It was bound with a strip of leather. His clothing was nothing out of the ordinary, a simple leather tunic covered with a heavy cape that would serve as a blanket if needed, and dark breeches tucked into high boots of sturdy leather.

Aside from the braid, which the captain instantly recognized as Wolf Nomadic in custom, the man carried a well-worn leather pouch slung over one shoulder and wore a heavy metal gauntlet on his right hand, the same hand that gripped the hilt of the sword. Clearly this man was not the sort he could simply take by force. This man would fight back. The captain would gladly have exchanged a full company of the drunkards he was generally forced to recruit, for one man of the caliber who stood before him.

The captain removed his hand from the hilt of his

own sword and smiled at Mika in what he hoped would be perceived as a friendly manner. He made a curt gesture behind his back and heard his men stomp out of the tavern, dragging the unwilling recruits with them.

"Pardon the intrusion," Houck said pleasantly, beckoning the gaping barmaid to him without taking his eyes off Mika. "There is no cause for alarm. Will you join me in a small libation?"

Uncertain as to what had just transpired and taking note of the barmaid's frightened features, Mika made no reply and did not remove his hand from the hilt of his sword. Tam pressed against his leg, and a low growl rumbled deep in the wolf's chest, confirming Mika's suspicions that the man's words were not to be trusted. But Mika had no objection to drinking with him; his head was still throbbing and he knew no better way to learn the truth of a man's actions than by oiling his tongue with a liberal coating of liquor.

They sat at a small, rough table and studied each other as the barmaid poured out large mugs of honeyed ale.

"Why do you wear that heavy gauntlet?" Houck asked. "It must be very uncomfortable."

Mika stared down at the heavy metal glove that had become all but second nature when he was around strangers. With a sly grin, anticipating the man's reaction, he slowly removed the gauntlet, finger by finger, revealing the hideous green, scaly skin, the bent knuckles, misshaped joints, and the curved talons, the color of old ivory.

Houck's reaction was all that Mika could have hoped for and more. The man gasped sharply, and all the color drained from his face. He rushed from the table, flung open the back door, and emptied the contents of his stomach into the stinking alley. When at last he returned to the table, he sat down heavily and stared at the hand, concealed once more by the heavy metal gauntlet. "How did it happen?" he asked. "Was your mother cursed before your birth?"

"My mother? No, it was I who was cursed," Mika replied reflectively. "It—my hand—was the gift of a demon named Iuz." Out of the corner of his eye, Mika saw Houck draw a protective symbol in the air before him. "I thwarted the demon's plans for a beautiful princess from the island of Dramidj. Perhaps you have heard of her. Her name is Julia."

"Aye, I've heard of her, but she was long before my time," said Houck, his eyes narrowing as he looked at Mika with suspicion. "She was princess of the isle in my mother's time. There was a great to-do over her disappearance. Did you have something to do with that?" Once more his hand crept toward his sword.

But Mika was paying him no heed, looking inward, remembering Princess Julia and her incredible beauty. He had first encountered her when he and his companion Hornsbuck, an older, grizzled Wolf Nomad warrior had been ordered by their chief to accompany the wagons that carried her to the Wolf Nomad capitol of Eru-Tovar, not knowing that they were carrying her to her death at the hands of an evil demon.

The princess was locked in the grip of a magical slumber, and it was not until Mika was doing battle with the demon that she had wakened. Not realizing that he was her savior, the princess had used a powerful magic gem in an attempt to kill him, and it was only by wrestling the gem away from her that Mika had defeated the demon and changed the princess into a wolf to save his own life.

But defeating the demon Iuz had not solved Mika's problems, for it had only been doing the bidding of its own master, Maelfesh, a demon of much greater standing. Maelfesh's displeasure was truly awesome, and he had rewarded Mika with a demon finger, promising that the hand would continue to change should Mika disobey his orders.

Those orders required Mika to take the princess to the walled city of Exag, where Maelfesh would make his wishes known. Unfortunately, things continued to go awry, and Mika's hand continued to change until it had become a full demon hand.

Even worse, TamTur and the princess, still in wolf form, had mated, and in time, the princess gave birth to two cubs, neither wolf nor human, but bearing attributes of both. Mika himself was the unhappy recipient of a harpy's lust and was forced to mate with her against his will.

The only good thing to come out of the entire adventure was the acquisition of the magic gem, which allowed Mika to perform magic far beyond his normal limited abilities. It had saved his life on numerous occassions, and he had been most reluctant to return it to the princess.

But the princess had other things on her mind, namely, reclaiming her throne. And so it was that the princess and her cubs, accompanied by Mika, TamTur, Hornsbuck, and Lotus Blossom, Hornsbuck's female companion and a warrior in her own right, returned to the island of Dramidj.

Once on the island, they encountered the princess's father, who had given her to the demon in trade for power. Once again, the old king seized the initiative and, taking the cubs hostage, demanded that the princess and her party journey into the bowels of the earth beneath the island and seek out the magical mate to the gem Mika wore.

Unable to deny the threat to the cubs, and anxious to gain the magical gem for reasons of their own, they had descended deep into the earth and fallen into a trap set for them by Maelfesh. There they lingered for twenty years while on the island above them, the old king died, and their children, Mika's half-human, half-harpy daughter Chewppa and the princess's cubs, TamSen and TamLis, grew into unhappy adulthood.

Mika, Hornsbuck, Lotus Blossom, the princess—now returned to her human form—and the wolves TamTur and RedTail, remained frozen in the magic pillar, alive but unable to move year after long year, until TamSen and Chewppa, united by strange circumstance and deeply in love managed, with the help of a city of dwarves, to free them. A great battle had ensued, and the demon Maelfesh was defeated once and for all.

The princess had regained control of her island home, and Hornsbuck and Lotus Blossom had elected to remain as well. Chewppa and TamSen, heroes of the island, had found acceptance at last and had married. TamLis, feeling herself ignored, and resenting the young and beautiful mother who had not aged inside the magic pillar, left Dramidj, some said to raise an army. Of her whereabouts, nothing was known. Mika had been allowed to keep the powerful magic gem and was invited to remain on the island and enjoy a position of power and prominence, but that had soon palled, for there was no excitement in it. Taking his leave of Hornsbuck and Lotus Blossom sadly, he had left the island to seek adventure elsewhere.

The magic gem, now cloaked in a setting of common silver and appearing to be no more than a chunk of worthless quarzite, hung from a heavy chain around Mika's neck. But there had been little or no excitement on the journey until now and even though Houck appeared to be a ready listener, Mika wondered how he could explain what had gone before. And even if the story were told, he doubted that Houck would believe him. Besides, no possible good could come of revealing the magical properties of the gem. No, the story would have to remain a secret, for it was too dangerous to tell.

"I asked you a question," hissed Houck, his hand now firmly clasping the hilt of his sword. "What do you have to do with the princess of Dramidj?"

Brought back from his reverie with a crash, Mika smiled at the man, his lips crooked in a rueful grin. Raising his mug he said, "Not as much as I would have liked to," and winked lewdly.

Houck stared at him with suspicion for a heartbeat longer and then relaxed his grip, realizing that there was no way Mika could have caused the princess to disappear, being no more than twenty-six summers old himself.

"Your health," the captain said pleasantly, lifting

his mug and downing the contents in three long, swift gulps.

Mika was impressed at the man's capacity. Fond as he was of liquid refreshment, he was more accustomed to taking his liquor in small but constant doses. But it would not do to let the fellow get the better of him. Lifting his own mug, Mika swallowed the thick brew in two long swallows.

The captain smiled grimly and ordered another round, as confident of his ability to drink any normal man under the table as he was of his ability to "recruit" his monthly allotment of men for the Tusmitian army.

But there was no way for him to know that Mika was no normal man. Clutching the gem, which hung from a heavy silver chain around his neck, Mika stroked its multi-faceted surface while mentally reciting the words of a low-level heal spell. The words had scarcely been thought before his head and body were cleared of all debilitating effects of the alcohol. Smiling grimly at Houck, Mika began the long, dirty job of drinking the man under the table.

It was necessary to use the gem twice more throughout the course of the evening before the captain slumped over the table, his head resting in a pool of golden ale, rumbling snores thundering from his slack lips.

Mika was impressed. Never had he met a man with such a great capacity for liquor who was not a Wolf Nomad. Mika peered blearily at the fellow, wondering if he were about to mistreat a fellow Wolf Nomad. But the man had no braid, and no self-respecting Nomad, not even one of the scurrilous Tiger Nomads, would be seen without his braid. No, the fellow was just another human, and under different circumstances, Houck would have made a boon companion. Unfortunately, it was not to be.

Through the course of the evening, Mika had feigned drunkenness and learned that Houck was in charge of all recruiting for the Tusmitian army. Some of their recruits were voluntary, but large numbers were required and Houck was often reduced to scouring the taverns for "volunteers."

The captain also had revealed that a large number of grushniks were available as an inducement in the case of one already skilled in the use of arms, one who did not need to be trained or used as cannon fodder.

Mika had few if any needs that he or the gem could not provide, but working under the assumption that one can never have too many grushniks, he swept the captain's fat purse into his own pouch, then withdrew the few remaining coins from the man's coin belt.

Almost as an afterthought, he dragged the unconscious figure into the alley behind the tavern and stripped it of its clothes. Returning to the tavern, he beckoned a fat drunk into the alley and exchanged the man's tattered, reeking garments for those of the captain, adding a copper coin to still the drunkard's questions. But the bewildered drunk did not bother to ask, merely accepting the money and the clothing and hurrying away, his fat, pale buttocks quivering as he disappeared into the gloom.

The trickery had filled Mika with a sense of accomplishment. Feeling more alive than he had in some time, Mika rubbed the captain's face with dirt, obscuring the man's distinctive features and tugged a hat down over Houck's ears. Next, he loaded the limp body on the man's own stallion and rode to the edge of town where he was hailed by the guards who manned the town gates.

Mika cooperated fully, showing the guards his credentials, which identified him as a trader, free to come and go with impunity across most of the borders in Greyhawk.

"And who is this one?" asked the guard, pointing with disdain to the captain, who was draped across the horse's hindquarters, still snoring and reeking of alcohol.

"He is unknown to me," Mika said with a shrug. "I met him in a tavern where I was fortifying myself for the cold night ahead. He said it was his last night of freedom. Said something about wanting to join the army. I did not want to leave him there while he was in this condition; the place was full of unsavory characters who might well have taken advantage of a man who could not defend himself. I feared he might come to some harm. . . ."

"We'll take him off your hands, sir. The army can always use another volunteer," said the guard, his nose wrinkling with distaste at the sour smell that rose from the captain's clothes. "We'll toss him in the dungeon and let him sleep it off for a few days."

"Good idea," said Mika. "Oh, and one other thing: The fellow seems to have some sort of problem. During the time I spent with him, he claimed variously to be the long-lost son of a king, a rich merchant, and a famous wrestler. Just before he passed out, he said that he was the captain of the guards, someone by the name of Houck."

"Don't worry," said the guard as he tugged the stallion's reins, "we get all sorts. A few days in the dungeon without food or water straightens them right out."

Mika tipped his hat to the man and, whistling for Tam to follow, rode out of the city feeling as though he had performed a good day's work.

Chapter 3

MIKA WAS BORED. What's worse, he had absolutely no idea what to do about it. Normally, he would have rounded up some friends, found a few accommodating lasses, and headed for the nearest tavern. But thanks to his last adventure beneath the island of Dramidj, he had spent the last twenty years imprisoned in a pillar.

Thanks to the demon and the pillar, he had lost touch with all of his old friends, aside from Hornsbuck and Lotus Blossom, who had been imprisoned in the pillar with him. But they had decided to remain on the island, and in truth, their friendship had suffered from the time they spent in the pillar, since they blamed Mika for the unpleasant occurrence.

With Hornsbuck and Lotus Blossom gone, there weren't too many other choices. All of his old friends were probably either dead or doddering gray-beards, and all the lovely Wolf Nomad lasses with whom he had consorted, old and sagging. He himself, as well as his faithful old companion, TamTur, had remained unchanged by the passage of time, with the single exception of the hideous demon hand that had replaced his own right appendage, a final lasting gift from the demon and a constant reminder of the danger of his escapades.

Oddly enough, he had grown accustomed to the awful thing, with its scaly green skin and curved yellow talons. It was far more powerful than his own hand had been and served admirably as a conversation starter. Men were impressed by it and, contrary to early fears, he was pleased to discover that women found it curiously attractive and often irresistible.

As a Wolf Nomad, Mika owed his allegiance to his clan and his homeland to the north, but after an absence of twenty years he was probably thought to be dead. Since there was little or nothing left for him at home other than memories, he had decided to explore some of the vast land that was the world of Greyhawk.

He and TamTur had sailed from the island of Dramidja and made landfall in the ancient port city of the Caliphate of Ekbir. Having drunk his fill of all the native wines and drawn the attention of a number of friendly and beautiful young women, as well as their less-than-friendly fathers and husbands, Mika soon decided that he had seen enough of Ekbir and left the city under cover of night.

Entering the neighboring state of Tusmit, Mika had drunk himself into a state of deep inebriation. Never had he been in a worse state. He had a purse full of coins and a magic gem that could obtain almost anything he desired. One would think that such a thing would make a man happy. But Mika was depressed. The magic gem had made life too easy for him, had taken all the excitement out of his life. Somehow it was very depressing knowing that no matter what happened, the gem could set it right. Yet to give the thing away was unthinkable.

Thinking of the captain languishing in a dungeon cheered Mika considerably over the next several days. In fact, it cheered him so much that when he next found his services as a fighter eagerly sought by another band of recruiters in yet another Tusmitian city, he happily accepted their offer to sit down and share a mug of ale.

Conversation gathered over large quantities of ale informed Mika that the pasha was perpetually fearful of being absorbed by one of his larger neighbors. Border clashes were not uncommon, and fatalities were high among the ranks of mercenaries who were recruited to fight these battles.

True stability was acquired by clever political manipulation of the countries that surrounded the tiny principality. With Ekbir, Zeif, Paynim, Perrenland, and Ket at each other's throats, no one of them had time to spare for Tusmit. Though he was unwilling to shed his limited supply of precious blood in the service of an unknown pasha, Mika cheerfully agreed to join the Tusmitian army. After accepting a second heavy purse for his commitment, he drunkenly excused himself for a call to nature and vanished into the night.

Common sense told him that gem or no, he could not hope to linger in Tusmit without encountering one or more of the angry recruiting teams. Hard riding through the Tusman Hills brought Mika into the frontier state of Ket. Here he hoped to settle for a time, for the rough and tumble character of the place appealed to him.

Acting as a trading center for all of the eastern lands of the Flanaess and the greater world beyond, Ket was a rich melange of cultures where a man might easily lose himself. Fortune and love would be easily found and just as easily lost. Unfortunately, Ket proved even more warlike than Tusmit.

Keen-eyed patrols of pikemen roamed the town, keeping strict order among the varied races and watching for those who might prove troublesome. Those branded as troublemakers were warned once. Those foolhardy enough to ignore such a warning were likely to wake up one morning and find their head perched atop a pikestaff.

Wondering if there were any place left on Oerth where a fellow might find a good time without having to worry about winding up dead or in the army, Mika and Tam soon left Ket behind them as well.

The Yatil Mountains presented a barrier that could not be avoided, so, having purchased enough wine-skins to ease the discomfort of the long journey, Mika and Tam entered the mountains.

The path was clearly marked yet seldom traveled, for no one lived in the mountains save a few hardy humanoids, a sprinkling of antisocial dwarves, and countless numbers of dangerous monsters and wild animals.

The moon, which had been full and bright the night before Mika's journey, promptly extinguished itself, leaving Mika to endure nights as dark and cold as a witch's heart. But they were not silent. Huddling beneath his blanket, afraid to light a fire for fear of what it might attract, Mika attempted to calm himself as well as his trembling horse. He spoke in quiet, measured tones, seeking to reassure the beast, telling him that the moans and howls, the cacophony of demonic cries that seemed to surround their tiny camp, held no danger.

Not for a moment did Mika believe his own words, and, apparently, neither did the horse, for after one particularly horrific screech, the creature nearly bolted.

But the terrible sound had terrified Mika as well as the horse. Tam needed no convincing; his fangs were bared and he growled ominously into the darkness that surrounded them. As Mika seized the horse and flung himself into the saddle, Tam's eyes narrowed until they were but slanted slits. His ears were plastered flat against his head, and his tail was curved under his belly. The three of them tore down the path as fast as their feet could carry them, with never a look behind them.

The morning found them cold and exhausted, but alive, which was more than could be said for the grisly remains of another party, which they found strewn around the still-glowing brands of their fire.

Little was found of the victims, merely a few scattered bits of bloodstained clothing and an occasional gnawed bone. The tracks, what few could be seen on the hard ground, were neither human nor animal but some awful combination of both. Not even the horses had escaped, but oddly enough, the baggage had not been touched.

Gaining courage from the light of the day and seeking relief from the hard, unforgiving saddle, Mika descended from his nervous steed and tied it securely. Tam exhibited more curiosity than fear, sniffing the gory remains and following the invisible trail of scent that seemed to lead directly to the edge of the steep precipice. Peering cautiously over the edge, Mika ascertained that the enemy had possessed either wings or strong magic.

The thought of magic made him nervous and his hand went to his throat, making certain that his own powerful amulet was still in place, and then to his waist, where his precious book of spells hung in its familiar leather pouch.

The son of a magic-user and healer, Mika had paid little heed in those early, carefree days when his father had tried to teach him all he knew. But since that time, he had learned the value of such knowledge, and although his rakish attitude often belied the fact, he had become a magic-user of some skill. The magic amulet enhanced his abilities, allowing him to perform feats normally impossible for one of such young age.

Reassured by the presence of both pouch and amulet, Mika approached the scattered debris with care in case a trap had been laid for whoever might follow. Probing the air and ground ahead of him with a low-level detect trap spell, he found the area to be free of any unseen dangers.

Stepping carefully to avoid the bits of bloody flesh that dotted the ground, he reached the first of the baggage, a large, leather trunk with a domed top.

Opening the lid with the tip of his sword, he found it to be full of women's clothing of a large and voluminous nature. Hidden in a fold of material, he found a small leather sack filled with trinkets of dubious value and a large diamond brooch surrounded by sapphires and emeralds. Mika tucked the sack and its contents away in his pocket for safekeeping.

A second trunk produced only men's clothing, equally large. It seemed unlikely from the sheer dimensions of the clothes that the monsters had gone away hungry. There seemed to be nothing else of interest in the trunk, but as he gave the contents a final pat, Mika's fingers brushed against something hard. Reaching into the pocket of a long leather vest, Mika withdrew a small, round object. It was black, no larger than an unripe yarpick—the size of a small apple—and carved in the shape of a skull. Diamonds winked up at Mika from the sockets, and black pearls shaped the ghostly grin.

Unnerved by the spectral find, yet knowing that the object was probably valuable, Mika placed it in his pocket. More careful searching revealed a second pocket, cleverly hidden in the hem of the vest, easily reached by the wearer of the garment, yet certain to go unnoticed by the casual observer. Mika discovered a set of knucklebones in this secret fold, which, when rolled, had the uncanny habit of turning up twos and sixes.

Tam had begun to growl and, with a sinking feeling burning in the pit of his stomach, Mika turned around and saw a pair of hands—long, white, and nearly fleshless—tipped with curved, yellowish talons, reaching over the edge of the precipice. The horse reared and, braying a harsh cry of fright, ripped the reins loose from under the stone that held them and raced headlong down the path with a clatter of steel on stone.

Cursing the stupid animal and all of its small-brained ancestors, Mika rushed to the edge of the cliff and sliced through the pale, white wrists with his sword, severing them from the horrible hands. But the hands continued to creep toward him even though they were attached to nothing.

A ragged mop of black hair appeared over the edge, followed by a pair of dull black eyes that showed little sign of intelligence. Long, skinny arms bereft of hands, dripping yellow ichor, looped over the edge of the cliff and began to pull the hideous creature upward. The disembodied hands, not to be outdone, had nearly reached Mika and were plucking at the air with their long, skeletal fingers. Mika leaped back and slashed at the hands, cutting them into tiny bits, all of which continued to crawl toward him with singleminded determination.

Trolls! Mika thought bitterly. Lately, it seemed as though he was confronted by the awful things at every turn. Now that he possessed the magic amulet they were more of a nuisance than a deadly menace, but one that he could gladly have done without.

The troll had succeeded in pulling itself onto the cliff, while Mika was busy ruminating on his bad luck, and was now tottering toward him with outstretched arms. Hand to his throat, Mika said the words to the magic spell that would cause the troll and all of its severed body parts to disappear as though it had never existed.

In one heartbeat, Tam was snarling and snapping at the gruesome crawling fingers, and in the next, they had vanished. Tam whined and sniffed at the ground in a puzzled manner. Mika, relieved that the hideous thing was gone, sighed and started off down the path in search of his horse. Wild barking caused him to turn around, wondering what dreadful thing had occurred.

Trolls, at least a score of them, were slithering over the edge of the cliff, their sickly white bodies looking like mounds of migrating grubs. Where had they all come from? Mika thought fast. He could not use the spell that had caused the first troll to disappear. That was one of the drawbacks of magic-using that not even his wonderful amulet could change. Once a spell was used, it was as though it vanished from Oerth as well as from the magic-user's memory.

Fortunately, Mika had a goodly number of spells at his command that would rid him of the nasty creatures. Calling Tam to his side, Mika grasped the amulet with his demon hand and leveled the other at the trolls. Speaking the magic words, he watched with satisfaction as the trolls burned with an eternal flame and dropped back into the abyss from which they had emerged.

Careful watch revealed no more trolls. Hoping that he had used up his lifetime supply of the hideous beings, Mika uttered a a string of colorful curses and resumed the search for his wayward steed. The animal was found grazing peacefully in a small valley some distance away from the site of the massacre. After a token trot, it allowed Mika to pick up the trailing reins as though nothing had ever happened.

Exhausted by the event of the day and by his enforced wakefulness the previous night, Mika was determined to get a good night's sleep. He created an ample fire using a magic spell, wishing to sleep warmly despite the great elevation, and drank a full wineskin under TamTur's baleful gaze. Relenting at last, warmed by the wine as well as the fire, he poured out a generous portion for the wolf, who wasted no time in lapping it up. Then, enunciating clearly, although his tongue twisted and curled around the words in a wayward fashion, he used a spell to erect an invisible barrier around the camp that no monster could penetrate unless it possessed magic greater than Mika's, which Mika considered highly unlikely.

Wrapping himself tightly in his blankets, he cradled his head on a full wineskin, and with the pleasant sounds of gurgling and sloshing shutting out the less pleasant sounds of monsters gnashing their teeth and wailing on the other side of the barrier, he fell into a deep and soundless sleep.

LULLED BY THE COMFORTING effects of the wine, Mika slept soundly throughout the night. He awakened occasionally, roused by high-pitched howls and angry snarls, as monsters and wild animals tried to penetrate the invisible shield without success. Smiling, he hugged the wineskin to his check, tugged the blanket higher, and drifted back to sleep as though the gruesome noises were but the sweetest of lullabies.

It was the sun that finally broached his slumber, shining down on him from directly overhead. Stretching and yawning widely, Mika froze in open-mouthed amazement as the rich scent of yarpick coffee filled his nostrils. Leaping to his feet in one fluid movement, he drew his sword, tripped over his blanket, and sprawled face-forward on the ground.

He found himself looking at a pair of boots, scruffy leather that had been mended and patched many times over in the boots' long lifetime, until the original color and design were all but impossible to determine. A low, pleasant chuckle directed Mika's gaze upward past a pair of bowed legs covered in thread-bare red tights, knobby knees, a leather jerkin as patched as the boots, and a blouse of some rough-spun, coarse fabric whose color also was no longer discernible.

Eyes as bright and merry as those of the first sparrow peered at him from under a pair of bushy white eyebrows. A bulbous nose and cheeks as rosy as an overripe yarpick were all that could be seen of the face, the remainder of which was covered by a huge, white beard that cascaded halfway down the little man's chest.

Mika was so surprised to see the fellow where none should be that he allowed the man to help him to his feet and place a mug of coffee in his hand before he was able to form the words and ask where he had come from and how he had penetrated the magic barrier.

"Och, laddie, there was no barrier, none that I could see, anyways," said the little man, who had seated himself before the fire as though he belonged there and who now was stirring the contents of a blackened pot with a long-handled wooden spoon. He gestured with the spoon at a mule that stood nearby, watching with a mournful demeanor.

"Melba an' me, we was just amblin' along, nice an' peaceful, eyes peeled sharp as they has to be in this dangerous place, when I seen ye lyin' here in the light o' day. At first Melba here kinda thought ye was dead. But the closer we come, I could tell that ye was still a-breathin'.

"Melba here couldn' understan' why a body

would be so foolish as to nap in such a place, but I figgered there were a reason, so I set up the kettle an' the coffee an' waited. Melba an' me don't keep no regular schedule, so we can afford the time, 'specially if there be a good story to be heard."

"But . . . but how did you get past the barrier? And Tam?" Mika asked in alarm, shocked to discover that his defenses had been broached so easily, even if it were by but a harmless old man. If an old man could get through, so could trolls and any number of other dangerous creatures who would not wake him in such a pleasant manner. Mika glared at Tam, who carefully avoided his eyes by gnawing industriously on a large, meaty bone.

"I saw no barrier, lad," said the old man. "Melba an' me, we just walked up an' found ye snoozin' away. Yon wolf greeted us real pleasantlike an' we gave him a bone to be hospitable."

Mika directed his attention to the space where the barrier should have been and was horrified to discover that it was just as the little man had said. There was no evidence of a magical barrier, no almost invisible shimmering of air! Somehow, the effects of his spell had vanished.

Carrying his steaming mug in an unfeeling demon hand, Mika walked over to the edge of the camp, where the barrier should have been, and found the perimeter to be heavily imprinted by claw, talon, and multi-digited hooves, clear evidence that the camp had been the scene of much interest by roving monsters throughout the night.

Mika ran his fingers through his hair, badly shaken by the failure of the magical shield, all too aware of the fate that might have befallen him. At least the barrier had held through the night and kept him safe in his drunken stupor. When it had failed and why were other matters. But perhaps the barrier had not failed. Maybe the old man was more than he appeared to be. Cursing his sluggish brain, Mika put a smile on his face and turned back to the fire.

"I must be getting old," Mika said with a rueful grin. "I bought a spell from a peddler in Tusmit. He said it would protect me while I slept. Guess I should have known better. Nothing protects you so well as a good, sharp sword, and I can thank the gods that nothing came along wanting an easy meal."

"Aye, there's plenty that would oblige ye, gobble ye down without a second thought," said the old man as he scooped up a thick dollop of the contents of the black pot, plopped it into a battered tin bowl, and handed it to Mika.

Mika had not thought himself to be hungry, but the aroma rising from the mixture awakened his belly and he was soon scraping the last of the tasty stuff from the bottom of the bowl.

The little man had finished his own meal and was now filling a pipe and settling back against a large rock, as comfortable and content as though he were sitting in his own parlor, rather than on the windswept wilds of a hostile mountain range.

"Where be ye heading, lad?" he asked casually. "Maybe me an' Melba can travel along with ye, there bein' more safety in numbers."

Mika gave only a moment's thought to the fact that the old man could scarcely provide much help if they encountered danger, as he realized with a sense of shock that he was lonely. He had been talking to Tam more than usual and had even caught himself talking to his horse! It had been a long time since he had been on his own, and it would be nice to have the old man along for company. Besides, one as old as he would not stand a chance against the dangers that lurked in these hills.

Feeling proud of himself for exhibiting such noble qualities, Mika said, "We're not heading anywhere in particular, just drifting along, seeing the land. But first we must get through these mountains, and if you wish to join us on our journey, I would be glad for the company."

"Well said, laddie," the old man wheezed, "an' thankee kindly. Maybe old Taurig can do ye a good turn before our journey is done."

Camp was quickly broken, and together they set out upon the rugged path. The land on each side of the campsite was clear of any obstacles other than the occasional rock, but it rose up precipitously on all sides, forming a long, deep valley. Toward afternoon, the peaks before them took on a deep blue cast, then became nearly purplish black as evening drew near. The wind, which had been cold but mild, began to blow in fitful spurts that tugged at Mika's cape and set his stallion to prancing nervously.

"Storm comin'," Taurig noted quietly as he clamped his pipe tighter between his teeth and nodded toward the distant peaks.

"Maybe we should look for shelter," he said, stroking his beard pensively before continuing. "Little bit o' water never hurt no one, but Melba here, she don't take too kindly to lightnin' an' thunder. That is, if ye don't mind."

Mika stared off at the peaks and waited a moment before answering, for he did not wish to seem a coward. But, in truth, he was no lover of thunder or lightning himself and knew all too well the dangers that could creep in under such turbulence.

"Well, now, animals have their foibles, just as we humans," said Mika, earning himself a nasty look from Tam. "Maybe we can find a cave in those hills ahead until the storm passes."

As though in answer to their needs, they found what they were searching for shortly after entering the hills. It was a cave, large enough to allow Mika to walk upright, deep enough to hold them all comfortably, and showing no sign of habitation by wild beasts or monsters. The presence of the cave, just when they needed it, seemed almost too good to be true. But Mika was not one to look a gift cave in the mouth, and soon Taurig had a fire going, despite the fact that the valley was barren of trees and bushes.

Mika, who had resigned himself to a cold camp because he was unwilling to exhibit any magical abilities before the old man, looked at the newcomer speculatively, wondering again if he had misjudged the fellow. The old man seemed to be no more than he claimed—an old peddler. But what was that he held gleaming in his weathered hand? Could Taurig be a wizard in disguise? Mika's eyes narrowed, and his hand crept close to the hilt of his sword.

"Now, now, laddie, calm down," Taurig said with a chuckle as he noticed Mika's gesture and guessed the reason behind it. "There be no magic in this old body. 'Tis but a magic stone I have, given to me in my youth by one who was grateful for a good deed, performed without benefit of thought. It has served me well all these long years, and I have thanked the gods many times over for causing me to act instead of thinking of my own safety."

Mika looked at the old man with new eyes, wondering what he might have looked like in his youth, trying to imagine him strong and well-muscled, swinging a broadsword. But the picture faded before it was formed, and Mika shook his head, unable to envision such a thing.

The night fell swiftly, total darkness blanketing everything outside the mouth of the cave. A high wind began to keen, causing Tam to pace nervously, whining deep in his throat. Mika looked up, alert, seeking danger, yet saw none. He crept to the mouth of the cave and looked out, hand on his sword, but there was nothing apparent save the cold, driving wind and pelting rain that stung his skin like drops of fire and made him shiver violently. A bolt of lightning coursed across the sky, briefly illuminating the harsh landscape, and in its cold glare, Mika saw no sign of danger.

"It's nothing, Tam, merely the storm," he said softly, touching the great wolf between the ears. But Tam drew no comfort from Mika's words and shrank back from his touch, snarling and baring his teeth. Mika started back, surprised at the wolf's actions, wondering what would cause him to do such a thing. Angry and hurt, Mika returned to the fire and sat down next to the old man, snatching up the mug and the bowl that were offered to him, not even pausing to wonder at the source of the generous—and seemingly endless—supplies that kept emerging from the man's flattened saddlebags.

The brew appeared to be no more than weak tea, but somehow, it loosened Mika's tongue and he found himself regaling the old man with tales of his exploits, some real, some but figments of his imagination.

"Who are ye, then, truly?" asked the old man, his blue eyes gleaming as he leaned toward Mika and poured him yet another cup.

"Me? Why, I'm Mika, a prince of a fellow," slurred Mika as he flung his arms wide to emphasize the point, emptying his cup of more than half its contents.

"Oh, you're a prince now, are ye?" asked the old man, his eyes gleaming still brighter.

"Aye, that's me," mumbled Mika, "a prince of a fellow, as Houck and Iuz and Maelfesh and many others could tell you. Let's drink to Mika, the rescuer of Dramidja! Mika of the Wolf Nomads, a prince of a fellow by any name!"

And as the old man leaned over and refilled Mika's cup to overflowing and then toasted him with his own, Mika was startled to notice how brilliantly the man's eyes glittered and, moreover, glittered at him as though he were some prize specimen about to be collected. But he waved the thought aside like an unpleasant smell, lifted his cup, and drank.

Some part of Mika's mind was still working as he babbled on about his longings and desires. It shouted out a warning. But the old man proved such a receptive audience and seemed so harmless that Mika could not stop his tongue from yammering on. Indeed, his tongue seemed to have a life of its own and went on wagging long after Mika should have laid his head down and slept.

At last the telling was done, and the old man beamed at Mika as though he were a prize pupil who had outdone himself on a difficult test. And then, exhausted as though he had fought some great battle, the fatigue reaching deep into his muscles and his brain, Mika curled up into a ball beside the fire, tugged his cloak over his ears, and tumbled into a deep, deep sleep.

Then, so deeply asleep that he felt as though he were drifting underwater, he felt a touch on the back of his neck, so soft the touch that it might have been but the gossamer whisper of a drifting spider web. But it was not. Mika turned, slowly, sluggishly, in the heavy element that surrounded him, dragging at his naked body like winter-thick molasses. Blue crackles that looked like lightning danced along the edges of his body but did not burn him. He saw a beautiful woman clothed only in dancing beams of moonlight. She held out her arms invitingly and beckoned him to her with a single delicate finger.

Mika stared at the woman and tried to obey her as some small part of his mind raged at him, wondering where she had come from. But Mika closed his mind to any doubts. It was enough that she was there, for she was the most beautiful woman he had ever seen in all his travels.

Her hair was the golden blonde of a summer sun glowing on a hillside of dandelions. And curls—curls that cascaded over her slender shoulders and hung to her tiny waist, teasing him with the brief glimpses of seemingly perfect breasts.

She smiled at him, and his heart all but stopped. She pouted and beckoned him forward yet again, as though bemused by his lack of haste. But try as he might, he could not seem to free himself of the feeling of heaviness that clung to him, slowing his every move as though there were heavy weights holding him back. The blue lightning clung to his limbs, leaping and sparking, spawning small fireballs that drifted off like tiny constellations. He fought against the strange flame and the clinging weight, so that he might hurry to her side. But it was no use; he was no longer able to move at all.

Mika stared at the woman with chagrin, wondering why life was so unfair. Here he was, being presented with the most perfect female he had ever seen, naked and inviting him to her side. Yet for some unknown reason, he was unable to move and was forced to stand anchored to the spot while lightning licked at his limbs as though he were some bizarre lightning rod.

The woman stepped toward him slowly, tantalizing him with the nearness of her charms, which he was unable to do anything about, other than stare. The woman, however, was not limited to staring. With a sense of shock, Mika watched as she reached out to touch him. Her fingers grazed the line of his jaw, her touch more fiery than the blue flames, then dropped slowly until they came to rest on his chest. Mika's whole body jerked spasmodically, and he felt as though he had fallen naked into a bed of stinging nettles.

The woman grinned wickedly, as though sensing his helplessness, a mischievous light filling her cornflower blue eyes, as she reached out for him again. It was with a sense of shock that Mika saw where she was reaching. Much to his surprise, the touch was as soft as duck down, and shivers of pleasure rippled through his body until he wished that he could fall on the ground and give himself up to the blissful experience. But that was not to be, and he remained as upright as an ironweed tree throughout the remainder of the long and seemingly endless night. Somehow, despite the reality of the vision, Mika knew that he was still asleep, and his fevered mind cried out for him to waken, to break the magic spell, but in this, too, he was powerless.

It was torment such as he had never before experienced. There were long, burning kisses that excited him, enflamed him, yet filled him with fear that his very essence would be sucked out of him and he would be left as nothing more than an empty shell.

The woman's caresses were a mixture of fiery agony and incredible sweetness, and never could he anticipate which it was to be. And then a curious thing happened. After a time, the two sensations became almost indistinguishable, and both were capable of rousing him to the near regions of ecstasy. Near regions—that was the key. For although the woman satisfied herself, using his immobile but not unresponsive body to satisfy her own needs numerous times, never once did she allow him to complete his own fulfillment. Each time it seemed that the glorious feeling would reach its inevitable peak, the woman withdrew, leaving him alone with his frustration and rage. He wept, he cried, he screamed silently, unheard, and all for naught.

It was humiliation beyond bearing. Never had Mika been treated so cruelly. Used. The woman was using him without thought or care to his needs, much as he had used countless woman during his lifetime. He wept unseen tears of rage and shame, but for whom or what he could not have said.

Time and again she returned and roused him against his wishes, raised him to the heights of ecstasy against his wishes, and then left him there until he was reduced to a sniveling heap. And then, finally, almost unbelievably, she ministered to him, brushing his bared lips with her own full, pouting lips, caressing his heaving chest with the softness of her own and fitting her loins to his.

Then it began, the long, rapturous experience that went on and on, far longer than he had ever lasted in full consciousness. Higher and higher they were swept, riding the crest of emotion, then gliding down into the pleasant valleys between the peaks. On and on it went, and Mika began to fear that once more it would end with the woman's own satisfaction, but not his.

But then all such thoughts were swept aside as they began the glorious assault on the final peak of pleasure. Almost unbelievably, they rode the wave together all the way up the steep slopes and plunged over the edge, balanced on a razor's edge between ecstasy and the yawning void of nothingness. Slowly, slowly, wrapped in the warmth of bliss, Mika allowed himself to be swept along on the diminishing waves till he came to rest on the distant shore, empty, but at peace. The crackling flames faded to pale blue, silver, and then extinguished themselves like stars fading with the coming of dawn.

He slept then, slept as he had not since he was but a babe in the cradle. Slept with the beautiful vision of the woman filling his mind. When he awakened at last, at peace with the world and himself, it was to turn with a full heart and arms that yearned to hold the woman of his dreams and keep her safe for a lifetime. But they found only emptiness where there should have been beauty and warmth and love.

Mika came awake instantly and sprang to his feet, looking around him wildly, searching for the woman who had become his whole universe in the passage of but a single night.

But there was no woman. Nor was there an old man and his mule. Nor was there a fire nor any sign that there had ever been one. The cold was so intense as to pierce his naked body, penetrate his bones and set his teeth to chattering.

Mika closed his eyes, squeezed them shut till explosions of brightness burst beneath his lids, attempting to recapture sleep, regain the dream. But it was no use; hard as he tried, the dream was gone, vanished forever, leaving him alone and bereft of comfort. And even though he had known, even in the depths of the dream, that it was magic and not truth, the harsh reality of it was shattering.

Mika collapsed on the hard, cold ground and felt tears trickle out of the corners of his eyes. It was no mere dream that he had lost. The woman had been everything he had ever wanted, and more.

Mika forced himself to remember, to bring back

the details, to picture her beloved face. And then, somehow, he knew that this was no mere dream, no trick of magic. The woman was real, of that he was sure. She existed somewhere here on Oerth, and lying on the cold ground of the cave, he vowed to search the world over until he found her.

Chapter 5

MIKA WAS NO LONGER BORED. As a matter of fact, life had become almost too hectic since the night that the old man had vanished so mysteriously. He had searched the cave thoroughly, yet found no evidence to prove that the old man had ever existed, save in his own imagination. Tam was no help and seemed cold and withdrawn, as though Mika had angered him in some way, but wolves were prone to such moods. Wrapped up in his own concerns, Mika spared Tam little thought.

Mika had gathered his few possessions, saddled the stallion, and was on his way by first light. He had found no sign of the old man and the mule during the remainder of his journey, although it seemed curious that they had vanished without leaving even the faintest of signs. Nor had they ridden back the way they had come, for the valley was open to scrutiny and there was no sign of man nor mule. It seemed that his suspicions had been correct, the old man had been a magic-user and had been responsible for the magically induced dream, although for what reason Mika could not have said.

Then all thought of the old man and his mule vanished, for coming around a turn in a narrow, rocky defile Mika was beset by a party of orcs traveling toward some unknown destination.

The orcs grinned broadly at the sight of a lone man mounted on a well-fleshed stallion and accompanied only by a lean, snarling wolf. Their flat, piglike faces lighted up with joy, and they licked their snouts in anticipation of the feast that was to come. Lowering their spears, several of them charged toward Mika while the others hung back to watch the fun.

Mika was in no mood for orcs. He had business to attend to. Searching the whole of Oerth for the dream woman might take a long time. Almost without thinking, he grasped the amulet and uttered the words to a low-level spell that even he did not need to memorize. With a deep, rending groan, the stoney ground opened beneath the feet of the startled orcs and swallowed them whole, leaving only their squeals of alarm and the stink of unwashed, sweaty bodies as evidence of their presence. When the last of them had vanished, the ground closed silently and settled itself with only one small gaseous rumble to show that anything untoward had happened. Mika smiled grimly and rode the snorting, skittish stallion across the patch of ground, with Tam following nervously behind.

During the course of their journey through the dangerous mountains, they were similarly attacked and ambushed by a band of hostile dwarves, several ghouls, and a very large and extremely unpleasant ice giant. These Mika defeated swiftly with the aid of his magic amulet, determined to win through and continue his search for the maiden of his dreams.

Tam began to look askance at him, and although his bonded wolf companion had always been aloof, now there was a separateness between them, a gulf of silence that had never before occurred.

Gone was the sense of fun that was the touchstone of their friendship. Gone were the tangible and intangible bonds that bound them together against all others. It was as though Mika had died or Tam had ceased to exist. Tam had attempted to solve the problem by placing himself close to Mika on the rare occasions when Mika allowed them to stop and rest, pressing close against the nomad's knee. But Mika had not acknowledged his presence, had not even seemed to be aware of him. Tam had whined and pawed at Mika's hand, demanding attention. But Mika had merely patted him on the head in an absent-minded manner and said, "Good boy," as though Tam were but some tame dog to be easily assuaged. Thereafter, Tam had kept his distance.

Mika was vaguely aware that something was troubling the wolf, but he did not think of it overly much. Other things pressed more heavily on his mind. Heavy thinking had brought him the realization that the woman, the vision, had been a succubus, a ghostly manifestation that had been leveled against him by powerful magic.

At first the realization had numbed him, and he feared that he would never see her again. Then the fear vanished, for he seemed always to see her lovely face before him like a mirage superimposed on reality. This was, to say the least, disconcerting, but it was preferable to her total absence.

Occasionally, he stopped to wonder who or what had hated him so much to send the magic-user and inflict this misery on him, but the list was too long to single out any one name, and after a time, he ceased to care. In any case, they had done their work well, for the woman was all he cared about, no matter why she existed.

The image—the mirage—seemed to beckon him forward, and once, when he had taken a turning of the trail, a turning that would carry him north, the image vanished. He became terrified at the loss and yanked on the reins, causing the horse to rear wildly. Galloping back toward the division of the trail, he hung his head and breathed deeply when the vision reappeared before him, pouting and pursing her lips in a flirtatious moue as though to say, "See what you almost lost?"

Knowing that she was but a vision, a magical summoning, a succubus, Mika also knew that he had the power to cause her to vanish using the magic gem. But such a thought was agony. The mere thought that he might never see her again nearly brought him to his knees.

Sleep was no better and offered him no escape. For it was then that she visited him as she had that first night, only now there was no satisfaction in their embrace, only unrelenting demands on his body that he was powerless to resist and left him drained and exhausted. It was almost as though the woman knew that he could banish her with the saying of a few simple words and fought back using the only means at her disposal, urging him, willing him, commanding him to need her. And well she succeeded, for Mika found it impossible to say the words that would cause her to vanish.

Yet in order to retain his sanity, he fought back by avoiding sleep, pushing on long after he was mentally and physically exhausted, until Tam and the horse left a trail of bloody footprints on the stoney oerth.

And this was not the least of their problems, for they were being followed. This Mika had ascertained on the morning after the old man's disappearance.

Mika had spotted a cloud of dust rising from the trail behind, and although it disappeared from time to time, it always reappeared. Mika could not think of a reason why anyone would wish to follow him, but he could not argue with the fact that they were.

Not wanting to stop and confront the unknown pursuer, Mika rode with all possible speed through the remainder of the mountains.

It was a difficult trip. Aside from the dangers of the wandering monsters and the nagging worry of the unknown pursuer, Mika was bedeviled by exhaustion and the recurring vision. He came to know every turn of her head, every graceful move of her beautiful body. Her eyes spoke eloquently, and passion smoldered behind her thick lashes. He had become a man obsessed.

He thought of her constantly, and his journey took on the feeling of a quest after some holy relic or priceless artifact. Gone was all thought of drifting aimlessly, wandering the country in search of adventure. Now, he had but one goal, to find the woman of his dreams.

Then a curious thing happened. Realizing that he was coming to the end of the awful mountains, Mika removed his map from his pouch and studied it carefully, trying to decide which way he would go.

His route would deposit him in the foothills of the Canton of Krestlav, one of the many small city-states that made up the whole of Perrenland. Although he would pass close by, he could see no reason to stop at the city, which was named Krestible, imagining it to be a primitive place with little to offer. Some leagues distant was the city of Schwartzenbruin, situated on the shores of Lake Quag, which he knew to be a city of some size, a far more likely place to begin his search.

Yet even as he traced his route on the map with his finger, a strange tingling seized his arm. Prickling fiercely, covered with the same strange blue flames that had marked his encounter with the succubus, his finger moved, seemingly of its own volition, and placed itself squarely on the city of Krestible. Nor could Mika move it; the finger remained firmly planted on Krestible as though it had taken root.

Now, Mika did not need to be hit over the head with a hammer before he was able to understand a point, especially one that was being given him rather forcibly. Someone or something wanted him to go to Krestible. Perhaps it was the woman herself. Perhaps she was a wizard or possessed some great magical power.

That thought was nearly enough to cause Mika to turn tail and run in the opposite direction, for his encounters with women possessing magical abilities had not exactly been of a benign nature. But try as he might, he could not seem to make himself turn away from the lovely vision. Of late, her expression had taken on a mournful air, her large, expressive eyes conveying great sadness, urging Mika, pleading with him to find her.

Nor was he anxious to turn back, to retrace his path, for he somehow knew that the persistent cloud of dust behind him held no good news.

As soon as he resolved to head for Krestible, his finger fell from the map, the flames extinguished. His interest roused, Mika tried to recall what little he knew about Krestible, but even though he searched the darkest corners of his mind, he could not remember anything at all.

Perrenland itself was a fairly small kingdom loosely ruled by a king who wore the title of voorman. The kingdom comprised a number of city-states, called cantons, each of which was ruled by a hettman, a title roughly equivalent to that of a prince. Legally, a hettman might aspire to become the voorman, but in truth, it seldom occurred, as the ruling voorman personally chose his own successor. Not surprisingly, each of the last four voormans had been the son of the voorman before him.

Perrenland had enjoyed relative peace for a very long time. Mika could not even remember hearing of a war in which Perrenland had been involved. The Yatil Mountains provided an effective barrier between them and their more warlike neighbors, Tusmit to the west and Ket to the south. Lake Quag formed their northern border, and the wild Latspur range shielded them on the east. A small portion of their northern lands touched on the southernmost border of the Wolf Nomad territory, but the Wolf Nomads had more than enough lands of their own to concern them and had never seen fit to acquaint themselves with their neighbors so long as those neighbors stayed quietly behind their own borders.

Once free of the wild and desolate mountains, the land descended quickly, gentled, and became green. Small hills rose and fell on either side of the well-groomed road. Here and there Mika saw small, neatly thatched huts with well-tended gardens and small holdings of livestock.

Now the vision of the woman, that constant reminder of her presence, faded until it was no more than an echo or a memory tucked away at the back of his mind. Mika was not alarmed, for the image had not vanished, but merely receded to a level that allowed him to function comfortably and take note of something other than his own lovelorn condition. In contrast, even the most common of sights seemed vivid, and Mika looked around him with interest.

Occasionally, he met wagons moving in either direction. Some were loaded with wheat or hay, but others carried a stranger cargo, humans and their possessions, the children silent and large-eyed as though they had witnessed some terrible tragedy, the women red-eyed and tight-lipped, the men hangdog and watchful. Even though Mika nodded and called out greetings, there was never any reply.

Mika could not understand what would cause so many people to take to the roads, other than a plague or some other natural disaster, of which there was no sign. The people turned away from him as though ashamed. The farther he went, the greater the number of carts and wagons, and often he saw farmhouses standing vacant even though there were animals in the corrals and crops in the field.

As evening drew near, he stopped at one of the farmsteads, hoping to barter for fresh goods. The farmer emerged from his barn, holding a sharp, pointed, wood hay rake before him, casting anxious eyes at the well armed man on the dancing stallion, and at the huge wolf who strode beside him.

Mika stopped well short of the man and greeted him politely, keeping his hands clear of his weapons. Once the farmer grasped the fact that the stranger wished him no harm, he was only too glad to trade eggs, cheese, and a plump hen for news of the world beyond.

After a time, the man's wife, clad in plain homespun garments, her mouse-brown hair gathered in a tight knot at her neck, crept out of the house and, hiding behind her husband's back, listened avidly. Soon after, three wide-eyed, tow-headed youngsters joined their parents and patted the stallion with shy hands. One, bolder than the rest, even dared to hold out his hand to Tam, who set the child to squealing when the wolf licked the boy's palm with his great tongue.

Eagerly, they listened to Mika's talk of his travels in Tusmit and Ket, and questioned him closely about his journey through the mountains, glancing nervously at the dark bulk that cast its ominous shadow over them as evening fell.

After a time, the farmer seemed to lose his fear of Mika, and invited him to join them for the evening meal and to stay the night. Touched by the man's gesture, knowing that these people could not have much to spare, yet anxious for the company of others after his long and lonely sojourn in the mountains, Mika accepted gladly.

The woman exclaimed softly and ran inside to begin preparing the meal. Mika dismounted and removed the heavy saddle, turning the stallion into the small enclosure beyond the barn, where it mingled with the farmer's ancient, swaybacked mule and a few scrawny, spotted cows. He hoped that his steed would attract no undue notice from the road.

The evening was a strangely pleasant affair, for the woman shed her shy nature, and although she had no more than an open hearth to work with, she provided a meal that was among the best Mika had ever eaten.

Several fat hens had surrendered their lives and swam in a rich broth surrounded by mounds of tender and tasty vegetables. Biscuits so light they nearly floated from the fingers were piled high on a platter. These were smeared with freshly churned butter, and were used to swab plates clean of the last bits of meat and gravy. Large bowls at either end of the table held sweet fruit compotes, and clay pitchers contained generous quantities of thick clotted cream.

Mika contributed one of his wineskins to the festivities, and the children drank from large mugs of warm, frothy, milk straight from the cow. Softly glowing candles shed warmth over the scene, concealing the harsh reality of the life within the rude hut, making it appear a warm and happy place.

Mika looked at the faces around the table: the farmer, roughened and weatherbeaten from long, hard years spent working in sun and rain; the wife, making do with the little that was her lot; and the children, their clean and shining faces wreathed with happiness. Reality struck Mika with the force of a blow as he realized that even though hardship was their life, the family was rich in spirit and love. For one bitter moment, he envied them.

While the woman cleared the dishes away and the children made ready for bed, Mika and the farmer filled their pipes and settled back to smoke in companionable, comfortable silence, while Tam crunched on a platter of bones set before the fire.

When the children were in bed, but still awake from the glint of the firelight on their eyes, Mika began to speak, unbidden, of all that he had seen and done since leaving the Wolf Nomad lands. Finally, as the last child's eyelids drooped and his breathing settled into slumber, Mika came to his landing in Ekbir. When he mentioned his mysterious pursuers, the farmer and his wife exchanged fearful glances.

There was silence for a time, and the woman, who had finished her chores and moved closer to hear better, sighed deeply as though sad that the tale had ended.

"Those followers," the farmer said quietly, clearing his throat and looking away with an embarrassed air. "They probably be from Tusmit, bounty hunters or some such like, following you because of the way you left."

Mika was startled, for never once had he given thought to the captain of the guards after accepting the heavy purse.

"Surely you are mistaken," he said. "No one

would follow a man through those mountains for the matter of a few coins!"

"Them may be paltry to you, sir," the farmer said politely, "but they be enough to care for a family until their man returns from doin' his time. That be the only reason most men join the army, to take care of them that they love, for it be hard to earn a living from the land. And if they fall in battle, as many do, they know that the pasha will see to it that their family be taken care of.

"But the Army, it don't take kindly to them that takes their money and then changes their minds, no offense to you, sir. They can't be havin' that, don't you see, or every man would do it, and then where would they be? So when it happens, which ain't often, the bounty hunters are sent to bring him back and plant his head on a pike as a warnin' to others."

"I never though they'd take it so seriously!" muttered Mika, who had no wish to see his head on the end of a pike, having grown accustomed to finding it atop his neck each morning.

"Don't worry sir, they won't find you here," said the woman in a soft voice, and Mika could read the admiration in her eyes. Warmed by the tone of her voice, Mika looked at her closely for the first time and saw to his surprise that she actually looked quite nice in the soft candlelight. If one could loose her hair from that ugly knot and strip her of those dreadful clothes . . . Mika slapped himself mentally and retreated hastily from the thought as he dipped his head in gratitude at the unvoiced offer of protection.

"My thanks to you, but I'm sure that it will never come to that," he said. "We Wolf Nomads are trained in the art of traveling without leaving a trail. They'll have lost the scent long before they reach this point. Now, forget about them and tell me about Krestible. What kind of place is it? Who's the head of state, and what sort of fellow is he?"

"Oh, sir, Krestible hasn't got no leader right now," said the woman, "and it's all on account of that stupid game."

"Hush, Hilda, it don't do to criticize," said the man, looking around nervously as though he half-expected to see someone lurking in the shadows of the room. "I'm sure them that are in charge knows what they be doin'."

"Hmmmpf!" scoffed Hilda with a disbelieving toss of her head. "Would you wager everything we owns, the farm, the land, the critters, an' even the clothes on our backs, in some stupid game?" And from the look in her eyes, it would have taken a braver man than Mika to answer, "Yes."

"Of course not, Hilda," her husband answered gently as he covered her rough, chapped hand with his own. "You know that you and the children always come first with me, but maybe them royal folks think different."

"Can't be too different," remarked Hilda, although her tone softened as she looked into her husband's eyes. "The Hettman Dorbin has lost everything he owned. He ain't got no title, no castle, no lands, no nothin', and all account of that stupid game.

"Now you tell me, Gemmy, what's he going to do? That man's been hettman all his life. He don't even know how to work. He don't know how to do nothin' but be rich an' order other folks about. He'll starve, most likely, an' it serves him right, but what's to become of the Princess Linea?"

"From what I hear, the Princess—"

"Now Gemmy, if you can't say nothin' nice, just don't you be sayin' nothin' at all," warned Hilda, and her husband's voice trailed away into silence.

Intrigued by their words, none of which he understood, Mika broke into the conversation. "What's this game you keep talking about, and what's happened to the hettman? And who is this Princess Linea?"

Husband and wife stopped talking, looked at each other in surprise, and then back at Mika as through he had suddenly become a two-headed rooster.

"Why, The Game, sir. You know, *The Game*," said Gemmy, as though speaking louder would somehow make the meaning of his words more clear.

"I'm afraid I really don't know what you're talking about," said Mika, completely bewildered.

"The Game . . . it's called just that: THE GAME," said Gemmy, watching Mika's face for some sign of recognition. But Mika just continued to stare at him blankly.

"You really ain't never heard of The Game?" Gemmy said in amazement. "You mean, folks don't play it where you come from?"

"I have absolutely no idea what you're talking about," Mika said rather irritably. "I've never heard of this game before, nor have I ever heard of anyone else playing it. Now, will you please tell me what this is all about?"

Realizing that they had come close to offending their unusual guest and that he was not lying to them, the farmer and his wife both began to speak at once.

"It's a game of chance . . ." said the farmer.

"It's a stupid game," said his wife, and both of them looked at each other in exasperation. Finally, Hilda gestured for Gemmy to speak.

"What it is, is a game, but it ain't really no game like any other, 'cause what you win, you win for keeps, and when you lose, it's gone for good."

"Well, of course," Mika said with a nod, wondering what all the fuss was about. Winning was winning and losing was losing in any game, no matter where you were.

"No sir, you don't understand, it's not just money," said Gemmy. "It be a bit more complicated than that. See, there's a board . . . looks kinda like this." And grabbing up a hard coal from the edge of the fire, he began to draw on the clean scrubbed surface of the wooden table, too engrossed in his project to hear his wife's sharp, indrawn breath.

Swiftly the drawing took shape until it revealed a playing board as long and as wide as a man's arm from fingertip to elbow. A border edged all four sides and was filled with shapes that looked somehow familiar. The interior of the board was a checkered pattern of alternating light and dark squares.

Mika shrugged, for other than the border, it looked no different from scores of other gameboards he had seen in his lifetime, and even though he had no wish to offend his hosts, he said exactly that.

"Ah, but it *is* different," said Gemmy, "for in other places, them other games is no more than that, games, where you win or lose a few grushniks. Here, the stakes be much greater.

"The Game is played like most. Each player has his own 'men' and a set of knucklebones. They roll the knucklebones and go ahead or fall back, accordin' to the numbers. But The Game don't end with the winning or the losin.' "

Noticing Mika's confused expresssion, Hilda broke in, thinking perhaps that she could explain better.

"Say you were to play The Game, sir, may the gods protect you against such foolishness," she said under her breath. "In the beginnin', you risk but a few grushniks and, if you lose, a few hours of your service to the winner. But The Game don't end when it ends; you carry over your win or your loss to the next game. If you win, you play another winner and move up in the ranks. If you lose, you drop down and play another loser and hope to win again. And it keeps on goin' like that. It be all right if you win, but if you lose . . . it can be real bad."

"See, there be two kinds of winnin', the right-then-an'-there kind, an' more important, the for-life kind," said Gemmy, taking over for his wife.

"When you keep playin' and winnin', you get higher 'points', but your risks get bigger, too. If you lose a lot, things can get real bad, like losin' your life or being a slave to the winner if you ain't got nothin' left to wager."

"Used to be just a game," said Hilda, her eyes fixed firmly on her husband's face, which had grown quite animated. "Everyone plays it. Fact is, that's how we got the farm here. Gemmy won it from someone who didn't play so good. But he promised me on the books of the gods that he wouldn't never play no more. Gods know where we'd be if he lost this place to someone who plays better'n him and the gods know . . . you can't win forever. And don't the Hettman Dorbin know it to be true, may the gods bless his poor, troubled soul, wherever he be."

Gemmy sat back and took in a deep breath, and the bright light faded from his eyes. "It's true," he said. "The playin' can get to be a madness, and it be hard to quit. When you win, alls you can think of is what you might win next. An' when you lose, you can't hardly wait to play again, so's you can win back what you done lost. But I gave my word to Hilda, and I ain't never goin' to break it."

The two clasped hands tightly across the crude board, smudging its outlines.

"But the nobles, and other folks, they ain't learned their lesson like Gemmy done," said Hilda, "The Game, it's become more than just a game with them. Now you ain't nobody in court unless your 'points' be real high.

"The Game has done turned the entire country upside down. Everywheres, property an' animals an' crops that ain't even planted yet, are bein' wagered. Folks are losing the work of a lifetime and set to wanderin' the roads, wonderin' what's to become of them."

Now the meaning of the vacant farms and the wagonloads of wandering people began to make sense. Memory stirred, and reaching into his pouch, Mika rummaged around and brought forth the strange black skull with the glittering diamond eyes and the polished set of knucklebones. Dropping them on the table, on top of the smudged game board, he asked, "Do these have something to do with The Game?"

It was as though he had thrown a coiled snake, poised to strike, into their midst, for no sooner had the grinning skull rolled to a stop inside one of the darkened squares than Gemmy and Hilda jumped back from the table and clutched each other tightly, their faces drained of color, their eyes locked on the skull.

"What's the matter?" asked Mika, leaping to his feet as well and staring down at the skull, trying to see what had alarmed his hosts so terribly.

"It's a black skull . . . a—a death piece," stammered Gemmy, looking at the skull with horror while Hilda buried her face in his shoulder, unable to look at it any longer. "It means that whoever was playing The Game lost, and his opponent chose for him to die. Where did you get it?"

"In the mountains," said Mika, struggling to understand, and he related the circumstances under which he had found the skull and the knucklebones.

"It don't do no good to run," Hilda said in a dull voice. "Once you get the black skull, death will find you no matter where you hide." And thinking back to the gory remains of the skullholder, Mika could only agree.

"But what has happened to the Hettman Dorbin?" asked Mika, anxious to change the subject. "Did he receive a black skull as well? Is he dead?"

"No, but he might as well be dead, for all the good his life will bring him now," said Hilda. "He wagered everything—money, possession, throne—and lost."

"Well, too bad. I mean, I'm sorry for him and all," said Mika as he picked up the skull gingerly and returned it to his pouch. "But what about the winner? Isn't he the new hettman?"

"No," replied Gemmy. "The man who won was clever, as he should be, bein' as how he's the prime minister, Travail. But he's no better'n us, a commoner by birth, an' only royalty can rule."

"And then there's the Princess Linea," added Hilda. "She didn't play—girls ain't allowed to play—and no one can wager another's life, so she's still princess. But she can't inherit the throne because she's only a hettentochter, a woman, instead of a hettensohn, although I can't see how a woman could do worse than men have done rulin' the country."

"So, what happens now?" asked Mika.

"War, most likely," Gemmy said glumly. "Krestible is fair game to any of the other cantons, unless someone of royal blood can be found to marry the princess."

"Well, that shouldn't be so hard," said Mika. "Unless she's old and ugly, and even then, with a canton for a dowry, I don't imagine she'll be too hard to marry off. Well, what's this? Why all the long faces? Is she really that ugly?"

A look passed between husband and wife that Mika could not interpret. Some silent message must have passed as well, for Gemmy stood up, moved into the darkness beyond the circle of candlelight, and when he returned, he held a single gold coin in his hand. He dropped it onto the table where it rang out sharply, then circled until it landed inside one of the darkened squares. Mika bent forward to examine it and felt his heart stop within his breast, for imprinted on the coin was the face in his vision, the woman of his dreams.

GEMMY AND HILDA OFFERED MIKA their own bed, a narrow affair of boards covered with a thin straw tick. Unwilling to take further advantage of their hospitality, Mika declined, saying that he and Tam preferred to sleep out of doors. It was that lie that saved his life.

The men came in that silent hour of deepest darkness before dawn, swinging their swords and tossing fiery brands onto the roof of the house and barn, which were quickly engulfed by roaring flames.

The bawling and bleating of terrified animals competed with the screams of the humans trapped inside the terrible conflagration. No normal man could have withstood their cries without attempting to rush to their rescue. And that would have spelled death as well, for the men who had created the disaster were waiting with swords poised to strike down anyone who sought to escape, rescue, or interfere.

But Mika was no normal man, nor, in some instances, was he stupid. He and Tam had taken one sniff of the tiny barn and decided to make their bed in the thick of a fresh haystack mounded just beyond the barn. The succubus, perhaps taking pity on his exhaustion, had contented herself with wrapping her arms around his neck and fitting her body to his as he drifted off to sleep. He had awakened instantly at Tam's first low growl of warning, despite the amount of wine he had consumed.

He had crept along the hedgerow, keeping the riders in sight, his hand clenched around the hilt of his sword. There were eight of them, dressed in the hardened hide armor of Tusmit, their face hidden behind molded leather helms that covered their heads from crown to throat and gave them a frightening, inhuman appearance.

Mika had watched as they turned into the yard on silent, muffled hooves, and observed as they struck the flint and lighted the oil-soaked brands, then flung them onto the dry, wood structures.

As they milled about the yard, swords and pikestaffs at the ready, waiting for the first of their victims to emerge, Mika was fast at work as well. At the very first sight of the flint stones, the very first scent of the oil-soaked brands, he had drawn his spell book out of its pouch and leafed rapidly through its pages until he located the spell he was searching for. He waited tensely until the buildings were completely aflame, yet judging the interiors still free of fire and death-bringing smoke. Then he raised his hand, clenched the magic gem in his demon hand, and recited the words to a seventh-level magic spell. Normally, that spell would have been beyond his capabilities, but with the added strength of the magic gem, his own powers were greatly enhanced, allowing him to perform the spell easily with no chance of error.

Hoping that the riders would not notice that the flames repeated their patterns over and over and that the cries of the trapped humans and animals bore a certain repetitive refrain, Mika slipped behind the invaders, and before they even realized that he was there, he had slain two of them, his long sword striking their heads from their shoulders.

As their headless bodies slowly toppled from their saddles, the horses, taking fright at the feel of the lifeless corpses and the salty stink of blood, bolted forward, driving the other horses before them toward the flaming house. Startled, the six remaining men twisted in their saddles, cursing, and saw Mika standing in the middle of the road with nothing but a book in his hand, his sword, and the heads of their former companions lying in the dirt at his feet.

Yanking the reins harshly, they tried to turn their steeds around to face Mika, calling out threats and raising their swords high to strike down the all-too-easy target. But as they urged their horses forward, gouging the animals' flanks with cruel spurs, Mika raised the demon hand, the hand that clutched the magic gem and, pointing at them with his other hand, uttered a short string of words, shorter than the refrain of a lullaby.

The riders had nearly reached him. So close were they that the hot breath of their horses gusted against his arms, and he smelled the rancid stink of unwashed bodies beneath the heavy leather armor. So close were they that when the lightning spat from the cloudless sky, it singed the hair on his head and coursed down the tips of the upraised swords, dancing along the sharp edges and outlining them in pale blue. Then it surged through their bodies, boiling their blood, exploding their brains inside their skulls, and stopping their hearts, all in the space of a single heartbeat.

Stopping only long enough to make certain that there were no survivors among the Tusmit raiders, Mika left Tam to round up the terrified horses and raced toward the burning house. Once again he hurriedly flipped through the pages of the book, found the spell he was searching for, grasped the stone, and spoke the words.

Then, out of that same cloudless sky that had offered up lightning such a short time before, there came a downpour of rain out of all proportion to the season, a downpour that would grow in size and mystery until it took on the dimension of a miracle to all who experienced it. And of course, one of the side effects of the great rain was that it extinguished the flames that were devouring the house and barn.

Amazingly, the house and barn still stood and exhibited only the slightest signs of scorching. Nor were the inhabitants harmed, beyond a good case of fright. This too was taken as a miracle by all save the farmer and his wife, who looked at Mika with knowing eyes.

"I am sorry for the trouble that I have brought down upon you," he said over the roar of the heavy rain. "You were right and I was wrong about the followers. Take their horses to Schwartzenbruin and sell them. Bury the bodies deep, and keep nothing that will link you with them."

Gemmy nodded in understanding, the rain coursing down the sharp angles of his face.

"And take this as my apology," Mika said as he placed the Tusmitian heavy purse in the woman's hands, the very coins that had caused the problem. Gemmy made a sound as though to argue, but the woman placed her hand on his arm as she looked at Mika and silently nodded her acceptance.

Calling Tam, Mika saddled the stallion and rode off through the deluge, knowing that the purse and the money gained from the sale of the horses would drastically alter Gemmy and Hilda's world. But he also knew that he had barely averted a disaster that could have cost them their lives.

The downpour continued throughout the night, and the morning dawned wet and gray. The houses grew larger and larger, the fences sturdier, the fields more neatly groomed as he traveled east. Soon the houses gave way to larger wood-and-daub dwellings, then brick, and finally, grand manors that undoubtedly housed the demi-royalty that clung to the fringes of every base of power.

Mika was wet and miserable, with moisture permeating every inch of his body. Tam slunk at his side, tail curled beneath his belly, fur plastered flat against his skin. Mika was too drenched to show much joy as the walls of the city came into sight, but he banged the hilt of his sword against the great wooden gates, demanding entrance, and together, man, horse, and wolf entered the city of Krestible.

Chapter 7

BRADDLE WAS BORED. Nothing ever happened in Krestible, at least nothing that helped advance his career.

At first he had thought himself the luckiest page in all of Krestible when he was chosen to become the newest of the Hettman Dorbin's servants, replacing an older, less nimble man who had been unfortunate enough to trip and drop a flagon of wine. The wine bottle had shattered on the hard stone floor, staining the hettman's favorite robe and drenching an envoy from Ket.

That faux pas had earned the unfortunate servant an early retirement in the darkest of dungeons and left an opening that the opportunistic Braddle was all too happy to fill. Once he had thanked the hettman profusely, his first bit of business, performed under darkest of night, was to realign the bit of flooring in front of the throne which he had pried up only two nights earlier.

Having won himself an exalted position, Braddle

had settled in, prepared to take advantage of the many opportunities available to one who was as sharp as he. But once the position was secure and he accompanied the hettman every moment of the day from waking to sleeping, he learned of the hettman's precarious position in The Game.

He watched in horror as the hettman's future, and his own as well, began the long slide into obscurity. His joy turned to darkest despair, and he sought to extricate himself from the position he had plotted and schemed for all those long, lonely nights. Finding a suitable substitute was not difficult, for few were happy with their lives in Krestible. The dupe he chose to take his place was a lowly kitchen page, who could scarcely believe his good fortune.

Braddle was not surprised when subsequently the hettman wagered and then lost first his entire entourage and then himself to Prime Minister Travail in a single toss of the knucklebones. Thus was Braddle spared the ignominy of following Hettman Dorbin and the aforementioned page into an exile that would have put an end to his career.

While not unsympathetic to the plight of the hettman and the unfortunate page, Braddle was almost certain that the knucklebones had been tampered with. But Braddle was no fool. He knew that this was a charge that could be leveled only by one who cared little for his life or was more powerful than the prime minister. Since Braddle possessed none of these qualities, his lips remained firmly sealed over his suspicions.

He had protected his own valuable hide, but to what avail? He found himself back in the same hot kitchens from which he had begun his climb up the ladder of ambition so many years before.

Braddle rested his chin on his arms and sighed, unaware that two stories above him, the Hettentochter Linea was doing precisely the same thing. Having thought on the same subject countless times before, Braddle knew that his only chance of rising out of the kitchens—without following the proscribed route of advancement based on natural attrition, which could take many, many years—depended upon finding a patron, a personage of power in the court who could be persuaded to take on a new retainer.

Braddle sighed again. Such positions were few and far between. There were not many powerful personages to choose from lately, for the number of high-ranking members in the court was at its lowest point in years. Of late, their ranks had been thinned slowly but steadily as the prime minister, aided by his constant companion, the magician Seldom, had succeeded in winning his every turn at The Game. Those members of the aristocracy who were left had become extremely wary of anyone who was not in their confidence, wondering perhaps if they were spies in the prime minister's employ.

Lately, Braddle had been taking another tack, spending his own meager grushniks on certain scrolls and documents purchased from an old man in the marketplace who claimed that they were magic spells. And indeed, they had proved to be so, gaining Braddle a limited magical ability in some areas. He could, for instance, persuade a chambermaid to lie with him, whereas before, the wench would have turned up her shapely nose and stalked away. He also could cause the head cook to set aside the tastiest portions of the haunch and make certain that his ale mug remained full. But he could not influence anyone who was the slightest bit wary of him or already on guard against magic. Unfortunately, that included almost everyone in Krestible who could advance his position in life.

Braddle sighed again as he stared out into the rain, watching, without really seeing, the wet figure of a man accompanied by a very large, ugly dog as they entered the city gates.

It really was quite discouraging. In order for him to rise from the kitchens and attain the levels of power and wealth that he truly believed he deserved, he would have to find a newcomer to court, a total innocent, someone who needed him, someone who could be carefully guided and maneuvered until he, Braddle, had achieved his goals and usurped him. And where, he wondered in despair, would he ever find such a person?

Two stories above him, leaning on her own window ledge, the Princess Linea was wondering much the same thing. It appeared that her only chance for a return to her former comfortable life could be achieved by marriage. But not just any marriage would do. The prime minister, that ugly, fat toad with his bald head and multiple chins, had carefully explained to her that she would not be allowed to marry anyone other than a prince. And his constant shadow, the little man with the long, white beard, had nodded vigorous ageement to everything the prime minister said.

Once upon a time, that same white-haired magician had entertained her with the most amusing magical tricks, going to great lengths to coax even the slightest smile from her firmly compressed lips. But now that her father was no longer hettman, the magician did not seem to care about her at all, no matter how hard she cried or how loud she screamed.

Womble had growled at them, baring his sharp, copper-colored teeth, but the prime minister had hurriedly emptied his pockets of a variety of coins and metal objects carried for that very purpose, and the two of them scurried from the room before Womble had finished eating their meager offering.

Linea sighed as she watched the city gates open to admit a stranger. His sodden clothes clung to his muscular body, and she sighed again in a petulant manner, her lower lip jutting out at a dangerous angle that once would have sent her maids scurrying in a desperate attempt to prevent a tantrum. But, of course, now there were no longer any maids and no one to care whether she screamed or not.

Well, things would change; she would see to that. She would marry. The thought even managed to cheer her briefly. But then her face clouded as another thought came to her. If the prime minister and his tame magician thought that she would marry some miserable, ugly worm chosen by them, they had another think coming.

Spoiled princess she might be, but Linea, just like the lowliest of scullery maids, had an inner vision of the man who one day would win her heart. He would be tall and handsome and strong, sensitive to her every mood and even her silent, unspoken desires.

He would look at her with knowing eyes, and they would recognize each other instantly and fall in love forever.

Linea sighed again, wondering not for the first time where such a man would come from. She knew of every eligible prince in all of Perrenland, and none of them interested her in the slightest. They were insensitive boors, every last one of them, and besides—and perhaps more to the point—none of them seemed to like her very much, either.

But marriage was the only route open to her unless she wanted to spend the rest of her days washing her own hair and lacing her own shoes. No, that would never do. She, Linea, Tsurin of Krestible, Hettentochter of Dorbin, Hettman of the Canton of Krestlav, would find a prince worthy of her, somehow, somewhere. Of that she was certain.

One level above Linea, resting their elbows on the wide window lintel, Travail and Seldom watched the man ride through the city gates, the rain pelting against his sodden clothing.

"I told you he would come," Seldom said with satisfaction. "He could not have done otherwise, once I planted the vision in his mind. I am sure that it has haunted him every moment, waking or sleeping, since I left him in that cave."

"But, Seldom, dear friend, I still do not know how we will control him," said Travail, sounding far less convinced than his smaller companion. "He looks, so, so . . . large. How can you be certain that he will do as we wish? What if someone tells him about the princess? What if he actually meets her and talks to her? May all the gods protect us against such a thing! And what if . . ."

"Please, Travail, calm yourself," Seldom said as he stroked his long, white beard. "Nothing will go wrong. I have chosen this man carefully. His body is far larger than his brain. He is vain and enamored of himself, thinking his abilities to be far greater than they really are. He will do as we wish. He will marry the Princess Linea and rule Krestible according to our dictates. The future, my friend, is ours."

Mika, wet, cold, miserable, and sneezing, barely glanced up a the tower of the castle that loomed before him, barely noticed the faces staring down at him so intently, never guessed at the number of hopes, dreams, and desires that were fixed upon his person. His only thoughts were fixed on wondering whether he would be able to find warm lodgings that would accept a wolf and whether it would be necessary to waste a heal spell on the cold he felt creeping through his bones. And so, on that coughing, sneezing, and sodden note, he entered the saviour of Krestible.

MIKA FOUND WHAT HE was searching for: a warm, friendly inn, fragrant with the rich scent of a roasting haunch. Once he had held up a gold coin for the inspection of the proprietress, her objections to the presence of a drenched man and a wet wolf melted away, and she welcomed Mika and Tam into her establishment as though they were long-lost lovers.

Her plump cheeks dimpled girlishly as she led them, wet and dripping, across the highly polished, wide-planked oaken floor of the great room. Still picturing the gold coin that was to be hers, she ushered them to the most comfortable nook in the room, one that flanked the roaring fireplace, completely ignoring the path of mud and water that marked their every step.

Serving up ample portions of the roasting haunch as well as a fluffy mound of potatoes and stewed yarpicks drenched in thick gravy, the woman brought Mika a huge flagon of foaming ale, smiling even more graciously when he indicated that Tam was to have the same.

Paying customers were few and far between in Krestible, thought Mistress Bonnie as she hurried to obey his wishes. She would have given a plate to the horse as well had he desired it! Since that cursed game had swept Perrenland, robbing the men of what few wits they possessed, living had become difficult and uncertain for the women, who never knew from one heartbeat to the next whether their men would wager all they owned on a stupid toss of the knucklebones. Only a man would have invented such a game, thought Mistress Bonnie as she ladled gravy atop Tam's food. No woman would ever do such a stupid thing.

Finishing not one, but two, servings of the well-prepared food, Mika sat back and took a long pull of the heady ale, gesturing for the woman to join him.

The sturdy chair creaked under her enormous bulk as she settled herself gracefully, delicately draping the ruffled hem of her gown over an ankle as thick as Mika's bicep.

"Thank you, mistress. I am certain that you have saved my companion and myself from a most awful death with your most delicious meal. It has been a long, long time since we have dined so well." He added a mental note of apology to Hilda even as the words dripped from his tongue. But his comments received the effect he had hoped for, and Mika noticed with pleasure the blush that rose from the woman's ample bosom until it covered her face to her hairline.

"We will be wanting a comfortable room as well," continued Mika, watching the glint of greed that lit up the woman's eyes, and knowing that he had judged her well. If he flattered her sufficiently, she would make certain that his needs were tended to, for the combination of greed and desire obviously burned hot in the woman's heart.

"Tell me something about this place, Mistress . . . ?"

"Mistress Bonnie," the woman said demurely, her plump cheeks and jowls quivering as she lowered her eyelids and fluttered her lashes at Mika in what she hoped was an alluring manner. "There being no master, as the good man perished some years back."

"My sympathies," . . . to the poor man, thought Mika as he smiled back.

"Now then, I'd be most grateful to you, Mistress Bonnie, if you would tell me something of this place, for I am a stranger here and know nothing of the town or its people. It always helps if one has the measure of a strange place, and I have an idea that you are just the one to tell me what I need to know."

"Strange is the right word, sir," Mistress Bonnie said, staring into the fire and forgetting to simper. "This used to be a real decent place to live. The Hettman Dorbin was a good and fair ruler, and life went on just about as you might expect. But then things began to change, and it was The Game that was to blame."

"I have heard something of this game," said Mika, "but I don't quite understand why it has taken such a hold on people."

"The Game! Pah!" she spat, and coming from her lips, it sounded like a curse. "Hold is a good word, sir, but poison would be a better one. Once this room was filled with people, eating and drinking and having a good time. I'd have had ten or more maids waiting tables, and even more pouring ale and preparing the meals. Now there's only you and me, and I'm grateful for that, if the truth be known. And all on account of that cursed game, for the men are all at home, counting their coins and waiting for the night's round to begin."

"How did it get started?" asked Mika, somewhat bewildered as to how a mere game could so totally seize the minds of those involved.

"It's simple, really," said Mistress Bonnie. "If they win, then greed drives them on, hoping to win more. If they lose, then they have to play again, hoping to regain what they've lost. They hoard every coin, spending nothing if they can avoid it. We merchants—we who have not wagered ourselves out of existence—we are the ones who pay the price.

"Then, too, there's the simple folk, those whose lives belong to the players. If the player loses, he's merely discomfited. But the lives of all those under his rule are thrown into chaos. They are uprooted from their homes and their lives and given into the care of a stranger to whom they are nothing but pawns to be wagered in the next game."

"But why did the hettman not put an end to it?" asked Mika. "This game is obviously disrupting the livelihood of the entire kingdom."

"The Hettman Dorbin was the biggest fool of them all," Mistress Bonnie said sorrowfully. "He couldn't even stop playing himself, so how was he to forbid others from playing?"

"I hear that he's in a bad spot," said Mika, lowering his voice to a confidential tone.

"You could call it that, all right," answered the woman, her cheeks and jowls shaking with grim humor. "He's lost everything except his life, and he's lucky the prime minister didn't play a black skull and ask for that, too."

"So, this prime minister fellow . . ."

"Travail's his name," said Mistress Bonnie with tightly compressed lips.

"Right, this Travail, then, with the hettman removed from power, he's in charge of the country?"

"A caretaker, sort of, caretaker of the canton," Mistress Bonnie said in a disapproving tone. "But that's only until the Princess Linea is married off and then the power will transfer to her husband."

"Well, then, your problems will surely be solved!" cried Mika. "For I have seen her image, and surely the town will soon be swarming with suitors hoping to win her hand and the kingdom."

"You don't know our princess," said Mistress Bonnie, and her deep, booming laugh washed over Mika, nearly bowling him from his chair with its volume. Wiping tears from her eyes with the back of her hand, the woman sought to gain her breath, pressing a hand against her massive bosom. "Our Linea," she said with a chuckle. "Well, let's just say that she'll need a special kind of man!" And no matter how hard he pressed her, Mika could elicit no more information about Princess Linea from Mistress Bonnie.

She showed him to his room and grimaced as Tam leaped up on the featherbed, marking it with his muddy paws. Gently touching Mika on the cheek, she murmured, "I expect that you'll join the ranks of those fools soon enough, no matter what I say, but if you'll take the advice of an old woman, stay away from that game."

Mika lay on the bed after she had gone, sharing its deep comfort with Tam, who was lying on his back, snoring. As the pale, transparent image of the princess paraded back and forth in front of his eyes, demanding his attention with seductive posturing, Mika thought of all that he had learned.

The Princess Linea was his to win. Never before had he wished to marry, and he had gone to great lengths to avoid that dread situation in the past. But she was literally the woman of his dreams. Never had he seen such perfection or desired another more.

His vision of her had grown stronger and stronger as he approached the city, until he saw her face before him at every turn. Just knowing that he was in the same city, that she was somewhere near, was almost more than he could bear. His body burned, calling out for him to act, to seek her out, to find her, to hold her in his arms. But his brain told him to wait, to watch, to think, to plan, and then and only then, to act.

Closing his mind to the demands of his body, he thought about the problem at length. Sheer force would undoubtedly work. He could seize her and be gone before anyone could react. But that was no way to treat a princess. She had been sheltered all her life and would require gentle handling. No, rough stuff was out. That left only diplomacy, which had never been Mika's strong point.

Becoming a member of royalty was no problem. Mika had donned many guises in his lifetime. This would merely be another. But it would seem that

Prime Minister Travail was an important figure in this game, and he would be well-advised to win the man to his side. But hard as he tried, Mika could think of no way to do so.

Time and again, despite Mistress Bonnie's warning, his mind returned to The Game. Mika liked to think that he was fairly good at games, especially those that involved the use of knucklebones. This game was unknown to him, but how hard could it be? And he had several advantages that set him apart from the locals: the loaded dice that he had acquired in the mountains, and his own magical abilities.

As he settled into sleep, Princess Linea's lovely face shimmering before him, her slender arms wrapped around his neck and her body pressed against his own, he smiled, knowing that the gods were with him this time. For once, it seemed that he could not lose.

FROM FURTHER CONVERSATION with Mistress Bonnie, Mika learned that the games were held every night in different locations all over the city. But only those players with the highest standings, those with the most to win or lose, played at the castle itself. Although he had never played The Game and had no standing whatsoever, Mika decided at once that he would try to join the gaming at the castle.

If he were to pass himself off as a prince, something would have to be done about his appearance. A quick moment's work with the magic gem and his spell book transformed his plain, sturdy leather clothes into an elaborate outfit of blue silk trimmed with softly tanned doeskin dyed a darker shade of blue. Tall boots, soft as a glove and the color of the midnight sky, clung to his legs, rising to his knees. A long silk cape swirled behind him, and a wide-brimmed hat trimmed with a trailing feather completed the outfit. His beard, matted and tangled from the long journey, had been trimmed close to his jawline, giving him a rakish air.

Tam paced the room nervously, unused to being closed up in such small quarters. Mika stared at him for a long heartbeat, noting the long canines and the slanted, glinting eyes. There could be no doubting him for anything other than what he was: a wild wolf. Something would have to be done if Tam were to accompany him.

Whistling casually, Mika picked up the spell book once more and leafed through it as though studying it. Then, before Tam realized what was happening, Mika quickly spoke the words on the page before him, and in an instant, Tam had been transformed from a prowling wolf into a dog, long and lean and sleek, with great swags of glossy fur, a thin, regal head with floppy ears, and slender, delicate legs. A fitting companion for a prince.

Tam stared at Mika for one long moment, then looked at himself, threw back his head, and howled, a mournful sound that ran shivers down the backs of all who heard. Then he attempted to crawl under the bed.

"Come on, Tam, it won't be so bad. You look good," said Mika as he tried to pull Tam out of his hiding place. "I want you to go with me, and you can't go if you're a wolf. These people probably don't allow wolves in their castles." Unable to burrow under the bed, Tam finally emerged from his hiding place and slunk off at Mika's heels, tail curled beneath his belly.

Their fine new looks gained them an astonished glance from a speechless Mistress Bonnie. Her eyes, all but buried in folds of flesh, opened wide in amazement as Mika doffed his hat and bowed to her before exiting with Tam still slinking at his heels.

The castle was not hard to find, for it was by far the largest building in all of Krestible. The merchant establishments were all closed for the night. The only lights to be seen came from the edges of the shuttered windows and barred doors. The cobblestone streets were practically deserted as well. A few people scurried toward games of their own, with leather pouches holding game pieces and knucklebones clutched in their fists.

The castle was an immense affair constructed entirely of gray stone. It was ringed by high palisades, but dwellings and shops had been built right up to its walls; some that were actually taller than the walls themselves enabled the occupants to look over the walls onto the castle grounds. Two guards stood before the gates, looking as though they wished they were any place other than where they were.

Mika strode up to the gate and greeted the guards pleasantly, asking for admittance.

"Can't go in without an invite," growled one of the guards. "You got an invite?"

"No," replied Mika, "but I am certain that I will be welcome."

"Come back when you got an invite," said the guard, his interest already fading.

"I'll do that," said Mika as he nodded pleasantly and strolled off in the opposite direction. Leaning against the wall, he took his spell book out of its pouch—which had been magically transformed from the tattered furskin it had always been to blue velvet embroidered in gold thread—and gesturing casually at the guards, he read out the words to a spell.

The guards remained slumped in their original positions; they had not changed in any way, nor did they appear affected by Mika's spell. Mika strolled back toward the gate and once more requested admittance.

"Got an invite?" the guard asked again. "Certainly," replied Mika. "Wouldn't think of appearing without one." He waved his hand in front of the man's face as though he held a document.

"Go on in," said the guard, "and good luck to you."

Mika nodded pleasantly and entered the castle grounds, looking around him with interest.

The property was larger than it appeared from the outside. The grounds were extensive and even though it was night, Mika could tell that they had once been meticulously tended. Now the sharp outlines of topiary trees and bushes were growing blurred, the grass on each side of the path was nearly knee-high, and vines and creepers were beginning to edge over the path itself.

The moat beneath the bridge was scummy and foul, and the scent of moist rot filled his nostrils. The castle was brightly lit, and Mika could see that there were at least four levels. The original structure, a square block and a tower, had been added to time and again, until there were as many wings and towers as there were styles of construction.

A large, round tower dominated the easternmost corner of the building, and large windows opened onto each level. Mika stared up at the tower, and even though all was dark, he wondered if the woman of his dreams was to be found behind one of those openings. His heart began to pound, and his breath grew ragged. Tam whined and pawed at Mika's leg and brought the Wolf Nomad back to his senses.

"Onward, Tam," he said in a low tone. "There's never been a woman or a game I couldn't master. The sooner begun, the sooner done, as my mother would have said."

So saying, he strode purposefully across the bridge toward the entrance, which loomed before him. There seemed to be a kind of added awareness that prickled around him, and the transparent image of the woman that was always with him grew momentarily brighter. He shivered, knowing in his heart that the woman was near.

There was no guard at the main entrance to the castle, merely a young page curled up in sleep on the wide steps. Mika stepped over the slumbering form and pushed the heavy doors with his gloved hand. The door swung wide, revealing an enormous hall brightly lit by chandeliers and sconces dripping with thick candles.

The hall contained numerous tables. Mika could see that each table was the playing ground for two players and a large number of observers. Advice-givers and hangers-on were crouched behind the players of their choice.

No one seemed to take any notice of him, so involved were they with the games. But the room was not silent. There were gasps and moans, gleeful shouts, and shrieks of grief from the players and their factions. And throughout, there was a palpable undercurrent of tension.

Mika made his way through the room, observing the players, pausing at one group and then another, taking note of the various methods of play, one hand fondling the knucklebones that he had taken from the death site in the mountains. At length, feeling that he had gained a rudimentary grasp of The Game, he looked about him, wondering how he was to get into the action. It appeared that all of the players present had advanced to this point after winning levels of competition elsewhere. How was he, who had never played before, to gain access to The Game? He had no desire to waste valuable time making his way up through the ranks.

He took up a position against the wall, where he could observe the players and decide where and how he might make his move. As he leaned against the wall, he was all but overcome. He grew faint, the room swam around him, and a feeling of nausea rose in his throat. Then he felt a warm tingling at the base of his spine. All of the symptoms were similar to those one experienced when one was the target of magic.

Mika put a trembling hand to his forehead and blinked to steady his vision, looking around him to ascertain the source of the disturbance, attempting to find the spellcaster.

Again, the woman's image burned bright before him, and he focused on it, clinging to it as he was buffeted by further waves of nausea.

After a time, probably no more than a few heartbeats, although it seemed much longer, the terrible feeling passed, but still there was no sign of the person responsible. No one stood out in the crowd, nor was there anyone who appeared even slightly interested in his presence. In fact, none of the people in the room had so much as glanced his way since he entered; it was almost as though he were invisible.

The last of the tingling sensation left him, and Mika shook his head, alert to the possibility of danger but dismissing the likelihood. None of the players had the look of a magician, and Mika prided himself on his ability to sense magic-users. No, these were but normal folk, and his imagination was the only thing at work, or perhaps a lingering effect of the cold rain or the nearness of the woman of his dreams. Concentrating on the alluring image before him, he told himself that there was no reason for anyone to suspect him. He was but a casual observer, his presence of no interest to anyone other than himself.

Unfortunately, Mika was wrong on that score, as well as several others. His presence was of great interest to a number of people in the room.

"I told you he would come," said Seldom as he tugged on Travail's voluminous sleeve. "Is he not everything I promised?" They were eyeing Mika from a far corner, careful not to attract his attention.

"He is tall, handsome, and wears his clothes well," agreed Travail, his multiple chins wobbling as he nodded his head. "And if he is as easily manipulated as you claim, I will be very pleased indeed."

"Believe me," Seldom said with a chuckle, "this fellow was asleep under a log when the gods passed out brains. And what's even better for our purposes, he fancies himself to be rather bright."

"That's quite an outfit he's wearing," commented Travail. "Did he think he was coming to a dress ball?

And whatever is that creature at his side? I thought you said it was a wolf?"

"He must have gotten rid of it and replaced it with a dog, although why he chose one so ugly is beyond my understanding."

"It does not matter," said Travail, staring fixedly at Mika. "The fellow is handsome enough, and, ugly dog or no, one glance should be enough to please our young princess. No doubt she will fall head over heels in love, especially since she knows that he is her only hope of escaping the tower. People are such pathetic creatures, allowing love to shape their lives. I am glad that I am above such petty emotions."

Blinded by the light of his own brilliance, the prime minister missed the look of pity that came from the only person he could call friend. Then, happy in the knowledge that they had found their man, Travail and Seldom turned aside to discuss their plans, thus missing entirely the spell of dizziness that caused Mika to slump against the wall.

Other eyes than those of the prime minister had spotted Mika as well. Braddle had taken notice of him the very instant he arrived. Braddle was threading his way through the crush of players and their entourages, carrying a tray of empty ale mugs, when Mika pushed through the doorway. Braddle was so taken by surprise that he stopped short, nearly dumping the tray and its contents onto a nearby gaming table. The angry outcry of the players brought him to his senses, and he hurried away to the warm, steamy kitchen, where he remained until he was able to bring his shaking nerves under control.

The person he had hoped for, even prayed for, had arrived. The figure in blue was no ordinary player, nor a citizen of the city, for Braddle knew everyone who was anyone within the city's gates. The man looked more than a little intelligent; his dark eyes were not those of a fool. He could be taught, with a little bit of help, all of those intricacies of The Game. And with the help of some magic, the fellow would win and take Braddle with him as he climbed the ladder of victory. Here, with careful planning, was Braddle's passage out of the kitchens, his passage to freedom.

Forcing his heart to return to its normal pace, Braddle thought about what he had to do. First, he had to place the fellow under his control so that he would be open to Braddle's suggestions. But the spell was tricky. It had to be done just right, or it could backfire.

For instance, he had to be certain that no one else was actually touching the man, or they would be affected, too. Nor could anyone be focused on the man, thinking about him, or even watching him, or the spell would include them as well.

But how was he to isolate the fellow? It seemed almost impossible. There was no way to get him alone, and Braddle could not risk allowing him to leave the castle before the spell was placed. He had no choice. He would have to cast the spell, and hope that no one else was watching.

There was still one other factor to be considered; Braddle had been warned against using the spell on another magic-user, for it was a middling powerful spell and if it were used on a magic-user more accomplished than himself, it would have little effect on the stronger man and the spell would double back on itself, killing Braddle.

Braddle thought about that possibility longer than the others. But in the end, he decided that the man in blue was not a magic-user. Everyone knew that magic-users were always little old men dressed in tattered rags, supporting themselves on staffs, and wandering around the country croaking out dire warnings. After all, hadn't he purchased his spells from just such a person? Having convinced himself that he was making the right decision, Braddle prepared to cast his first spell.

"Here, Braddle, why do you be hiding in the pantry?" cried one of the serving maids. "What mischief be you up to now?"

"Nothing, Scylla, my love," Braddle said quickly, seizing the pretty girl around her slim waist and kissing her full on the mouth. "I was just nursing my broken heart and hoping you'd come along and help me mend it. When are you going to stop saying no to me? It's not fair to flaunt your beauty and then deny me. I expect I shall die soon, unless you say yes."

"Oh, Braddle, you do go on," Scylla said with a breathless laugh. But her checks were flushed a deep crimson, and forgetting what she had come for, she rushed back out of the pantry, petticoats and curly tresses flying.

So attractive were Scylla's charms, so wonderful the feel of her soft body against his, that Braddle nearly forgot his own purpose. Then it returned to him in a rush. Taking the tiny scrap of scroll out of his breast pocket, Braddle studied the words for the hundredth time, then, calling up the vision of the tall figure in blue, he spoke them aloud with as much feeling as he could muster, imbuing the spell with all of his hopes and dreams.

As the words were spoken, they vanished from the page of the scroll, leaving him holding an empty scrap of parchment that began to crumble instantly, then fell to the floor in a tiny shower of dust. As the last word left his tongue, a powerful jolt shot through Braddle, hurling him against the stone wall of the pantry with enough force to knock the air from his lungs and leave him gasping for breath. A blue current penetrated the top of his skull, coursed through his veins, and exited his toes. His body was outlined with a bright blue nimbus, like a ring around the moon, that faded away slowly, leaving him frazzled and shaken, feeling as though he had been struck by lightning. He raised his hand shakily and touched the top of his head, half-expecting to find a hole burned in his scalp. Every last red hair was standing on end, but his head was intact.

Unable to comprehend what had happened, yet knowing that contact had been made, Braddle staggered from the dark pantry, too groggy to come to his own defense when the cook accused him of drinking.

The Princess Linea had observed Mika's entrance as well, from her own window in the tower, hidden behind an intricate screen of carved stone that allowed the woman to view the goings-on below without being seen. At first, she had scarcely believed her eyes, for the figure in blue was like none she had ever seen before. Even Womble, crouched obediently at her side, left off gnawing on the chair struts and whimpered as though sensing that something of import had occurred.

All of the hettensohns who had courted Linea in the past had been either too old or too young, too fat or too thin, too stupid or just too boring for words. And none of them seemed to appreciate her as much as she felt they should. Linea knew her own worth and refused to settle for someone too stupid to accept her personal appraisal.

It was obvious that this one was no boy. His figure was tall and quite mature in stature. The soft silk clung to his body, showing off his adult and most masculine features to their very best advantage. Linea's heart fluttered faster as she watched the play of his muscles beneath the soft blue garment.

Then a peculiar thing happened. As Linea studied the man, wondering who he was, a tingling sensation crept over her body, starting at the very top of her head. The tingling crept downward, filling her with a sensation of heat and a yearning to do . . . something, although she knew not what. It was as though a great magnet were calling to her, drawing her attention, yet she could not have said where she was to go or what she was to do. She only knew that there was something, something very important, that needed doing.

Then the feeling faded, leaving her slightly dizzy and very confused. She touched her hand to her forehead and wondered what had happened. She looked down at the court below and saw the man in blue leaning against a wall. Although he was still interesting, her mind could not seem to focus on him, and her eyes began to drift around the room as though searching for something precious that must be found.

And then she saw him, a tall, slender figure dressed in brown livery topped by a crown of bright red hair. Her heart leaped within her breast, and the same warm tingling spread through her body, leaving her slightly breathless. She gasped and pressed her hand against her heart to still its sudden thumping.

The man in blue was all but forgotten as Linea stared after the young man who seemed curiously unsteady on his own feet. He reached the doorway and turned briefly, and in that short heartbeat of a moment, Linea's cornflower blue eyes met those of Braddle's and the oerth rocked beneath her feet. Then he turned and was gone, releasing her from the power of his gaze, if not the power of her own emotion.

Linea's mind raced. Who was he? And why was he dressed in the common clothing of a servant? Her mind considered and then discarded the possibility that the man was actually a servant of the castle. It could not be. It was impossible that she would fall in love with a menial. For whatever the reason, the man was undoubtedly traveling in disguise.

Instantly, Linea began to construct elaborate scenarios in which the unknown man figured prominently. He was a prince from a far-distant kingdom. He had seen her from afar and fallen in love with her. Or perhaps his father and hers were lifelong enemies, and he was forced to travel incognito.

Being a young and impressionable woman much given to romantic daydreams, Linea had no difficulty arriving at any number of possibilities, none of which were true. Yet that did not deter her. She knew in her heart that she had found her own true love. For the moment, that was enough; the truth could wait until later.

For now, all of her attention was focused on finding and meeting the man in brown. That was imperative. But the how and the when of it, and what was she to do about her clothes and her hair, were enough to make her cry. Her eyes filled with tears, and for a heartbeat she almost lost herself in another tantrum. But she caught herself in time, knowing that there was no one to hear her and no one to care, other than Womble.

No. If she wanted this man, she would have to manage it herself. It seemed an overwhelming task, but she was Linea, Hettentochter of Dorbin, Grand Voormann of the Canton of Krestlav. True love and her entire future, were at stake here, and if there was a way to get what she wanted, Linea knew that she would find it.

Chapter 10

MIKA WAS SOMEWHAT TAKEN ABACK. Even though he had been forewarned by Gemmy, Hilda, and Mistress Bonnie, well, a game was still a game. He had expected great volumes of noise, excitement, and enthusiasm. Instead, there was only the intense silence, broken occasionally by the muttering of the players and their hangers-on, and the occasional order given to serving maids and pages who scurried about the stone floors carrying food and drink.

He had been warned, but he had not accepted what he had been told. No one paid him even the slightest bit of attention, and as time passed, he began to wonder just how he was to inject himself into the gaming. How could he win the princess if he couldn't even enter The Game?

Then the tingling came and went, and as he perused the players and onlookers, wondering at the feeling's cause, he was approached by two men who made their way toward him through the dense crowd.

The man in the lead was immense. He was taller

than Mika, which was tall indeed, but his height was offset by his girth, which was truly heroic. Mika had never seen a man so huge. It was as though the man had devoted his entire life to eating. His body, although encased in garments of the finest quality, would have weighed more than six large peasants. The fabric in his cape alone would have served admirably as a small tent or the sail of a two-man boat. So great was his girth that his legs seemed almost too small to support such a great weight, and his feet were as slender and as delicate as a young maid's. So vast was his body that it took a while for one's gaze to rise above it and focus on the face.

But the size of the body became inconsequential when one looked on the man's face, for it was undoubtedly one of the most cheerful faces on all of Oerth. It was pear-shaped, just like the body, small and almost pointed at the skull, which itself enjoyed only the barest covering of silver-gray hair, before descending in ever-widening ripples of loose fat, the jowls completely covering whatever chin and neck there might have been. His eyes were pale blue, the hue of the most innocent of summer days, and were greatly magnified by thick, round lenses, which perched on the very edge of his ridiculously small bump of a nose. The eyes twinkled and danced like moonlight on freshly fallen snow, and seemed to promise laughter, friendship everlasting, and banishment of worry.

Mika felt his heart leap within his breast and the burden of his quest, the search for the woman of his dreams, lighten at the man's approach. Somehow, he knew that this man would become his friend, his mentor, his guide, and that his search would soon be over.

So rapt was he that he barely noticed the smaller man trailing in the larger man's wake. Some tiny part of Mika's mind, that which was still functioning, took in the facts of the man's appearance: the bald head, the diminutive size, and the long, flowing, white beard. An alarm bell sounded in the distant recesses of his befogged brain. But still suffering from the effect of Braddle's magic spell and the hypnotic power of Travail's gaze, Mika failed to respond to the warning, and it faded into distant memory.

Linea saw Travail and Seldom wend their way through the ranks of The Game players toward the man in blue. Vaguely interested, she watched as they greeted the stranger, and she knew from their motions that they were introducing themselves. Then, Travail took the stranger by the elbow and looked deep into his eyes and spoke intently. The three of them stood silent and still as though they were considering a weighty topic.

The moment was broken abruptly, and Linea caught her lower lip in her teeth and gasped sharply as the red-haired man, still dressed in the suit of brown livery that set off his slender form quite nicely, boldly approached the group without being summoned and offered them mugs of honeyed ale as though he had been doing it all his life.

Linea was all but overwhelmed at his boldness, at his daring, thinking to pass himself off as a servant while approaching the most powerful man in the kingdom, now that her father had been deposed.

Linea watched him with admiration as he conversed with the men. Although she could not hear the words, she knew without a doubt that the handsome young man was enacting some plan that would bring them together.

Evidently his plan was working, for instead of reprimanding the man for his boldness, the trio accepted the ale and then seemed to include the young man in their discussions.

Linea was dying to know what they were saying. After all, it was her future that was at stake. She stamped her foot in a fit of pique, causing Womble to leave off his metallic munchings and whine as though wishing he might help her. Linea ignored him completely and pushed up against the carved stone screen in a futile attempt to hear their words. Were they talking about her? Surely they were. But what were they saying? Once or twice she thought she saw them glance up at the stone screen that sheltered her, and she cringed back, frantically combing her bedraggled hair with her fingers even though she knew that she could not be seen.

The screen had been built by a long-dead hettman to allow the women of his household to view the revelry below to which they were not invited. Linea was grateful that such was no longer the case, for these were enlightened times. In more normal days, dances and parties had filled the grand ballroom rather than these stupid games, and she had whirled and spun about on the highly polished floor in glorious gowns with her hair beautifully dressed, instead of hiding behind the stone curtain for fear of being seen.

Then it happened. In reality—no figment of her

imagination—Travail, Seldom, the man in blue, *and* the handsome, red-haired stranger all stopped talking and looked upward, directly at her window.

Linea pulled back in confusion, nearly tripping over Womble, feeling her face go crimson and the blood shiver in her veins. She felt dizzy again and wondered for a moment if it were the return of the strange feeling that nearly had overcome her a short time before. It was a peculiar, jangly tingling that made her feel as though she had been stung by a million wasps. But the feeling passed, and she withdrew from the window and ran back to her room.

Womble followed at her heels, pausing only long enough to consume a few silver doorknobs. When he entered her room, Womble found the princess, she whom he adored more than anyone else in the world, lying flat on her rumpled bed, sobbing as though her very heart would break.

Womble was at a loss. He would have done anything, even if it involved physical pain, which he abhored, if it spared his beloved mistress suffering.

Womble rubbed his great head against Linea's shoulder and purred softly to let her know that he was there. She flung her arms around his neck and, burying her face in his fur, began to recite her tearful litany of sorrow.

But large as his heart was, Womble's brain was no larger than it needed to be to satisfy his few needs, obtaining food and enough metal to still his ever-present hunger.

Dimly, he heard the words, "blue stranger, dog, Travail, and Seldom." Dimly he matched the words to the images he had seen while crouching behind the screen with his mistress. Dimly he perceived that these creatures had caused his mistress pain, were the cause of her sorrow, and as he kneaded his paws against her shoulder with his sharp claws carefully sheathed, a rage began to burn in Womble's heart, a great anger directed at those whom he perceived to have caused his mistress such great grief. Then and there, Womble took his mistress's pain to heart and decided that somehow he would put an end to her suffering.

Braddle could scarcely believe his luck. It appeared that the spell was actually working! Until that moment, he had been uncertain as to whether or not the old peddler had been what he claimed to be and whether the spell really would work when used. Braddle's small pile of grushniks had been hard-won over the years, and he had feared that he had squandered them foolishly on a scroll that would prove worthless. Not until he was stricken by the jolt of power had he begun to hope, to dare to hope, that the scroll really worked.

Confusion battled with excitement, and without even thinking what he was doing, he wandered into the grand ballroom, needing to look once more on the person who was to liberate him from the shackles of his life.

Trying to appear casual and, in truth, still slightly dazed by the after-effects of the magical spell, Braddle turned to look at Mika. His eyes rested briefly on the man in blue, but then, for some reason that he could not have explained, his eyes were drawn upward, past Mika, to the carved stone screen where the women of the castle had once watched festivities.

So far as Braddle knew, the room was no longer used. But his eyes were drawn there as though by some powerful force, and even then, though there was nothing to see, he felt himself seized once more by that same strange feeling, a tingling, electric awareness that left him breathless and dizzy.

There was another sensation as well, one that usually only surfaced in the very darkest moments of night, a feeling of intense loneliness and grief. It was at these moments that he groaned aloud, knowing that something important was missing from his life, something that not even power could cure. Only now, he had the strangest feeling that he was no longer alone.

A feeling of warmth came over him, filling him with certainty that something important had changed. Somehow, he was no longer alone. All but staggering under the implications, Braddle turned and lurched out the open door and leaned against the outer wall until the pounding of his heart returned to normal.

Filled with the knowledge that his spellcasting had worked, Braddle was seized with euphoria, and risking the attention of the guards, he leaped into the air and crowed wildly into the night sky. Then, returning to the kitchen, he seized a tray of drinks that were not even his to serve and made his way into the heart of the grand ballroom, ignoring the angry cries of the page whose tray he had taken, as well as summons from thirsty guests. If he were wrong and the spell had not worked, Braddle knew that he would be in big trouble.

Pushing his way through the crowd, Braddle approached the small group standing in the far corner of the vast ballroom and, holding up his tray, made ready to offer them mugs of honeyed ale. He did not know how they would respond nor what he would do if they refused him. Then, much to his surprise, he saw the prime minister raise his hand and quirk a finger, summoning him to his side.

"Here's a likely fellow," said the prime minister. "I've had my eye on him for some time now." Braddle could only stare in surprise, for he had no idea that his life was of interest to anyone other than himself.

"I think young 'Whosits' here would serve you very well. As I recall, he was once a member of the Hettman Dorbin's court, if only briefly." Braddle's heart lurched within his chest, and the tray tilted at a precarious angle, nearly spilling the contents of the mugs as he wondered worriedly what the prime minister knew.

The man's eyes were free of guile, and his laugh was so good-natured that it seemed impossible that he could mean anything other than what he actually said. And yet . . . something was wrong; all of Braddle's senses told him so. But he could not afford to miss the opportunity. He would take his chances with the danger, no matter what it was. He could not do otherwise.

"Braddle," he croaked. "Braddle's the name, good sir. And I will serve you gladly. You have but to command me."

"I wish you to serve my lord, Mika, a prince of the

Wolf Nomads who has graciously accepted our invitation to spend some time with us here in Krestible. Prince Mika tells us that he is interested in sport and, although not very proficient in gaming, would like to try his hand in our humble tourneys.

"It appears that he has heard something of our young princess's beauty as well, and he has come to present himself and make her acquaintance."

Braddle felt as though he had been struck in the stomach by a heavy object. The pain radiated throughout his body, although he did his best to prevent the others from noticing. The very thought of the man in blue coupled with the princess caused him extreme anguish, although he could not have said why, for he, like all those who lived in the castle, had often felt the fury of her displeasure, as well as her incessant demands.

Yet trouble him it did. For a heartbeat he found himself remembering the exact shade of her blue eyes, the tilt of her chin, and the gleam of her honey-blond hair, although he had never before even thought on it. After all, the Princess Linea was not a woman to be thought of like any others; she was the princess, and well it was to remember that.

That was obviously the problem here. His intuition had not been mistaken. Braddle knew that he had not imagined the feeling of danger and warning. The prime minister's eyes fairly sparked as he spoke of the young princess, and unbidden, all of them turned and stared at the carved stone screen behind which it now seemed likely that the princess was hidden. Although he did not know the reason, the stranger turned as well, his gray eyes probing the stone screen above them.

Braddle knew without words being spoken that he was being given the opportunity he had sought, to rise up out of the kitchens and serve as the stranger's page—only, and it was a big only—*only* if he could keep his mouth closed about the princess and her demanding, arrogant, petulant personality.

The princess was of no concern of his, despite the peculiar feeling that kept coming over him, a warm, tingly feeling, whenever he thought about her. Nor, he reminded himself sternly, did he care to acquaint himself with the full extent of the prime minister's plans. If the prime minister wished him to squire the stranger about and remain silent about the princess, then that was exactly what he would do.

"Sir," said Braddle, turning to Mika and bowing low, "I would be delighted to serve you. I will instruct you in all that you need to know." And keep from you all that you do not need to know, he thought, his eyes meeting those of the prime minister, who beamed down at him with unspoken approval. "Rest you easy, sir, for you have come to the right man."

MARCOVITTI, THE PASHA OF TUSMIT, paced back and forth in his chambers, his hands clasped tightly behind his back. His advisors, that august body of oldsters who had guided his every decision since he had come to the throne as a young man without the barest trace of down on his soft checks, watched him with worry in their eyes.

"I tell you it is time!" thundered the pasha, his dark eyes flashing with anger. "I am tired of playing Ekbir against Zeif and Perrenland against Ket.

"We do not have to fear war any longer. We can defend ourselves and more. We have been recruiting steadily, and our army is strong and well-prepared, far better prepared than our neighbors, who have grown soft and careless over the years."

"But Marco . . ." one of the advisors whispered softly, holding out a hand as though to still the dangerous torrent of words.

"No!" screamed the pasha, the veins standing out in his temples and throat like writhing snakes lying just below the surface of the skin. "No!" he screamed, putting his hands over his ears. "Say no more. I do not wish to hear your words. They are feeble and mewling like those of newborn kittens. I am Marco! I am the Pasha! Tusmit is mine to rule, and from now on, I will do as I wish. No more will your words confine me!"

"What is it that you wish to do, sir?" asked another old graybeard, his eyes covered with a blue-gray opaqueness, his skin so fragile as to be nearly transparent.

"What I should have done long ago: invade Perrenland," snapped the pasha, ignoring the gasps of horror that arose from his advisors. "They have grown lax of late, allowing this game to control and influence their every waking moment. It has infiltrated and taken over every level of their society, from hettman down to the lowest, most common peasant.

"My spies tell me that the Hettman Dorbin himself has been toppled from power because of The Game. His downfall has left the country leaderless, except for that daughter of his, who is next in line but must marry royalty to pass on the crown.

"We have just cause for such an invasion, gentlemen. One of our captains was assaulted by a Wolf nomad mercenary, and he and another recruiter were tricked out of all their gold. This nomad was followed to the border of Perrenland. A party of trackers was sent after him but has not returned. We suspect that the nomad has done away with them as well. Such a slaughter could not go unnoticed, not even in Perrenland. The nomad must be in Perrenland's employ.

"If we allow this outrage to go unpunished, we must expect more of the same in the future. Already recruitment has fallen off, and several captains have been attacked and their purses stolen. We must curb this now and punish the offender. If it goes unchecked, others will think us fools. We will be perceived as weak and attacked from all sides. I say we must attack Perrenland now!"

"How would you go about doing such a thing?" one of the ministers asked hesitantly.

"Send in the army," the pasha replied without a moment's pause. Moving to a table, he unrolled a large, oiled parchment scroll and weighted it at all four corners. "Here," he said, stabbing the map with a blunt finger. "Here is where we'll strike them and drive a wedge straight for Krestible. Once Krestible falls, the rest of the cantons will surrender without a spear being thrown."

"But my lord," said one of the advisors, "you are forgetting the mountains. No matter what your rationale for attacking Perrenland, our army will have to go through the Yatils, and even a large, well-armed force is not safe from the horrors that roam those hills. We would lose twice as many men traversing the passes as we would fighting in Perrenland. No country, no matter how large, can afford such losses. And our tiny country could never bear such a loss of life."

"Is that your biggest objection?" asked the pasha, a curious smile quirking the corner of his mouth.

"Aye," admitted the old one. "If not for that, I would say that the plan appears sound, but never could I agree to such a massacre. Our men would stand no chance against the awful horde of monsters and unnatural creatures that inhabit the dark defiles of those mountains."

"The orcs," said the pasha, nodding in agreement.

"The ogres," added the minister.

"The kobolds," said another.

"Not to mention trolls, ghouls, and wights," shuddered still another.

"And you cannot forget the hippogriffs and the hobgoblins," said a fourth minister.

"Cave bears!"

"Gorgons!"

"Griffons!"

"Gnolls!"

The advisors' voices added to the din as they gleefully listed all the monsters their army would likely encounter, certain that the litany of horrors would bring their young leader to his senses and prevent him from making a mistake that he might not live long enough to regret.

"Is that all?" asked the pasha, smiling at them patiently, like an adult humoring a child. "Any other objections? Speak then now, or never!"

"Giant lynx and manticores," said one of the advisors, although a bit feebly, for now it seemed apparent even to the dimmest of them that the pasha had a plan.

"Stone giants," said the pasha in the most quiet of voices.

"They're the worst," agreed one of the ministers, shivering at the mere mention of the horrible creatures' name. "The way they can just pick up boulders as big as houses and hurl them at people . . . it's enough to give you nightmares."

"I have signed a pact with the stone giants," said the pasha, continuing on as though the minister had not spoken. "They have agreed to aid us in our mission. They will not harm our army. Our men have free access through the passes, nothing will harm them. When we attack Perrenland, the stone giants and all of those monsters you have mentioned, and others even more ghastly, will join us. Our army will be invincible."

There was a long moment of silence as the ministers stared at their young ruler with eyes filled with horror. Their blood ran cold, and they looked at each other with fear. What dreadful thing had happened without the wisdom of their counsel?

"I have made a pact with the stone giants," the pasha repeated, giving voice to their innermost fears, driving the words like poisoned arrows still further into their hearts and brains. "All monsters living under their dominion will be ours to command. Perrenland cannot stand before our advance. We will be victorious!"

"And what happens if we are not victorious?" asked the oldest of the advisors, his strange, blind eyes probing deep into the heart of the pasha, who turned away as though he had not heard the question.

"What happens if we lose?" thundered the old one, now more certain than ever that he did not want to know the answer.

"Tusmit," muttered the young pasha, all evidence of his earlier bluster and rage gone as though it had never existed.

"Tusmit?" queried the old one, as though he had not understood the answer. "Tusmit? What about Tusmit?"

"They get Tusmit if we lose," whispered the pasha. "But don't you see," he added, his voice rising, shaking with passion. "It cannot happen! We will win, you'll see, we will win! And once we are victorious, I will wed the hettman's daughter and unite Tusmit and Perrenland. Together we will be invincible!"

"Pray that you are right sir," whispered the old graybeard. "Pray that you are right."

The pasha turned away, unwilling to meet his advisors' eyes, now filled with a mixture of condemnation and pity. He did not wish to see those eyes, and he had lost all desire to share with them the knowledge that it was he who had introduced The Game to Perrenland.

Chapter 12

MIKA MADE HIS WAY back to Mistress Bonnie's in the dark hours, long after the mid of night had passed. Mika's mind was awhirl with all that had happened; it was more than he could have hoped for. Two paces behind him trailed the young page, Braddle, who had been given to him by the prime minister, and slinking along still further behind was Tam, who seemed to have no love for Mika or the young man.

At first, Mika had suggested that Braddle remain at the castle, knowing that the page's presence would inhibit his normal way of life. Until he knew the page far better and had decided whether or not he was to be trusted, Mika's skills as a magic-user and the secret of the magic gem would have to remain just that: secret. It was always wisest to keep something in reserve against the time when it was needed, even if one was among friends, and as yet, Mika had no idea whether he was among friends or enemies.

Braddle followed Mika into the inn, and both of

them were surprised to find Mistress Bonnie slumbering in a large chair beside the open hearth. She awakened at their first step, even though they had tried not to disturb her.

Her relief at seeing Mika alive and well was touching. "Oh, sir!" she cried. "Nothing happened to you. Are you all right?"

"Of course, mistress," Mika replied gently. "Why should I not be all right?"

"Well, things sometimes happen up at the castle, and what with The Game and all . . . I was worried. Did you play?"

"No, mistress," replied Mika. "Not yet. This young man has been given into my keeping so that I might learn my way around the town and be tutored in The Game. Do you think that you might find him a place to sleep?"

"But my lord!" cried Braddle, his freckled face becoming flushed and his red hair all but standing on end. "I am to stay with you! His Excellency, the prime minister, has decreed it to be so. I must do as he has ordered!"

"Braddle, do you intend to follow me into the bath?" asked Mika.

"No, no, my lord," stammered Braddle.

"Do you intend to accompany me to the privy?"

"Of course not!" replied Braddle, his face growing even redder.

"Then I think that I might be trusted to sleep by myself," said Mika. "I have managed it up until now, and while there are occasions when I choose to sleep with others, this is not one of those times, if you get my meaning."

"B-but the prime minister . . ."

". . . does not have to know everything that goes on between us," said Mika, deftly cutting off any further protests. "Now sit you down, and let us talk."

Braddle was confused. Things were not happening in the way that he had pictured. Had the scroll not worked after all? Surely the fellow was not supposed to be so hard to control! But it must have worked, for here he was out of the kitchens!

Thinking quickly, Braddle decided that he would obey the stranger as best he could, while not actually defying the prime minister's commands, those orders which the prime minister had whispered in his ear while Seldom showed Mika around the room, explaining The Game as he went, pointing out examples of play from one table to the next.

His orders were to teach Mika how to play The Game but not to show him any of the techniques and ploys by which one might win. He was to escort Mika anywhere he wished to go, inside the city gates or out, tell him anything he wished to know, with one single exception. Never, *never* was he to breathe even one word about the Hettentochter Linea that was not complimentary.

Normally, Braddle would have found that a difficult order to obey, but now, somehow, every time he thought of the princess, all he envisioned were her brilliant blue eyes, the color of sapphires. Or her hair. Visions of her hair, great curly blonde clouds of it softer and more mellow of color than the earliest of buttercups, flowed through his mind. He imagined the silky feel of it as it cascaded through his fingers.

Braddle blinked and shook the image from his

head. Was he losing his mind? Where did such thoughts come from? Never before had he imagined the Princess Linea in such a manner! He looked around fearfully; if thoughts could be read, he would be in *big* trouble.

Mika sat staring at the young page, slowly sipping the hot, mulled ale that Mistress Bonnie had brought them, wondering what he was going to do with the fellow. It would certainly be a help to have someone show him around the place and fill in all those bits of information that he would need to know about The Game and the princess.

But it would also be dammed awkward, and he would have to be on his guard at all times, for the youngster did not look half stupid. Then, too, it had to be assumed that Braddle was the prime minister's man, for Travail had chosen him out of all others available. The prime minister had seemed a friendly and open sort, but those were always the ones with the most to hide.

"Tell me about yourself," Mika said pleasantly, settling back into the chair and putting his feet up on the grate to warm them. Tam lay at his side, still clearly disgruntled.

"There is little to tell, sir," replied Braddle with an empty gesture.

"Where do you come from?" asked Mika. "What are your goals, and what do you wish to make of your life?"

"I, I don't come from anywhere. Uh, I mean, I come from here," stammered Braddle, surprised by the question and wondering what Mika was getting at. "I have never been anywhere other than here. I have served in the kitchens since I was big enough to fetch and carry."

"Your entire life . . . in the kitchen!" exclaimed Mika, unable to imagine such an existence. "And what are your ambitions, boy? What do you want to do with yourself?"

"I want to get out—and stay out—of the kitchens, sir," replied Braddle, unwilling to concede any more of his dreams to the man whom he hoped would be the means of furthering them.

"Well, that should be easy enough," said Mika, wondering if anyone's hopes could be that limited. "I will see to it that you remain out of the kitchens and a good deal more, if you help me learn how to play this game well and tell me all you know about the princess, for it is my intent to win The Game as well as her hand in marriage."

Braddle could scarcely keep from leaping out of the chair and attacking Mika! Hearing him speak of his intentions toward the princess was almost more than Braddle could bear. For a heartbeat, he paused to wonder why on oerth he even cared. Until this moment his only concern had been how to avoid the princess and her incessant demands. Briefly, he recalled the day he had run up and down the stairs at least two hundred times, carrying first hot then cold, hot, cold, hot, hot, cold buckets of water, attempting to equalize the temperature of her bath, only to have her toss her curls and order him to bathe Womble! He still wore the scars from that encounter. But then he ceased thinking of it and gave himself up to his emotions. He looked down and ran his hand over the lower half of his face as though he were thinking, although in truth it was to keep Mika from seeing him grind his teeth together and muffle the groans that slipped through. Mika would not have her!

Braddle thought quickly. Mika seemed a pleasant fellow, and he was Braddle's way out of the kitchen. Further, Braddle had been instructed by the prime minister himself to teach Mika The Game and talk to him about the princess. Very well, he would do just that. But there was no law that said that he had to teach him well, and the princess, well, that was another matter entirely. One could say a lot by not saying anything at all.

Still and all, he was threading a treacherous path between the prime minister and the nomad for reasons of his own, which he still did not understand. Things could hardly be worse! Braddle felt the blood begin to pound at his temples and the hot ale twist inside his belly like bitter poison.

It seemed obvious now that the spell had backfired in some way, leaving Mika untouched and uncontrolled. Whatever was he to do about it? Even if he taught Mika all he knew about The Game, it seemed unlikely that the man could win, for even the best of players frequently lost. Nor could he tell Mika everything he knew about the princess, or the man would surely vanish before morning, leaving Braddle to face the prime minister's wrath.

"It's too late to start teaching you The Game now," said Braddle. "We will start on the morrow."

"The princess, then," said Mika, gazing at the transparent image which floated before his face, taunting him with her nearness. "Tell me about the princess."

Braddle thought fast. There *had* to be something he could say about the princess without lying. If he were clever, he could fill the man's ears with words, yet not say anything that would reveal her true nature, her pettiness, her terrible temper or her extravagent spending.

"She is very beautiful," Braddle said cautiously, giving himself up to the image of her beauty, allowing the picture of her to fill his head, knowing that the Princess Linea was the most beautiful woman he had ever seen, even more beautiful than Scylla, which was very beautiful indeed.

"Yes," sighed Mika. ". . . beautiful. Her eyes?" he prompted.

"Her eyes are dark blue, like the sky before a storm," said Braddle, leaving out that her temper was like the storm itself.

"Her nose . . ." Mika began.

". . . is tiny and shapely and turns up slightly at the end," said Braddle, surprised at himself, unaware that he had taken notice of such minute characteristics.

"Her lips," Braddle said, anticipating Mika's next question, "are pink, all of themselves, requiring no artificial color, and the lower lip is full and slightly pouty so that it is easy to wonder what it would be like to kiss it." Startled at his own words, Braddle sat up straight in his own chair and continued in a more gruff, businesslike tone.

"Her hair is long and shiny and the color of corn silk, and is fashioned in waves and curls and falls to her waist. It is very lovely. Her figure . . ."

". . . is not a matter for discussion," Mika said

brusquely. For one who had spent all of his days in the kitchen, Braddle knew far more about the princess than he should, Mika thought.

Braddle was also very disturbed, for he had been unable to say anything that might put Mika off on the subject of the princess. He had waxed eloquent like a lovesick fool! He kicked himself mentally and made a vow to say something terrible about the princess at the very next opportunity.

"Now, about The Game," said Mika, breaking into Braddle's thoughts and changing the subject abruptly. Feeling themselves to be on safer ground, they began discussing The Game in general terms, Braddle talking and Mika listening until the first cock crowed. Mika yawned finally and, stretching his arms wide, proclaimed that they had done enough for the first night. Taking a gold grushnik out of his pouch, he flipped it to his young tutor. "Take this and buy yourself something, perhaps some new clothes to denote your change in status. Get you to bed now before it is daylight, or I shall be accused of cruelty."

Braddle stared after Mika with an open mouth, holding the precious gold coin, the most money he had ever possessed in his entire life, clenched tightly between thumb and forefinger. To throw that much money away so casually all but put Braddle in shock. At that exact moment he decided to one day possess money, so much wealth that he would be invincible. He would make so much money that he could give whole bagsful away and never miss it. He would make so much money that he would be the richest man on all of Oerth!

Mika saw the strange expression come over the

young man's face as he tossed him the coin, and he wondered if perhaps he had done the wrong thing. He was unfamiliar with the economic climate in Krestible. Perhaps with the way The Game had been affecting their society, the gold coin was not worth as much as it would be elsewhere. Mika resolved to give Braddle more money at the very next opportunity. If he were to learn all he could about The Game, he would need Braddle's cooperation, and so far as he knew, grushniks were still the fastest way to anyone's heart.

Braddle awakened long before the sun had risen to its zenith and pushed aside the heavy down coverlet. He swung out of bed fully dressed, having slept in his clothes. He splashed water on his freckled face, ran his fingers through his unruly red hair, and gargled noisily. He was ready to face the day.

The marketplace was already in full swing. Peasant women from the country sat on the cobblestones, piles of yarpiks, baskets of mushrooms, freshly laid speckled eggs, bound bunches of fragrant herbs, new potatoes, twists of onions, and braids of garlic spread out for inspection on their colorful skirts.

Bread sellers hawked their wares in dulcet tones, holding aloft fragrant cinnamon rolls, sticky buns dripping with honey and bursting with currants, and crusty loaves of bread as long and as thick as a man's leg.

A seller of fresh fish shouted out the praises of his pop-eyed, gaping-gilled offerings, competing with the cries of his neighbor, a halfling who had brought a basket of flint down out of the hills.

Each and every seller had his own distinctive cry, bleated out every few moments, producing an overwhelming cacophony of sounds that assaulted the ears of the listener until it became a solid, indistinguishable babble that was all but impossible to understand.

But the seller for whom Braddle searched had no cry of his own, nor did he choose to make himself prominently visible. In fact, Braddle had often wondered if anyone other than himself ever saw the man, for he had never seen the oldster with another customer.

The old man crouched in a corner made by the juxtaposition of two large stone buildings, his head tilted back to take advantage of the full warmth of the morning sun. He was an old man, far older than anyone Braddle had ever seen. His face was seamed and lined like old parchment. His sparse hair drifted about his head, stirred by even the slightest breeze or movement.

His eyes were sunk deep in their sockets and were hooded by heavy eyelids. They were tired eyes, eyes exhausted from a lifetime of observing and being disappointed by the behavior of his fellow man. And it seemed to Braddle's fanciful mind that the worst of those images lay just below the pale blue surface of the old man's eyes, and if he were not careful he himself would see them, too.

Braddle was hesitant to awaken the old one, but he had to return before Mika roused, and the gold coin was burning a hole in his pocket. Braddle stood in front of the old man and hopped from foot to foot impatiently, wondering how long the old one was going to sleep.

"Do not wiggle about so," said the old one, his eyes still firmly shut. "I find it very annoying."

"Oh, sir, you're awake," said Braddle, grasping the edge of the old man's tunic and touching it to his forehead. "Please, sir, you must help me. The spell, it did not work. Well, it seemed to work, I mean, I read the words just like you told me, and the words disappeared off the page just as you said, and the paper crumbled and turned to dust, so that part worked the way you said it would."

The old one's eyes opened and stared at Braddle intently, the faded blue taking on a deeper hue.

"Did anything happen to you?" he snapped. "Did you feel anything?"

"Well, not really. It didn't kill me or anything like that, but there was this sort of shock like I'd been hit by lightning. It kind of slammed me up against the wall and knocked the air out of me for a moment or two. I thought maybe I'd been hit by lightning. It felt like there was a hole burned in the top of my head, but I was all right, so I guess nothing happened."

The old one's eyes were very alert now, and his body had gone rigid. "Something happened, all right," he murmured. "And you should give a generous offering to the gods for sparing your foolish life. Who was your target, and what was it you were trying to do?"

Braddle quickly told him, leaving out nothing.

"Describe this Wolf Nomad to me again," the old one said softly, and he listened carefully to everything Braddle had to say, quizzing him closely on a number of details. It also seemed to Braddle that the old one looked at him in a different manner, looked at him as though he really saw him. Finally, the old man was satisfied and sat back, wrapped deeply in thought.

"The spell did work," he said at last. "Unfortunately, you managed to pick a powerful wizard as your target. Never did I imagine this to be the case. I supposed your target would be no more than a kitchen wench, and the spell would work adequately for such as that. But it was not meant to deal with another wizard. You are lucky that you were not killed. The walls saved you, and the fact that you were some distance away. Had you tried the spell in close proximity to the man, you would have been killed instantly, burned to a cinder."

Braddle felt his knees go weak, and despite the warmth of the sun, his skin was covered with goose bumps. Then, marshaling his courage, he spoke up to the old man. "So you say. How do I know that the spell was even a real spell? How do I know that the spell was good and the man's a wizard? He does not look like a wizard. How do I know that he is not a normal, regular person, and it was the spell that was faulty, not worth the parchment it was written on? Can you prove what you say? I want to know before I give you any more gold. And if you are a real wizard, why are you selling spells in the marketplace like any ordinary merchant?"

"Good questions, little worm," said the old man. "Perhaps I was not mistaken in my judgment of you. Perhaps you do have a head on your shoulders, after all. You didn't need any convincing when you thought I was your only chance, but now, now that you think you have another option, you are more careful. Good, perhaps you will live long enough to use what you buy."

"What could I possibly buy that will work against a wizard?" Braddle asked in despair, no longer so certain of his suspicions. "If he *really* is a wizard, then surely he will know that I am using something against him and then he'll kill me."

"Not necessarily," said the old man after a long heartbeat of thought. "I have a charm that might work. It is very old and quite powerful and should be able to do the job while protecting you as well. Unless he uses a detect magic spell of his own he will not find out, as long as he does not suspect . . ." Here the old one fell into a murmur of ruminations, muttering to himself, arguing both sides of the issue, back and forth. Finally, he looked up, scrutinizing Braddle carefully. "Yes, I think you can do it." he said at last. "I have had my eye on you for some time, you know."

"How much will it cost me?" asked Braddle, trying to ignore the old man's statement, which only served to plunge him into even deeper confusion. How and when had the old man had his eyes on him? Surely the old man was mistaken; perhaps he was senile. Braddle's hand wrapped moistly around the coin hidden in the dark confines of his pocket, and he wondered, not for the first time, whether what he was doing was wise. Why could he not be content to live out his life in the kitchens?

"It will cost you no more than the single gold grushnik you hold in your hand," said the old one, "and a bit of daring. Without risk, there can be no gain. Remember that, young Braddle. And better to ask an eagle why it must fly to the heights than to question your own yearnings. You were meant for higher things, just as the eagle." Although he chuckled at Braddle's expression, his eyes held no laughter.

Braddle was so startled at the man's words and the fact that he knew his name, although Braddle had never told him, that he drew the hand that clenched the coin out of his pocket. "Guesses," he said, "or you heard someone call my name. There are many here who know me. Answer the question, good sir. How do I know you're not a charlatan? If you're really a wizard, why are you selling your charms and spells in the marketplace like a common merchant?"

"That's none of your concern," the old man said sharply, turning away from Braddle, his eyes losing their luster.

"All right, all right," Braddle said hastily, pressing the coin into the old man's hand. It was a small price to pay if it worked.

The old man took the coin and dropped it into the top of his pouch, not even bothering to look at it or test its purity with his teeth. Then he removed a small object from inside the pouch and handed it to Braddle with the softest of sighs.

Braddle held the object gingerly in his fingertips and examined it carefully. It was a small thing, no bigger than a cherry, and withered and dry and brownish black in color. It was shiny, as though it had been fondled often over the centuries.

"What is it?" asked Braddle, his voice almost reverent as he felt the power of the thing tingling in his fingers.

"A heart," replied the old man softly. "A heart

filled with power of the strongest sort. It will act as a charm for you and protect you against harm. But I must warn you: it can be used only for good. It will not work if it is used for harm or for evil. If it is used in such a manner, it will most likely explode, killing you and anyone else unlucky enough to be near you. Do not forget."

"Such a charm would surely be worth more than but a single gold coin," said Braddle. "Why, it must be worth at least ten such coins," he added, naming a figure larger than any he could imagine. "Why are you doing this for me?"

"That is none of your concern either. I have my reasons, and they will come clear to you in time," said the old man, looking older and somehow smaller than he had when first they spoke. It was as though the transaction had tired him, taken out all the strength contained in the small body. He closed his eyes and leaned back against the rough, gray stone wall, turning his face to the warm rays of the sun, dismissing Braddle without a word.

Though Braddle stood there a moment longer, looking at the old man and wondering what it all meant, he knew that there was no more to be said, no more to be learned. Closing his fist around the precious charm, he turned and hurried away.

BRADDLE AND MIKA ATE the morning meal in silence, each occupied with his thoughts, eyeing the other speculatively when he thought the other was not looking. Tam had remained in dog form, no more thrilled about his fate than he had been the previous night. He sprawled glumly beneath the table, refusing to be tempted by the bowl of scraps Mistress Bonnie put out for him after proclaiming him the ugliest dog she had ever seen.

As soon as breakfast was done, Braddle began the job of teaching Mika The Game. A table was cleared, and under Mistress Bonnie's worried glances, they began.

Braddle began by explaining that The Game, which had been played in Perrenland for as long as anyone could remember, had a deeper religious significance, as well as being a game of simple pleasure.

"It hardly seems to be a game of simple pleasure," said Mika.

"It has not always been so," replied Braddle. "It is

only within recent times that the changes began."

"Whose decision was it to make these changes?" asked Mika, wondering who had the most to gain, suspecting that it could only be the prime minister.

"I don't know," replied Braddle. "It started when those little men came to town. There are three of them. Odd fellows. They are the ones who post the new rules. At first it was just the one set of changes, and everyone learned them. Then the changes started coming more often, and now there are changes every morning. One or another of the little men post the new rules all over town, and people read them and make ready for the night's games."

"And you mean to tell me that no one has ever asked who these men are and who authorized them to make the changes?" Mika asked in astonishment.

"Oh, I'm sure that someone has done that, sir, but I wouldn't know who. They certainly wouldn't tell me," said Braddle. "But no one could do something that important without someone knowing about it."

But Mika was not so sure. He had seen many smart men make stupid mistakes, and he had observed governments topple because they had grown too large and unwieldly. Everyone always assumed that someone else knew what going on, while in truth that was seldom the case. Mika made a note to himself to learn the identity of the three old men who had brought such change to the people of Perrenland.

Once more, Braddle began to explain The Game.

"Try to picture the board as a picture of all the known planes of existence," said Braddle. "Each of the corners represents the four corners of the Oerth, while the squares are positions in both time and space. The pieces represent the gods as well as the demons of evil as they move through time and their houses of power."

"Where is the Great Wolf Mother, mother of us all?" asked Mika, looking at the playing pieces, which Braddle had placed on the black-and-white spaced playing board.

"The Great Wolf Mother is not one of our goddesses," said Braddle. Noting the tight line of Mika's lips, he added hastily, "Although I'm sure that it is a serious mistake, and no one would object if you substituted a piece in her honor."

Mika looked down at the board and studied the pieces. All the usual gods were represented, the god of plenty, represented by a cornucopia, the god of war with his thunderbolt, the goddess of peace with her lyre, the goddess of love holding a halved heart in each hand, and so on. A carved wooden cornstalk signified crops. A polished rock symbolized the land itself. A coin stood for wealth, and a small wood house represented the homestead. A fused pile of objects indicated all one's oerthly possessions. A cluster of figures indicated servants. And finally, a man standing alone represented the player. All in all, each player possessed sixteen playing pawns.

Frowning down at the board, Mika removed the fat, smiling man with a large, naked belly, thought to be the god who smiled down on and guided Perrenland, and he replaced it with a beautifully carved image of a woman with a wolf's face, the holy Wolf Mother herself, mother protector of the Wolf Nomads.

Braddle was somewhat disconcerted by Mika's

action but gave no outward sign, as he did not wish to offend or anger the man who had control over his life.

"Now what?" asked Mika.

"Well, the movement of the gods represents their movements through time and space," repeated Braddle, "and their positions on the board in respect to one another are an indication of your future.

"Everyone knows that the gods control our destiny," added Braddle, while thinking to himself that a man could give their decisions a little help now and then, "but you control their movement on the board by means of the knucklebones. The skill in The Game comes with the rolling of the knucklebones, and it is up to the individual player to interpret the numbers and decide the placement of the pawns. The outcome of The Game is decided by the final positions on the board and the gods remaining. This will tell you where you stand with the gods and what your future will likely be."

"Well, I don't understand," said Mika, sitting back and scratching his head, realizing that he had underestimated the complexity of The Game. "If that's all there is to it, how is it that so many people are losing everything they own?"

"Ah, well, it is possible to buy favor with the gods," replied Braddle. "And to convince them of your absolute sincerity and complete belief in them, and to honor them, you must compete with your opponent to wager the highest amount on the outcome of The Game, raising the stakes at every opportunity."

Realization dawned swiftly. "Ahhh," said Mika. "So, by wagering everything, possessions, wealth, land, and even yourself, you determine not only your status, but your future according to the will of the gods."

"Exactly," replied Braddle. "Originally, The Game was played only to determine one's status and predict the future. The new rules have changed all of that. New playing pieces representing material possessions have taken the place of some of the lesser gods."

"And how is The Game actually played?" asked Mika, although fairly certain that he could predict the answer.

"Well, it is quite simple, really," said Braddle. "Each player must move all of his pieces to the opposite side of the board, losing as few as possible to his opponent, while capturing as many of his opponent's pawns as possible. It is also possible to make side bets that one of your pieces will be able to capture one of your opponents. There are four safe squares in the center of the board, but it generally does no good to remain there. Movement, of course, is determined by the toss of the knucklebones."

"But there are so many pieces. How do you know which to move first?" asked Mika.

"You must decide which piece you wish to move first. Generally it is the god whom you consider to have the most influence over your life, or the one to whom you owe the most allegiance. You pick up the knucklebones and close both hands around them, shaking them back and forth. When you release the bones, you call out the name of the god, asking him to guide your hand and bring you luck.

"To begin, you throw a single knucklebone and

move your pawn forward according to the number thrown, until it passes the third row of pawns. After it has passed this point, you may make two throws: one to move the first pawn, and the second to begin moving out the second pawn. Only after it has passed the third line of pawns may you move out the next piece, and so on and so on, taking another roll of the bones with each pawn put into play."

"But that must get very confusing," said Mika, beginning to realize that The Game was far more challenging than he had first realized. "How do you keep track of everything?"

"On a slate," replied Braddle. "Each game has a slatekeeper, although this too is a recent development. It was never necessary before."

"What happens if you have two pawns in the same space?" asked Mika.

"No more than one pawn can be moved in a turn," Braddle answered firmly. "But I have noticed that the very best of players complete all of their throws before moving any one piece, then study their positions so as to establish a strong offensive as well as a good defense."

"Obviously, the most dangerous time will come when both players' pawns reach the middle of the board and begin to move into the squares occupied by their opponent."

"True," said Braddle. "Whenever you invade an occupied square, your opponent then loses the pawn and whatever it signifies—loss of that god's protection, if the piece is a god, or a material possession, if that is the case.

"Loss of a piece also means that your opponent

loses one of his throws and may not regain it until his lead pawn reaches or passes beyond the next row of squares. The Game is over when all pieces reach the safety of the opposite side and take up their starting positions, or by loss of your personal pawn, the pawn that represents you."

"And how is it determined what your fate is to be?" asked Mika.

"Slavery is assumed if the piece is captured and merely placed at the edge of the board. Banishment is indicated by placing the pawn face down on the table. And death is signified by replacing the pawn with a black skull," Braddle replied slowly. "That, of course, ends The Game."

"I would imagine so," Mika said dryly.

"It doesn't have to happen that way, of course," said Braddle. "There are alternatives. Instead of taking a player's life, you can merely banish him, exile him to wander without home or possessions so long as he might live. This is what happened to the Hettman Dorbin. Then, too, it's always possible to return and play again, assuming you can acquire another stake with which to wager.

"But the longer one is out of The Game, the more difficult it is to regain the vantage, for there are daily changes."

Mika made a mental note to learn something about the identity of the mysterious little men who wielded such power over the inhabitants of Perrenland. It was obviously of the utmost importance to stay abreast of the newest rules, even though the changes might be slight, for The Game could alter significantly, and woe be to the man who had not kept up.

Mika listened earnestly as Braddle talked on, explaining the intricacies of The Game. Soon, based on his knowledge of other similar games, it became apparent that the youngster was leaving out bits of information that Mika would need to know if he were to become a serious contender. These were fine points, and for a time, Mika was willing to believe that the young man was simply unaware of the more advanced moves. But as time went on, it became increasingly obvious that Braddle was leaving out their mention on purpose.

Aha! thought Mika, what was going on here? Was the boy leaving things out because he was so instructed by the prime minister, or was he following some secret agenda of his own? Whatever the reason, Braddle would have to be watched. Mika considered calling the boy on his duplicity but then reconsidered, realizing that he would learn more if Braddle did not know that he had been found out.

Their lives took on a routine. They played The Game from morning till dusk and then went to the castle each night, where they observed other games in progress. They studied each new addendum to The Game's rules as it was posted. And each night, Mika attempted to catch a glimpse of the princess, she who ruled his thoughts waking and sleeping, but that was all he ever got, a glimpse of her beautiful hair, shimmering in the candlelight, the hem of her gown, the elusive scent of her perfume, nothing more.

The vision of her still haunted him, and knowing that she was nearby, inaccessible, only made it worse.

Her image shimmered before his eyes through every waking moment, and she haunted his dreams at night, draining him emotionally as well as physically.

In what was truly a sign of his depressed state, Mika had even lost his voracious appetite. Mistress Bonnie chided him to no avail and raised a great clatter in the kitchen, cooking delicate morsels to tempt his palate. Each night after the games were over, Mika bid Braddle good night and stood outside the castle walls, peering up at the princess's window, hoping to catch sight of her.

He pondered the possibility of turning himself into an eagle or a spider or something of the sort and finding his way to the princess's chambers, but something held him back, an unwillingness to act in a manner that might upset her. At length, Mika realized with a sense of shock that he, Mika-oba of the Wolf Nomads, intrepid adventurer, wooer of women, had fallen in love with a woman whom he had never even seen in the flesh.

Joy battled sorrow as he took a close, painful look at the wreck he had become, and he was grateful that none of his old companions, or any of the countless women he had loved and left over the years, could see him now. Their laughter would be unbearable.

Even worse, Tam was angry with him, or perhaps it was disgust with his dog form, for after a fortnight he disappeared, leaving Mika with only a fragrant, steaming pile of dung deposited neatly in his shoe to remember him by. Mika missed him badly, but knew that Tam was probably better off without him, hunting in the hills and chasing female wolves unencumbered by the hated dog guise. Mika hoped that if he ever really needed him, Tam would be at his side.

Despite his restlessness and Braddle's incomplete teachings, it was apparent to both of them that Mika was rapidly reaching a point of skill where he would be able to enter into The Game at the castle. Braddle reported his pupil's progress to the prime minister, and it was decided that Mika would be allowed to play for the first time, and if he won, he would be permitted to meet the princess.

Mika was as elated by the news as Braddle was depressed. Mika stood in his room and materialized outfits, one after the other, trying to decide what to wear. But no matter what he visualized, it did not seem right, being either too fancy, too drab, too austere, or too elaborate. Finally, he settled on a wine-colored velvet doublet, with a high throat and puffed sleeves, trimmed in gold. His tights were a slightly darker shade, as were the boots and the glove that covered his right hand as always.

His spell book, the weighted knucklebones, and the black death skull were carried in a separate leather pouch and hung over his shoulder. The magic gem, still appearing to be no more than an ordinary bit of quartzite firmly encased in a solid silver fitting, hung from a heavy silver chain around his neck.

Braddle planned to wear a suit of russet brown, which complimented his thick, auburn hair and also accentuated the multitude of freckles that covered his face like snowflakes. He had Mika to thank for the new clothes, as well as a chest full of others, for Mika lavished coins and clothes on him as though by doing so, the Wolf Nomad might somehow impress the princess with his largesse.

The princess was not excluded from Mika's generosity, for he had realized early that even though he could not see her, there was no reason why he could not send her gifts.

And send them he did. He sent chests inlaid with gold and precious gemstones, filled to the top with beautiful garments fit for a princess. He sent an enchanted singing bird that did not need to be fed or caged and never repeated the same song twice. He sent a bouquet of sweet-scented flowers that bloomed endlessly and never died, and a pair of ruby earrings nestled in a cask of pure platinum. All were conjured by the magic gem. And all were carried to the castle by an anguished Braddle who knew that he had no hope of competing against such wealth.

Mika's generosity was causing the prime minister no end of distress. Travail's greed caused him to finger the presents, counting in his head what he could get for them. But wisdom won out, for he realized that Mika would be very angry should he learn that she had not received his presents. But with a quirk of mischief, the prime minister removed Mika's name from the cards that accompanied the presents and substituted Braddle's name instead. He had no real idea why he had done so or what he hoped to accomplish, but it was done.

Thus, Braddle was sent daily to the castle, bearing that day's offering of love. The princess learned to anticipate his visits and watched for him out of her window. Above all, she admired the play of the sun on his shiny red hair and the look of him in his handsome new clothes, never once recognizing the lowly kitchen helper he had been such a short time before.

In this instance, clothes did indeed make the man.

Not having any reason to think otherwise, Linea believed that the presents came from Braddle. When she peered down from behind her carved stone screen each night, it was Braddle she searched out, and the dark man at his side was beneath her notice. Above all, she admired Braddle because he alone was the only man who did not play the hated game.

Since they had never spoken, Linea invented dialogues in her head, and soon she came to believe that Braddle too shared her intense hatred of The Game and all that it represented. She yearned and dreamed of the moment when they might meet. Her dreams were realized on the night that Travail informed her that she was to make herself ready to receive certain visitors after the conclusion of the evening's games.

Linea was all atwitter. She rushed back and forth across her debris-strewn room, wondering what she was to wear and how she would fix her hair. Even though her confinement had gone on for some time now, she had not gained much proficiency in self-grooming. Her abundant hair flowed in all directions, bearing some similarity to a haystack, her shoes were mismatched, and her gown was buttoned crookedly.

It had been necessary to send the message to Linea through a kitchen maid named Scylla, for it had become too dangerous for the prime minister and Seldom to venture anywhere near the princess's quarters. Womble had taken an extreme dislike to them and had attempted to kill them on several occasions. They had escaped by sheer luck alone.

The first time it had happened, they had shrugged it off as a case of mistaken identity. Womble had often eaten the odd page or a scullery wench carrying silver to be polished or swords to be sharpened. The second time, there was no mistaking his intentions, and they had escaped only by tossing out their swords and daggers and emptying their pockets of coins. Womble had paused to devour the coins, being unable to pass up metal of any sort, and they had seized the opportunity and run away as fast as their legs could carry them.

"Let's get rid of the horrid beast," snarled Seldom, looking down at the long, shallow gouges that ran the entire length of his leg. "I can make him disappear. We'll tell the princess he ran away."

"No," said Travail. "She knows he'd never do that. He'd never leave her. I wonder what's gotten into the creature. He's never disliked us before."

"We never did away with the hettman before," muttered Seldom. "Or caused the princess to cry. Maybe he's smarter than we've given him credit for. Maybe he's figured out that we're behind the princess's problems."

"No, couldn't be," replied Travail, dismissing the thought with a wave of his hand. "The creature simply isn't that smart. It must be something else. Cut down on his metal rations. That'll soon bring him to his senses."

But Travail was wrong. All of Womble's animosity grew out of the princess's dislike for Seldom and Travail. She viewed them as being responsible for her father's downfall and, consequently, for her own sorry state of affairs, even though she had no way of proving it. She hated them more than she had ever hated anyone ever before. And that was more than enough for Womble.

Womble was disappointed that he had failed to kill Travail and Seldom. It would be more difficult now that they suspected his intentions and were on their guard. But Womble was nothing if not persistent, and he had no intention of giving up. His attempts grew ever more devious. Travail and Seldom saw his glowing silver eyes glowering out at them from every dark corner and heard his dank breath whether he was there or not. They grew to fear him greatly.

Once they were walking down a passageway, when suddenly, a massive oak door fell forward, crushing them to the floor beneath its great weight. Their terrified screams brought help instantly, and it was found that the hinges and the lock were missing. The wood that remained exhibited signs of gnawing.

There was no specific sign that Womble was responsible for the accident. But Travail and Seldom needed no proof. They believed it to be so and increased their watchfulness to the point of paranoia, hoping that Womble would become appeased as his mistress grew happier.

The great night came at last. Braddle and Mika made their way to the castle. Linea watched them come with a panic unrivaled in her short life. Travail had graciously allowed the servants to fill the large hip bath with hot water, which Linea had scented a bit too heavily, being unfamiliar with the necessary amounts. Somehow she had managed to shampoo her hair and bathe herself, both unfamiliar chores. She had gotten soap in her eyes and sobbed through the entire procedure, feeling sorry for herself at having to perform such a menial chore. But the awful job was done at last, and she climbed out of the bath, wrapped herself in a large towel, and attempted to comb out the snarled mass that was her hair.

In the end, it was Womble who helped, stroking her head gently with his paw. He was able to brush her hair with claws unsheathed, with so delicate a touch that her hair soon floated around her shoulders, clean, fragrant, and unsnarled. Linea praised him warmly and stroked his head, and had she not been fearful of covering herself in a layer of fur, she might have even hugged him. In her gratitude, she fed him two ugly silver bracelets, which she had always disliked, and a heavy gold choker that had grown too small. These he consumed with great relish, enjoying them even more than usual because they were hers.

Choosing a gown was far more difficult, but thinking that it might make Braddle happy, she wore one of the gowns that he had brought her. Womble was unable to manage the buttons, succeeding only in eating them, and Linea was forced to wear a cape that hid the gaping back of the garment. That night, as she took her place behind the carved stone screen, Linea's heart beat faster, and somehow she knew that something momentous that well might change her life forever was about to happen.

Travail and Seldom also waited the outcome of the evening with no small amount of trepidation. They wanted Mika to win, but not to win so easily that he would gain too much confidence. They wanted Mika to believe that he had much to lose and needed their assistance. It would not do to have the fellow become too sure of himself. To this end, they had bribed the player with whom Mika would be playing. He was to lose to Mika, but would do so only after putting up a long and hard defense. They had also promised to return whatever Mika won from him during The Game.

What was to follow after The Game worried them the most, for it was then that Mika would meet the princess for the first time. It was imperative that she not speak, for then, surely, Mika would be driven away by her sharp tongue and petty, pampered bearing which no spell, no matter how powerful, could hope to conceal.

Of them all, Womble alone looked forward to the coming evening without reservation, for he had decided that this was the night that Travail, Seldom, and the Wolf Nomad would die, putting an end, once and for all, to his mistress's sorrow.

THE GAME WENT SMOOTHLY—far too smoothly as far as Seldom and Travail were concerned. Mika did not even need to use magic to win. His opponent, a beefy, red-faced farmer, began to sweat after the first three moves, and his thick fingers trembled on the playing pieces.

Mika made it a point to appear calm and at ease even when his opponent managed to box him in early in The Game. His cheery whistling and confident smile only rattled the farmer further, which was undoubtedly part of Mika's strategy. The man had not expected Mika to be such an adept player, having been led to believe that he was but a novice. He threw an anguished look at Travail as Mika began his final assault a short time later, which soon resulted in the man's defeat.

Much to everyone's surprise, Mika scooped up the tokens that symbolized the man's home, his farm, his livestock, and his possessions and, instead of dropping them in his pouch, handed them back to his opponent.

The man stared at Mika in open-mouthed amazement, staring first at his hand then up at Mika, unable to comprehend what he was seeing. Never before in the history of The Game had such a thing happened! As word spread throughout the hall, players stopped in mid-move, advisors stopped their murmurings, scorekeepers ceased their scribbling, and even the pages and maids gaped at Mika in disbelief.

Mika was unprepared for the commotion. His action had been unplanned, a spur of the moment move. Then, using the silence to his advantage, he smiled his most charming smile and bowed low to the captive audience. Not knowing what else to do, they bowed in return, relieving the awkward moment, and soon a hubbub of busy talk broke out as they discussed what he had done.

Travail was dumbstruck! Never had he thought that such a thing could happen, for he had counted on Mika's natural greed to function as it did for everyone else. No one had ever thought to say no to the acquisition of a rich farm, many hectares of land, and all the animals and buildings it supported. Such a thing could not be permitted! Why, it might start a trend, and then what would he do?

All players who succeeded in reaching the final tournament of play then faced off against the prime minister, and he had never been known to lose. Travail did not want to even consider giving back all the farms and lands and chattels he had won. Such a thing was unthinkable!

"See here," blustered Travail, "we can't have this.

You must take what you have won!"

"But I have no wish to become a farmer," Mika replied pleasantly but firmly, unable to think of a fate worse than being tied down to the land, a slave to its relentless timetable, tilling, planting, harvesting, over and over again, season after season, year after year, until he was old and gray and bowed. The mere thought was enough to make him ill.

"It makes no difference what you want," snapped Travail. "Some things must be done without regard to feelings. You must take what you have won. It is the way it is done, the way The Game is played."

"I play for sport, not for gain," said Mika, beginning to feel the slightest twinge of anger growing at the back of his skull. "I do not wish to become a farmer. I stand by my actions, and while I do not wish to offend, nothing you say will change my mind."

Their every word had been closely followed by all those in the room. Heads swiveled back and forth from one to the other, and breaths were held as people wondered what the outcome would be and how it would affect them.

Up in her chamber, behind the stone screen, Linea was growing restless. She paced back and forth, wondering what all the commotion was about, what was causing such a delay. The Game was over, she could see that, but instead of coming to her chamber as agreed, they were all standing around that dark stranger, who was far less attractive than his red-headed companion. It was all the stranger's fault!

Linea's temper began to rise. What could he possibly be saying that would be so interesting? Whatever it was, Linea knew in her heart that Braddle could say it better. But wise fellow that he was, Braddle was standing silent, not filling the air with empty words that would delay his meeting with Linea.

Linea stomped her foot angrily and pointed through the stone grill at Travail, Seldom, and Mika. "Look at them, Womble. Talking! Talking! Talking! Don't they realize they're keeping me waiting? Oh! They make me so angry, I wish you could gobble them up, right down to their shoe buckles!"

This was good news for Womble and his ears perked right up, for lurking in the back of his mind was the concern that should he do such a thing, the princess would be very angry with him. Now that this last obstacle had been removed, he could begin his hunt in earnest. Linea turned away from the screen and stomped to the other side of the room, flinging chairs out of her way, overturning tables, and muttering to herself. Her face turned red with anger, and her hair frazzled around her face. As she turned aside, forgetting him in her rage, Womble seized his chance and slipped out of the room, his mind coursing through the maze of corridors that lay before him as he planned his ambush.

"The matter is over, sir, and I have won," said Mika, his voice taking on a hard edge. "And as agreed, it is now my right to meet the princess."

Travail was on the spot. It was true that that had been their agreement, and if he reneged, the fellow might actually lose his temper and attempt to do him some bodily harm. Perspiration broke out on Travail's forehead. No one had had the nerve to attack him in many, many years; he was too feared for that. But Mika did not seem the least bit afraid. Nor did he seem to be the simple, malleable fool that Seldom had taken him to be. Travail knew that he needed to do something. He could not continue to stand in the middle of the floor like a fool, with every eye and ear in the place glued to him. He needed to act, yet act in a positive manner, so that he would not appear to lose face to this nomadic nobody.

"Sir, you are unfamiliar with our ways here in Krestible, and although this is not how The Game is played, courtesy demands that we bow to your request and honor your decision." Making a second, low sweeping bow, which was difficult indeed for a man of his great girth, Travail smiled up at Mika with a grimace that showed many teeth and no humor. His eyes were cold and hard behind his thick lenses, and a lesser man would have taken heed of the warning and departed as fast as his feet could carry him. But Mika took no notice, bowing in return yet not as deeply as Perrenlandian etiquette required, thus turning his action into an insult.

"This way, sir," said Seldom, bustling ahead of Mika and Travail, talking as fast as he could and trying to head off a confrontation between the two men. "Come along, come along, we must not keep the princess waiting!"

Braddle's mind was in a turmoil. He had lived in the palace all his life and knew the Princess Linea all too well, yet not at all, and now his heart was beating as though it might burst. He was actually going to be close enough to touch her, to feast his eyes on her. But being a realist, he knew that with Mika there, she would not even see him. He knew with a great sadness that he would never exist for her. He was beneath her notice. Well, that was not exactly true. Although he had never actually spoken to her, she had called him an "ignorant, unwashed oaf" when they were both eight years old, and she had once thrown a shoe at him for daring to allow her dinner to cool between the kitchens and her tower. He now regarded both of those instances fondly, holding their memory to him like precious gems.

Braddle was no less human than any other young man his age. He thought the Princess Linea to be the loveliest woman he had ever set eyes upon, but her temper was a royal pain. Were she his woman and not a princess, he would have set her straight with a good deal of loving and a swat on her shapely, if royal, posterior when she got out of line.

But since she was not his woman and was slated for Mika, he could but continue to lust silently after her and grieve. Still, the thought of Mika and the princess disturbed him more than he might have imagined, and he found himself lagging behind the rest of the group, not the least anxious to reach the long-sought meeting. And it was this reluctance that saved him.

Leaving the Great Hall, the party entered the oldest part of the castle, the part that had been built by the princess's great-great grandfather when Perrenland was still covered with massive trees and farmlands had yet to be wrested from the wilds. The first castle had not been a castle at all, but a small, easily defended building of thick planks and hand-hewn beams joined together with heavy iron spikes.

As time passed and the castle grew in size and stature, much of the old building was either replaced or incorporated into the newer structure, which was built of stone. But in some places, such as the corridors they were now traversing, the original wood floors remained, waxed and polished, gleaming handsomely in the soft light of the wall-mounted braziers.

"I just know that you'll get along famously with the princess," Seldom blathered nervously, hoping and praying that it would be so. "But you must remember . . ."

But Mika never found out what it was that he was to remember, for at that exact moment the floor collapsed beneath them, tumbling him and Seldom and the immense waddling figure of the prime minister into a dark abyss.

They fell for but a short distance and landed with a thump that left Mika dazed and unable to breath. He felt as though he were about to suffocate. As he struggled desperately for breath, he heard a low, menacing growl just as he realized that the cause of his discomfort was the prime minister, who had landed directly on top of him! The growl came again, this time sounding even closer and more menacing. Mika fumbled for his sword, but his hand was pinned beneath him. He cursed Travail with what little breath remained to him and tried to reach the magic gem, but it was out of reach as well, buried beneath the huge mass of Travail's flesh.

A ghastly shriek ripped through the darkness, and Mika recognized it as belonging to the little man, Seldom. He kept screaming something that sounded like "Womble! Womble! Womble!" which made absolutely no sense at all. But perhaps the words meant something to Travail, for at the first scream, the prime minister rolled off of Mika and began scrambling away, hollering for help at the top of his lungs. Relieved of the great burden, Mika took several deep breaths before staggering to his feet and looking around for the source of the danger, wondering what a Womble was.

They had fallen into a room, perhaps an old dungeon, the planks of the flooring scattered around them like matchsticks. The prime minister and Seldom were pressed flat against the wall, staring at something still hidden in the darkness on the far side of the room. Seldom was mumbling words under his breath, and the hair on the back of Mika's neck began to rise as he recognized the words to a spell that would bring down a rain of fireballs. Seldom was a magician! Why had he not realized it before?

Mika quickly removed himself from the spot where he was standing, not wishing to be incinerated along with the Womble. The prime minister was doing a curious thing. He was stripping himself of jewelry and tossing it into the darkness where the Womble was. Rings flew, followed by heavy chains of silver and platinum hung with medallions and orbs of state. His sword went, as well as his dagger, and even the buckles on his pants and shoes, all of them tossed into the darkness.

Mika strained forward, trying to see what was hidden in the shadows, but the light did not reach that far. Braddle called down to him, calling his name over and over, and Mika looked up to see his hand extending into the pit.

"Quick, sir. Grab my hand, or Womble will get you!" Braddle cried with urgency.

Mika wasted no more time in wondering about the curious Womble but leaped upward, grabbing Braddle's hand and pulling himself to safety.

Seldom was reaching the end of the spell. The fireballs would soon be filling the small area of the pit. Mika would never have used such a spell under the circumstances, for it was too likely that everyone in that small area would be hit by the blazing bombardment. Travail had run out of jewelry and was doing his best to force his immense body up the face of the steep walls, a feat that went against all the laws of the natural world.

A segment of the darkness detached itself from the darker shadows and began to glide forward. Travail screamed with real terror and reached upward toward Mika, begging him with stricken eyes to help him out of the pit. But it would have taken a far stronger man than Mika, or even Mika and Braddle together, to raise the prime minister out of the pit.

Mika still had no idea of the source of the danger. But it must have been extreme for the two men to react with such fear. He could not wait to discover its identity, nor could he allow the fireballs to fill the pit, for that would surely kill them as well. Grasping the magic gem, he uttered the words to a simple levitation spell and breathed a sigh of relief as the prime minister and his cohort rose up out of the pit just as a great arc of flame materialized and filled the pit with a rain of fire.

The heat of the fire drove them back from the edge of the pit. A heartbeat later, there was a terrible cry, like that of a being in horrible pain. Then there was a rush of hot air, the stench of burned fur, and a blur of motion as something huge leaped up out of the pit, knocked them down like so many kindling sticks, and rushed past them down the corridor.

"What was that?" asked Mika as he picked himself up off the floor for the second time.

"Womble," groaned Travail as he rolled over and pressed his forehead against the floor. "He almost got us that time. If you hadn't gotten us out when you did, Seldom, we'd have been cooked meat."

Mika opened his mouth to speak, to tell them that it had been his action, not Seldom's, then he closed it again, unwilling to reveal his abilities to these men whom he did not trust.

Seldom raised his head groggily, wondering if he had cast a levitation spell. He didn't remember doing so, but things had happened so quickly, and they were here, up out of the pit, so surely he must have done so.

Mika opened his mouth to speak, to ask again what a Womble was, but before he could do so a whirlwind of fury descended on them, and for a heartbeat, Mika thought that the mysterious Womble had returned.

"You hurt him! You tried to kill him! How could you do such a thing? He's the only thing left to me, and you want to kill him, too! What's he ever done to you? Nothing, that's what. You're just a bunch of bullies, and I hate you! All of you! Except him!" said the princess as she whirled around, eyes bright with tears, chin trembling and pointed straight at Braddle! And then she hurried away after Womble, leaving only her heartbroken sobs behind her.

TRAVAIL STAGGERED to his feet, moaning. Seldom clambered to his feet, holding his arm, which dripped blood from four long grooves extending from elbow to wrist. Mika himself felt as though he had been run over by a large boulder with claws, and he could spare no sympathy for the two men whom he suspected were not entirely innocent of the princess's charges. Whomever or whatever this Womble was, it certainly seemed to dislike them heartily!

"Are you all right, sir?" Braddle asked anxiously as he helped Mika to his feet and brushed him off. Braddle was more shaken than he cared to admit.

"Yes, I'm all right," Mika said slowly. "What was that thing, that Womble? Where did it come from? Does it live in the castle? The princess seemed to think . . ."

The three men exchanged worried glances but before any of them could reply, a young page hurried up, his features contorted with excitement. "Sirs! Sirs!" he cried, and so feverish was his tone that

Braddle, Mika, Travail, and Seldom forgot their encounter and gave the boy their full attention. "Sirs," cried the page, "word has just come! We've been attacked! Perrenland is at war!"

"War! What are you saying? Don't be absurd. Who would attack us? We have no enemies; no one would go to war with us!" blustered Travail, his small blue eyes growing large behind the thick lenses and his jowls shaking with emotion. "You must be mistaken!"

"No, sire, there's no mistake," said the page, all but wringing his hands with worry. "I heard the messenger clearly before he died. But there's another one, only he was too poorly to move another step. Come talk to him if you don't believe me, he'll tell you himself . . . sir!" the page said, coming to a faltering halt, realizing whom he was talking to in such an impertinent manner. "But it's true, sir, I promise. Please come."

So earnest was the boy's tone, so frightened his manner, that there was little doubt that he was telling the truth, or at least what he believed the truth to be.

All thought of the princess and the Womble vanished from Mika's mind, as well as his companions' minds. Women were one thing, but war was quite another.

"War," mumbled Travail as he waddled back toward the Great Hall, his tiny legs bearing the huge, pear-shaped body toward its destination. Seldom hop-skipped at his side, trying his best to keep up.

"Who would attack Perrenland?" Mika asked Braddle in a low tone as they followed in the prime minister's footsteps. "I didn't think Perrenland had any enemies. For that matter, I didn't think you even had an army."

"Tusmit," said Braddle in answer to the first question. "That's the only country it could be. They're always scheming to bring us grief in one way or another, but the mountains have always stopped them from doing any serious harm. And no, we don't really have much of an army. The mountains protect us from everyone save the Wolf Nomads, and our truce has lasted longer than my lifetime or that of my grandparents. Why would the nomads seek war with us?"

"Why, indeed," muttered Mika, unwilling to believe such a thing of his kinsmen, for war was not a nomad concept, requiring far too much cooperation and the subjection of many to the rule of the few, which was contrary to everything nomads believed in. No, Mika discarded the idea immediately. Whoever had attacked the peace-loving Perrenlandians, it could not be the Wolf Nomads.

His thoughts quickly shifted to Tusmit. Tusmit, rife with hostility and poverty. Tusmit, literally overrun by the military and bristling for a good fight. It had to be Tusmit.

But the mountains, Mika mused. The mountains would defeat any army, no matter how large. The sheer number of monsters that inhabited the lonely peaks and dark valleys would prevent such an occurrence. The lone traveler, riding fast and maintaining a low presence, stood a good chance of slipping through unnoticed. And a small, well-armed party might fight its way through. But a large, slow-moving army with pack horses and heavily loaded mules would attract the notice of every horrid entity that called the mountains home. The army and their animals would be torn to shreds and carried off to lairs and dens to be eaten at leisure. Mika did not think that even Tusmit was so foolish or so bloodthirsty as to attempt such a venture.

They entered the Great Hall and saw that all the tourney tables were empty, playing pieces and knucklebones abandoned and chairs overturned, giving testament to the players' hurried departure.

They had not gone far but were clustered at the far end of the hall nearest the great entrance doors. There was no longer any doubt that the page had spoken the truth, and even though Perrenland was not his country or even his concern, Mika found himself running alongside Braddle, as anxious to find out what had happened as if he had been born and raised in Krestible.

Travail's voice cleared the way for them. Making his way through the crowd, Mika remembered the gory, ravaged messenger, flayed and tortured by orcs, whose grim tidings had begun his wanderings so many years before. A shivery tingle ran down his spine, and he wondered if it were some awful premonition of danger to come.

Fortunately, the sight that greeted him was far less grisly than that last occasion. One messenger was dead, a sword thrust to the belly the cause of his death. The second was still alive but barely so, his lips and chin stained with blood. "A healer's been sent for," whispered someone in the crowd.

But Mika could see that the man was too far gone for help. He himself could use the magic gem on the man, but even as he fumbled for it in a half-hearted fashion, knowing that using it would reveal his powers, the man's head dropped to his chest and with a soft exhalation, he died. Mika let his hand rest on the magic stone, regarding the man sadly. The gem was powerful, but not so powerful that it could pull a man back from the great and final abyss.

"What did they say?" Travail asked heavily as he stared down at the two dead men, still dressed in the bright red and green of the Perrenlandian army. No one replied for several heartbeats. The sight of blood, of violent death, seemed to have shocked them senseless. Finally, one man, made of sterner stuff than his companions, turned to Travail and said, "War. They said it was war."

"I know that, fool!" Travail snapped impatiently. "What I don't know is *who* or *what* attacked them. Did they happen to say? Did they give any hint of their attacker? Any small clue to let us know what we might expect?"

Travail's sarcasm was wasted on the man. The man looked at the prime minister gravely and said, "Monsters. Monsters and men from Tusmit is all they said."

"They said that the stockade at Finches Point were overrun an' everyone else murdered an' ate upon the spot," added a serving maid who repeated the words with curious relish. "Stone giants, they said, an' harpies an' griffons an' all sorts of other abominations," she continued, obviously enjoying the sound of her own words and the attention she was getting.

Mika's blood ran cold at the mention of harpies, remembering his own encounter with a harpy high above a distant spur of those same mountains, and for a moment he felt faint. Stone giants? Griffons? What kind of horror was he getting himself into? He had been bored, it was true. He had wished for adventure. But a war with monsters was more than he had bargained for.

There was little more to be said in spite of all the commotion. Under the circumstances, especially considering the unfortunate encounter with the mysterious Womble, a meeting with the princess now seemed totally inappropriate. Excusing himself to a distraught Travail, who scarcely took note of his words, Mika and Braddle took their leave.

At the inn, Mika paced the floor back and forth, back and forth, wondering if it were time to leave. The vision of the princess haunted him still, but perhaps with the help of the gem, he could erase her from his mind. She was lovely, and he knew that he could love her happily and well, but not if he were dead, and somehow he had a terrible feeling about the coming conflict.

Back and forth he paced all day. A dozen times he lifted the gem and began the words that might erase all memory of the princess from his mind. But in the end, he was unable to complete the spell.

In the loneliness of the late night, she came to him again, the form he had come to love and hate. She plied his body with her ghostly wiles, spinning her magic about him, causing him to groan aloud and beg for release from the delicious torment. And he knew that he could not say the words that would banish her. For better or for worse, his destiny was linked with hers and that of Krestible.

He would do his best to protect her and the country as well, even unto death, may the Wolf Mother, protector of us all, prevent it. For when all was said and done, he was a Wolf Nomad to the core. Wolf Nomads were loyal and true and honest and steadfast and brave and good. It was an aspect of his nature that he had attempted to deny, for it was a fact that being loyal and brave and steadfast generally got one killed at an early age.

Mika had done his best to avoid danger, conflict, and—above all—death, for as long as he could remember, preferring to consort with the lonely wives while their husbands were off getting themselves killed. And dead was dead, even if it was honorable.

But now all of that seemed somehow shabby to him, and he almost regretted his past actions. Good men had gone to their Wolf Nomad deaths, and he was still alive, protected from almost all forms of danger by his incredible magic gem. He was safe and alive, but it was a sad and lonely life, one that failed to comfort him in this hour of dark introspection.

He missed Hornsbuck, his old Wolf Nomad companion with whom he had drunk and adventured, and most of all, he missed Tam, who had been at his side since the day he had stolen the tiny wolf pup from its den.

And in that moment of self-scrutiny, Mika learned something about himself. He knew that he was a scoundrel and had often failed to live up to the code of the Wolf Nomads. But while he had failed to die, he had fulfilled one of the Wolf Nomad tenets: He was a stalwart and loyal friend. He had risked danger and, yes, even death for Hornsbuck and TamTur. To them, he had been loyal and faithful and true, even by Wolf Nomad standards. The thought cheered him considerably.

But cheer was not enough. Mika felt the need to *do* something, to prove himself to the princess, to prove himself worthy of her love. And above all, he felt the need to find Tam.

He thought long and hard about what to do and how to go about doing it. Then it came to him in a flash of inspiration, and he smiled to himself, knowing that his plan was right.

He would scout out the situation in the mountains, find out exactly what was threatening Perrenland, and give them the information so that they might take steps to protect themselves. And he would find Tam at the same time so that they might be together again, as Wolf Nomad and bonded companion should be.

Mika looked out the window and noted the position of the moon above the horizon. There was still a goodly span of time before dawn—time enough to change himself into something that would be able to traverse the dangerous mountains and return in safety. Mika may have discovered his conscience, but in no way had it diminished his desire to remain alive.

MIKA REVIEWED HIS OPTIONS. He needed to be something that could pass through the air without notice, without attracting the attention of anyone, man or monster, so that he could gather his information quickly and easily and be gone before he was discovered.

He disliked the thought of changing himself into something weak and helpless, like a sparrow or a bat. While having the advantage of being swift and ordinary, and drawing little attention, they were without power and could easily be killed by hawk or arrow. Mika had no wish to find himself eaten by a hawk or plummeting to his death with an arrow in his breast.

In the end, he decided to turn himself into one of the monsters themselves. The mountains were the home of every horrid creature west of the Veng River. Surely one more would drawn no special interest. If there really were an army of monsters and men, it was the safest guise he could choose. Now the only problem was to decide what monster to be.

He quickly discarded harpies out of sheer dislike. He also had a problem picturing himself as a woman. Nor did he wish to be an eagle; there were too many things that were bigger still. By process of elimination, Mika finally decided upon a griffon.

Griffons were larger than the largest of men and far, far stronger. They possessed the head and upper body of an eagle and were endowed with the eagle's keen sight, powerful beak, and sensitive hearing. The wingspan of an adult griffon was greater than two tall men lying head to foot, and griffons were able to sustain flight over long distances.

Their front legs were those of an eagle and were armed with razor-sharp talons capable of killing a full-grown horse and carrying it away. The hindquarters of a griffon were those of a lion, so powerfully muscled that they could launch the beast into the air, as well as carry its great weight on the ground. Its tail was capable of delivering a heavy blow, although men were divided on whether or not it possessed a poisonous stinger. So few escaped an encounter with a griffon that there were none who could give accurate information.

Griffons were greatly feared by men and beast alike and were to be avoided at all cost. Fortunately, griffons inhabited the loneliest and most desolate of places, making their nests high atop the most remote mountain peaks, so they seldom ran afoul of humans. Mika thought that the Yatils could easily provide good nesting sites for griffons, but if his luck held, he would not encounter any of them on his journey.

In his book he found the spell that would transform

him into a griffon, and he studied it carefully. The elements of the spell required the feather of an eagle and a bit of lion fur. Fortunately, his pouch was well-equipped with all manner of herbs and strange spell-making ingredients, so he was able to find the bit of feather and fur that he needed.

Turning back to the book, he studied the words to the spell until he had committed them to memory. Although the gem increased his powers, all but ensuring him the ability to perform the spell correctly, it was still possible to make a mistake, which the gem would enhance even further. He had no desire to find himself transformed into some awful form from which he had no recourse. Magic, even with a magic gem, was dangerous, and he had learned to treat it with the greatest respect.

Aside from the spell itself, there were other considerations. He could take the gem with him on his journey, but to do so was to expose himself to the risk of losing it. It had happened before when he coupled with the harpy over those same Yatil Mountains, and he had regained it only through the most incredible of circumstances—it fell into the hands of his half-harpy daughter Chewppa, who sought him out and helped rescue him from the pillar where he was imprisoned. He did not wish to test his luck a second time. Chewppa and TamSen, Tam's half-wolf half-human son had wed, and it was extremely unlikely that they would come to his rescue should anything go awry.

But to leave the stone unguarded while he journeyed in his griffon form was to take another sort of risk. What if robbers broke into his room and stole the gem before he could return? The thought of being parted from the gem made him very uneasy. Back and forth he debated the problem, but finally, realizing that he was losing valuable time and that it was unlikely that his room would be burgled, he decided to leave the gem behind.

Once decided, he made his preparations swiftly. Placing a spell on the door so that it could not be opened, he removed his clothes and tossed them aside. Lastly, he removed the heavy chain necklace that held the magic gem, and he thoughtfully gazed down on it. Its brilliance was dimmed by the spell of concealment that he had placed on it, making it appear to be no more than a hunk of semi-worthless quartzite. But of course the spell had not dimmed its power.

After removing the eagle's feather and a bit of lion's fur from his vials, there was nothing left to do but say the words to the spell and get on with it. The sooner begun, the sooner done, as his mother used to say. Squaring his shoulders, Mika faced the window, held the magic gem in his fingers, and spoke the words to the spell.

A feeling of sickness filled his belly, and he grew dizzy. The room spun around him like a whirlpool, and he fell to his knees, still clenching the gem in his fingers. There was a loud roaring in his ears, and blackness engulfed him. Then it was done, over, and a great calm descended upon him, filling his breast with a sense of peacefulness and his belly with hunger. Suddenly, he was overcome with the desire for horseflesh, hot, steaming horseflesh and blood, boiling hot blood!

Totally taken aback, Mika blinked in surprise.

Horseflesh had never been high on his list of gourmet treats, but now it was all he could think about. Blinking again, he saw the room and the window before him as though he were peering through a looking glass. Everything seemed very close and very large, but strangest of all was the absence of color. Everything was either brown or black or gray or white. There was absolutely no color at all.

Mika looked down over the large protuberance that poked out in front of his face and saw that his chest and legs were covered with feathers and that his toes had become talons. It was done. He had become a griffon.

Without intending to do so, Mika opened his beak and uttered a cry of triumph that was somewhere between the screech of an eagle and the roar of a lion. It was both loud and intimidating. Mika felt himself shrink back in fear from the awful sound until he realized that it had come from his own throat. A feeling of power swept through him, and, opening his wings, he flapped them experimentally. They filled the small room, brushing the walls on each side. There was no room for him here, and time was passing swiftly. He had to leave if he were to accomplish his mission and return before dawn.

He picked the magic gem up in his beak and placed it carefully in the center of the bed. Then, walking awkwardly on his newly acquired limbs, hearing his talons clack on the hard tiles of the floor, he crossed to the window, stepped up to the sill, spread his wings wide, and leaped into the air.

The powerful wings beat against the air, carrying him higher and higher into the dark night sky. His legs, both front and rear, were drawn up tight against his body, and his tail trailed behind him, performing much the same function as the rudder on a boat.

At last Krestible was but a huddle of buildings in the darkness below him. Turning to point himself toward the mountains that he had left so gladly such a short time before, Mika began his dangerous mission.

Linea stood at her window in the tower and watched the large-winged figure rise into the sky, growing smaller and smaller until it vanished. Briefly, she wondered what it had been. It was too large to be a bird. She almost wished that it had been a dragon come to carry her away; it seemed to be the only way she was ever going to get out of this cursed tower.

The evening had been a disaster. Fuming still, she twisted a long lock of hair around her finger and looked around for something on which to vent her anger. But there was nothing to be seen. Anything that could be broken, she had thrown long ago, and besides, it didn't seem to accomplish anything. The crash was satisfying and made her feel better temporarily, but then, after the rage faded, the object was gone, broken to pieces, never to be rejoined. She had lost some of her favorite things that way and had recently come to believe that such behavior was both futile and childish. But she was angry, and she wished there was something she could do about it. There wasn't even anyone to yell at. It was hard to sustain an anger when you were all alone. The anger kept drifting into tears.

It seemed to Linea, with her newly acquired perspective, that she had a lot to cry about. Granted, she was spoiled. Was she to blame for that? It was the way she had been raised. But the long hours alone with none but her own company had allowed her to know herself better, and she didn't really like what she saw. It was no wonder that others did not like her. She wasn't so sure that she cared for herself. The only one who really liked her, loved her unconditionally, was Womble, and now even he was gone. She didn't know what had become of him. He seemed to have vanished.

At first, she had been angry with the prime minister and the little toady who was always at his side, as well as the dark stranger, for it had seemed at first glance that they had tried to kill Womble for no good reason.

But then she had found the square head of one of the old-fashioned spikes caught in the fur at the corner of Womble's mouth, and she realized what had really happened. Womble had taken her at her word and had eaten the spikes out of the old plank flooring, laying a trap for Travail, Seldom, and the dark stranger. She had scolded Womble, ignoring the look of pain in his silver eyes, and went back to the hall to apologize for her words. But the men were gone, and the entire castle was now in an uproar with talk of war.

Sitting in her tower window in the dead of night, Linea admitted to herself that she was afraid: afraid of war, afraid that she would never see her father or Womble or Braddle ever again, afraid of being left alone with her own thoughts, and most of all, afraid that she would live out the rest of her days alone and unloved. Putting her head down on her arms, she began to sob, crying for the life that might have been.

Travail, situated one level above her, heard Linea's sobs but had no time to be moved by them, for he had troubles enough of his own. He was staring at a map outstretched on a wide table, weighted down along the edges with books.

"What do you think, Travail?" murmured Seldom. "Do you think the messengers were right? Could we really be at war? There has not been a war in our lifetime, and we would be ill-prepared for such an event."

"Tusmit. It has to be Tusmit." Travail replied between gritted teeth as he stared at the map. "No one else would be crazy enough to declare war on Perrenland. Or maybe it's not so crazy after all. We assume that everyone wants peace as much as we do. It makes life so much easier. But there are always those who prefer war."

"But why Tusmit?" asked Seldom, pulling on the end of his bulbous nose. "How could they possibly cross the mountains, and what have they got to gain?"

"It cannot be anyone but Tusmit," replied Travail, his blue eyes growing animated behind his thick lenses. "I don't know how they plan to cross the mountains, that will be the hard part. Once they get here, we will present no problem. If it is to be war, then they no doubt will win."

"How can you say such a thing?" Seldom cried, staring at his friend in dismay. "Why, we are twice the size of Tusmit and have twice the number of men in our army and, and . . . "

"And we have grown soft and lax over the years, while Tusmit has grown strong and hard. More than half of our army is in name alone. The men remain at home with their crops and their families and show up only for parades and affairs of state. They are farmers for the most part and know nothing of warfare. I doubt that many of them would even know what to do with a sword or a pike."

"Surely you are putting too black a face on things, my friend. Go to bed; things will look better in the morning," Seldom said kindly.

"You don't understand, do you?" said Travail, turning his immense bulk to face the smaller man. "Things would be bleak enough if that were all we had to worry about, but that's not all. There's The Game."

"The Game," Seldom repeated with a blank look on his face. "What bearing does The Game have on war?"

"It has everything to do with war!" shouted Travail, doing his best to hold his temper. "Don't you understand? The Game has disrupted the very fiber of the country, the thread that holds it all together. Men have lost everything, their homes, their farms, their possessions."

"Yes, yes! I know that," Seldom cried impatiently. "I thought you wanted it that way. You certainly never complained before when the majority of those lands and possession wound up in your name."

"Of course not," said Travail. "It was all part of the plan, but I never imagined war. Don't you see? All of those men who lost their lands were part of the army, a big part of the army. Even the soldiers who were without land played, and lost. Now no one has anything at stake, and men without something to lose will be most reluctant to fight."

"But you planned to give them a place to live and work when you had won it all," said Seldom, slowly grasping what his friend was saying. "They would have had a roof over their heads and land to till. It just wouldn't have belonged to them any more."

"It does not appear that we will have the time to implement that part of the plan," said Travail. "If war has really come to Perrenland, all will be lost. Everything I have schemed for, for so long will be lost."

"Surely there is enough of an army left that we can present a strong defense. How large an army can Tusmit have?"

"Strong enough," said Travail. "That young pasha—what's his name? Marco whosits?—is a hothead, from what I hear. I had thought that his circle of advisors could keep him under control, especially since I pay them a goodly number of grushniks to do so. But it appears that I was wrong and that they have failed.

"No, Seldom, if it is war, then our army will not be enough. We will have to rely on your magic."

"But, Travail!" stammered Seldom. "Think of what you are saying. How can I, one magician alone, stand off an entire army? It is impossible; I cannot do it! You must send to Schwartzenbruin for reinforcements, for more magic-users. We need help. I cannot do it by myself!"

"You must, old friend, you must. If the Tusmites

are already over the mountains and at our border, help will not arrive in time, and our poor remnant of an army will not be enough. You had best go dust off your books and ready your potions, for you are all that stands between us and disaster."

In the silence that followed, the two men looked at each other and were afraid.

Braddle had no such fears; he had only anger and despair. Just when it seemed that he was making progress, this happened! War! Why did men have to be so bloodthirsty? Why couldn't they just lust after normal things like women and a new suit of clothes or a nice haunch and a beaker of ale? Why did they have to lust after whole countries?

Braddle had never been to war, and he had no desire to experience it, now or ever. War interrupted plans, and getting killed would certainly put an end to his. He hoped that Mika would not give up and take flight. Braddle would have to do his best to convince Mika that the war would not interfere with his plans. And if Mika were determined to leave, perhaps he could be persuaded to take Braddle with him. Braddle loved Krestible. He would miss some people, the kitchen wench Scylla for one, but he would rather miss them than be dead.

Then there was the matter of the princess. For some reason, she had begun to occupy his thoughts more and more. In fact, she was seldom out of his mind. What would happen to her if war came to Krestible? She might even be used as a hostage! No, he could not leave her alone. He would have to persuade Mika to stay.

The more he thought about it, the more agitated he became. Nor could he sleep. After tossing and turning on his bed until the covers were churned up like waves on a storm-tossed sea, he decided to go talk to Mika and see what direction the nomad's thoughts were taking. He grabbed up the magic charm and slipped it into his pocket as he left, vowing that he would convince Mika to remain, one way or another.

Much to his surprise, there was no answer to his knock, even though light still showed beneath the bottom of the door. Braddle tried the latch and found the door to be secured from within, yet Mika did not answer even the loudest of knocks.

Braddle became alarmed, wondering if some harm had come to Mika. Perhaps he had slipped and fallen and knocked his head on the edge of his bed and was at this moment lying on the floor near death! Other horrible scenarios popped unbidden into his mind. Fearing the worst, Braddle rushed down the steps two at a time, out of the building, and into the lean-to that had served as a handyman's quarters, when there had still been a handyman. Taking the longest ladder, he eased it out of the tumbledown shack and carried it to the building, positioning it beneath Mika's window, which stood open, glowing with the soft light of the lamp.

Braddle climbed the ladder, his breath rasping in his ears, his heart pounding with alarm over what dread sight he might find when he reached the open window. But when at last his fingers grasped the edge of the sill and he peered into the room, there was nothing to be seen. The room was empty.

At first Braddle was relieved; at least Mika was not

dead. But then he grew agitated, wondering if Mika had already departed without even saying a word. Looking around the sleeping town to make certain no one was watching, Braddle clambered over the edge of the sill and slipped into the room.

A thorough search of the room and its contents left him even more confused. None of Mika's things were missing. Everything was still there, even the worthless quartzite necklace that the man always wore, but of Mika himself there was no sign.

Even more puzzling, the door was firmly latched; Braddle could not open it even from the inside, and he could not discover what was holding it shut. Nor could Mika have left by way of the window, for it was a goodly distance above the ground, and a man would risk a broken leg if he jumped. Further, all of Mika's clothes and boots were accounted for. None were missing. If Mika had left the room, he had surely left it naked.

More disturbed than before his ascent, Braddle climbed back down and returned the ladder to its niche. He did not know what to do. He thought about alerting Mistress Bonnie, and perhaps the prime minister, but then he certainly would be banished back to the kitchens. No, he would tell no one. He would wait until morning and see if Mika returned. Then, and only then, would he make a decision, or in the words of his dear old dead mum, "When in doubt, don't do nothin'."

Womble was the most miserable of all. He had laid his plan so carefully, eating the spikes out of the planking, then hiding in wait in the dungeon below, hoping that they would fall into his trap. And it had worked perfectly! He had just consumed the last of the ancient spikes, some coated with a delicious layer of rust, when the prime minister, Seldom, and the dark stranger had crashed through the floor and landed on the hard stone tiles.

Womble had hoped to get all four of them, for he did not share the princess's liking for Braddle. If all of them were gone, she would have no one else to love except him, and then things would be the way they had been so long ago.

He had taken his time, stalking them, enjoying the thought of devouring them. The spikes had taken the edge off his hunger, so he could afford to swallow the trinkets they tossed him as though they were appetizers. In any case, he did not relish the thought of their soft flesh and brittle bones, but he would eat them out of love for the princess.

Then, just as he began his final stalk, fire had rained down from out of nowhere, singeing his fur and burning his skin. He had lashed out in pain and clawed one of them, but then they were gone, lifted up out of the pit by some means that Womble did not understand. He had followed them quickly, avoiding the worst of the flames and making his escape down the corridor. He sought out the princess and buried his head in her lap, crying for comfort.

And comfort him she had, stroking his great head and soothing his distress. She had even tried to dress his wounds by dabbing them with perfume. How was she to have known that it would sting so badly? Incensed at his injuries, she had gone off to do battle on his behalf and had returned to tell him of her words.

It was then, as she cradled his huge head between her tiny hands, that she discovered the nail-head clinging to his fur and had realized what he had done. It was then that she realized that it was he who had attacked first.

He had thought that she would be pleased. But she began to yell at him, and she even struck his sensitive nose with her tiny fists, yelling and screaming and cursing, saying horrible things to him that made his head ache and his heart hang heavy in his chest. She yelled even louder and shook her finger in his face, saying that he was not to hurt one tiny hair on Braddle's head or she would never ever love him again. Then she had stomped her foot and stormed out of the room, too angry to bear his company for another heartbeat.

Womble had crept out of the room and made his way through the castle without meeting another soul. Ignoring the huge outcry that echoed through the Great Hall, he slunk out of the scullery, without even pausing to empty silverware drawers or nibble on an iron skillet, and slipped into the soothing soup of the fetid moat. He had remained in its dark waters throughout that long day, surfacing only to breathe, the princess's words causing more pain than his wounds.

When night fell, Womble slithered from the moat and rolled in the soft, stinking mud at the edge, coating his wounds with a thick layer of protection. Then he crawled into his lair, a den beneath the gnarled roots of a great tree at the water's edge, and began to plot his revenge.

Braddle, she had said; it was Braddle he must

spare. All of her anger had been on account of him. But she had said nothing about the other three: Travail, Seldom, and the man named Mika, the one with the huge, appetizing chunk of metal hung around his neck. These he would kill if it was the last thing he did.

As he lay there in the dark, covered with stinking mud, lonely and hurting, Womble's thoughts turned toward home, the only place he had ever been happy. He remembered the warm, furry breast at which he had nursed, and the others of his sort with whom he had spent his time before the humans came and took him away on a whim.

More and more his thoughts returned to that happy time; more than ever he yearned to return. But Womble did not have the faintest idea where home was. Hated and feared as he was, he stood little chance of reaching it even if he were to try, for he knew that without the princess to protect him, he would be hunted and hounded until he was dead. Whimpering softly and cradling his hatred to him like a blanket, Womble drifted into sleep, dreaming of revenge.

MIKA FLEW INTO the night with long, powerful sweeps of his wings. The ground passed beneath him like a magic quilt, this pale square a field of golden wheat, that dark square plowed oerth not yet put to seed. Houses and barns passed beneath his gaze, and pigs and cows standing in the fields looked like children's playthings. Then it came to him, rich and heavy and enticing: the scent of horseflesh.

Mika fought to control himself, knowing in his rational human mind that he did not wish to eat a horse and that there were far more important things to be done. But the scent drew him like a magnet, literally demanding his descent. Almost against his will, he allowed himself to be drawn downward, the scent growing stronger and stronger with every beat of his pounding heart.

Below him, cocks began to flutter nervously, shifting on the branches of the trees. Hens squeezed their eyes tight and tucked their heads beneath their wings, not wishing to know what was to happen, not even if it meant their own death, as though by shutting their eyes, they shut out reality.

Mika landed heavily, unused to the peculiar anatomy of the griffon. But even this did not stop him. He stalked forward on his heavy hind legs, his taloned forelimbs held at the ready, moving toward the delicious scent.

A barn loomed before him, a sturdy building, better built than most, its doors held shut with an immense bar. Even that could not dissuade Mika the griffon from his intent. Ignoring the nearness of the house, which lay in the shadow of the barn, Mika tore at the bar with his talons. His curved claws caught in the wood and ripped long slivers from its edges, but the bar did not move.

Inside the barn, he sensed the quickening of nervous hearts and heard a clatter of hoofbeats as the captives within paced frantically within their stalls, sensing the nearness of danger.

Driven on by the closeness of his quarry, he dug his claws into the wood and pulled, shredding it still further, frustration and desire beating at him like hammers. Then his demon hand, now a demon claw, grasped the bar and wrenched it free, tearing loose the iron brackets as well. The doors swung open, and Mika was nearly overcome with the heady scent of horseflesh.

Ignoring the lowing cows and the hysterical hens, the griffon strode directly toward the corner stall, which held an immense white stallion, surely the farmer's pride.

The stallion reared up on its hind legs and uttered a strident cry. Its front legs slashed the air, beating a rapid tattoo before they struck the wooden floor. It rose up again, its head as high as that of the griffon. It flung back its head and bared its teeth, eyes gleaming black with a rage of its own, for the stallion was king of its own small domain. Its large, square teeth had ripped chunks out of opponent's necks, and its hooves had pounded lesser contenders into the oerth. Even though the thing that paced toward its stall was like nothing it had ever seen, the stallion was not afraid.

But the stallion's readiness to fight and its lack of fear did nothing to prepare it for what followed. Reaching the stall, Mika pushed through, rending the boards as though they were no more than paper. Reaching up with his demon talon, he seized the stallion by its muzzle, closing its nostrils, and twisting its head at the same time, forcing the stallion to its knees.

The stallion fought for air, fought to breathe, fought to hold its head erect. It lashed out with powerful hind legs as the griffon forced it to the ground.

The hooves caught the griffon on its own hindquarters and on the rib cage, but so great was his blood lust that Mika did not even notice the blows, and he continued his relentless assault. Then there was a terrible cracking sound and the stallion's neck swung limply in the griffon's grasp. Its hooves beat the air in a final futile pattern and then fell lifeless against the ground

The griffon struck then, ripping out the horse's throat, the overlapping edges of the beak scissoring cleanly through the flesh. The stink of blood filled the air, and only then did the griffon become aware of the raucous cries of the barn's other occupants as they screeched, lowed, and blatted out their fear. In the distance, the griffon heard the cries of human alarm as the household stirred in reply to the fearful summons.

A lesser creature would have fled, fearing the humans' wrath, but not the griffon. Having won its prize, it would not relinquish it without a fight. Seizing the immense stallion in beak and talons, it dragged the animal out of its stall and over to the entrance of the barn. There it saw lamps aglow in the windows of the house and men carrying torches streaming toward the barn, shouting directions and curses. Some were carrying weapons.

That part of his brain which remained human, that part which was still Mika, screamed inwardly, raging at the portion that was the griffon, urging it to fly, demanding that it forfeit its prize if it wished to live.

But the blood lust was still on the griffon, blanketing its mind and washing its senses in red.

Ignoring the advancing men, the griffon seized the carcass of the horse firmly in its talons and then opened its wings. It began to beat them against the air in an attempt to rise, to leave the petty humans far behind.

Mika raged, a captive within the body he had assumed, a prisoner to his own machinations. He was divided. The men were coming closer. He could see their faces clearly, the hatred and fury glinting in their eyes, arms drawn back, muscles corded, ready to throw the spears that would rip into his body and end his life. Their bows were stretched taut, their arrows tipped with cruel steel pointed at his heart. He cringed, crying aloud, unheard, wishing that he could undo the spell and remove himself from this horrid danger. But, it was too late. The men were too close. The griffon would never succeed in getting itself and its great burden off the ground safely.

Mika screamed aloud, as did the griffon. The terrible screech brought the men to a halt as they stumbled and placed their hands over their ears, forgetting their weapons as well as their intent. Few of them had ever even seen a griffon, let alone approached one, and as the horrible cry burst over them, they were overcome with fear.

The griffon, knowing well the effect of its cry, used the moment to run forward, its great hind legs pushing against the oerth, adding to its momentum. The huge wings beat up and down, forcing the air beneath them, defying gravity, and then, almost impossibly, still holding the stallion in its talons, it rose above the men, above the roof of the house, and into the cold, dark sky.

Mika's mind, released from the terrible fear, shrieked aloud, giving voice to his wild joy at finding himself still alive. The griffon gave vent to Mika's feelings as well as its own, loosing a cold, hard, imperious screech of victory at the men below who had thought to thwart him. One man, braver than the rest, perhaps the owner of the unlucky stallion, drew back his arm and threw his spear at the griffon. But the weapon struck the dead flesh of the stallion instead and waggled there like an insult, until killer and victim alike were swallowed by the dark night and vanished from sight.

The griffon consumed the horse on the mound of a

tall, barren hill, where it was able to see in all directions. Never had a meal satisfied it more. Beak and talons ripped into the flesh of the stallion, reducing the beautiful creature to a pile of scraps, hooves, mane, tail, and other inedible bits. Then the griffon rose, heavily, once more into the night sky.

The blood thirst satisfied for the time, Mika turned his attention to the job at hand and studied the land below. He was approaching the foothills of the mountains, and as yet he had seen no sign of an army, human or otherwise. He was somewhat south of Gemmy's farm, in an area that appeared to be only lightly settled.

An army would find little in the way of provisions, and with a sinking heart, Mika realized that an army would choose the most populated area for its advance so that it might acquire food and supplies as it marched. Gemmy and Hilda's farm lay along the only road exiting the mountains. It was along this road that the army would come.

Mika could not erase the image of Gemmy and Hilda's innocent, tow-headed children from his mind. He hoped that no harm had come to them. And since it was the logical direction, he corrected his course and flew on.

He began to see evidence of the army's passage, burned buildings, charred posts, and tumbled rafters lifting their blackened remnants skyward as though to pray for a mercy that had not been granted. The pitiful, unwanted contents of the houses had been strewn along the ground and trampled into the oerth by careless feet.

Of the former owners, there was no sign. Nor was there sign of any living thing—not one person, not one animal. Not one bird croaked a sleepy sigh into the night, and it was this total absence of sound that caused Mika the greatest sense of dread.

It was obvious that an army had indeed passed. The destruction was too overwhelming to suppose any other cause. But Mika was disturbed by the lack of people. Where were the inhabitants? Not even his keen eyesight showed him any sign of survivors.

The farther he flew, the greater the swath of destruction. The houses and barns, or what little remained of them, grew in number, yet still there was no sign of life, human or otherwise.

Then he was above the land that had once held Gemmy and Hilda's small holdings. The house, the barn, and even the haystacks had been reduced to cinders. There was nothing left. Mika's heart beat hard in the griffon breast, and even his lust for blood was stilled at the loss of those precious lives.

Cold eyes glinting brightly, Mika set himself toward the mountains, determined to seek out the source of the bringers of death. He could not believe that an army of men had caused such destruction, but, until now, he had not been willing to believe the tale of an army of monsters. Now he could scarcely believe otherwise.

He did not give thought to the fact that the army would now be behind him, advancing on the city of Krestible. It would take them a while before they reached that great walled city, and by then, surely the alarm would have spread. No, it was his intent to search out the mountains and see the extent of the horror. Were they all advancing on the city, or was there a rear guard still to follow? This was a question that would have to be answered before proper plans could be laid. The griffon flew on.

The cold downdraft sweeping off the mountains forced the griffon to climb higher and higher into the cold thin air, and it was only as Mika rode the thermals that crested the peaks that he realized that dawn was breaking in the east. As yet it was but a thin sliver of light at the edge of the world, but even as he watched, it turned from silver to pink and caused the cruel peaks to glow.

Fear struck his human heart, for he had thought to be back before dawn. He did not know how long the spell would hold. The difficulty of different spells determined the length of their existence, and with the magic gem aiding his own small magical abilities, it was even more difficult to gauge. Mika examined his body and found no sense of weakness, no wavering edges that would indicate a dissipation of the spell.

Briefly, he toyed with the idea of returning to the city and venturing forth again that night with the spell newly placed. But what assurance did he have that the lure of horseflesh would not prove irresistible to him a second time and perhaps this time the farmer's spear would find its mark. No, he had best take his chances here and now, learn what he had to learn, and be gone.

He wondered how he would return to Krestible in broad daylight. Surely the sight of a full-grown griffon landing in the middle of the city would cause great alarm, but Mika shoved the thought from his mind. He would deal with the problems at hand first, then address the problems that were to follow. Now his only concern was the finding of the monster army, if it existed, and returning to Krestible with some useful knowledge. For Gemmy and Hilda's sake, it would be done.

THE ROUGH PATH that Mika had ridden through the mountains on his journey to Perrenland had been well-trod, that much was evident. Boulders had been tossed aside from the edge of the path, and smaller rocks had been crushed until the narrow route was enlarged to twice its normal size. Men and horses alone would not account for the size of such a passage, and Mika gave credence to the report of an army of monsters.

He saw the first monsters even as he was wondering how such an alliance had been formed. Directly below him was a large, heavily armed contingent of goblins. Even at that distance he could see the squat figures clearly, see the ugly faces with their bulging foreheads, broad noses, and gaping mouths as they stared up at him with small intelligence in their dull eyes. Disliking sunlight, they appeared to be building crude stone shelters to protect them from the coming light of day.

Mika swept over the goblins, taking count of their

numbers, shocked at the evidence of their existence, noting the lean wolves that prowled their perimeters and the bugbears standing guard.

The bugbears, undisturbed by daylight, were patrolling alongside the mangy wolves, their lusterless brown fur merging with the gray dawn. Taller than their smaller goblin cousins, the bugbears shambled about with their peculiar, awkward gait, which Mika knew was deceptive, for when bugbears wished to move quickly, they could do so.

Several of them looked upward, clenching their massive wood clubs set with iron spikes, and more than a few waved swords in his direction, challenging the griffon to descend. But the rising dawn glinted off the ragtag bits of armor they wore, and after satisfying himself with screaming out his hatred of them, Mika flew on.

Now he was beginning to grow alarmed. Goblins never moved in daylight if they could avoid it. Seldom were there more than forty in any one band. He had seen at least five hundred. Each band usually had its own chief, and although goblins were tribal, they were highly independent and would not have agreed to joining such a group effort without some strong incentive.

Mika could not even imagine what such an inducement would be. But he could easily imagine the death and destruction that would be unleashed on the hapless human population once the goblins and bugbears reached the lowlands. He could but hope that the goblins and bugbears were the worst of it.

But his hopes were soon dashed. Morning advanced quickly, and in the rising light he saw large bands of gnolls, taller than the tallest men, their greenish gray pelts covered with bits of clothing and armor taken from human victims. They lifted their hyenalike muzzles to the sky as he drifted overhead. They yipped and howled, snapping and gnashing their pointed teeth as though imagining the taste of his flesh. Gnolls were no lovers of light either, and the size of their numbers swarming down the mountainside astounded him. Greater and greater grew his alarm.

Before the sun reached its zenith, he had traversed more than half the width of the mountains and seen ample evidence of gnolls, goblins, orcs, ogres, wolves, zombies, trolls, kobolds, hobgoblins, and more than a few stone giants, all traveling in the same direction: toward Perrenland.

The majority of the horrible creatures were dwellers of darkness and had taken shelter from the rising sun, leaving only their animal companions—jackals, hyenas, and wolves—to protect them while they slept.

Their numbers were beyond counting. Scattered among the monsters were battalions of men, dressed in the drab gray livery of Tusmit. These battalions were armed to the teeth and had not stopped with the onset of daylight, continuing the march that would lead them, inevitably, to Krestible. The humans showed no sign of fear at his presence, and a few waved their weapons in a gesture of comradeship.

Accompanying the army of humans, towering over them, more than twice their height, was a battalion of stone giants, their gray skin and rock-colored clothing making them almost impossible to see even when in motion. Each was accompanied by a cave bear, sometimes several. Stone giants were not hostile to men, but they had little or no reason to align themselves with humans; Mika could not understand what possible incentive would cause them to do so.

His mind numbed by all that he had seen, Mika swung wide, circling, ready to return, to report on what he had observed, when suddenly a loud scream rent the cold mountain air, jarring his thoughts back to the present. There above him in the cold currents was a large figure with widespread wings, talons outstretched, claws curled in readiness for attack. With a sinking heart, Mika recognized a mirror image of himself, an enormous male griffon.

While the assortment of men and monsters below could see him plainly, they would have no reason to suspect that he was an enemy. But griffons were extremely territorial, and this one would know that he did not belong. There would be no chance for communication, no hope for an explanation, and no quarter given: it would be a fight to the death.

As the griffon descended, Mika saw that it was even larger than he was. Its talons seemed longer and sharper, and its body a third again as heavy. Briefly he wondered why he had not made himself bigger. Then the time for thinking was over as the griffon plummeted down upon him, talons outstretched, seeking out Mika's heart, going for the quick kill.

Mika tilted his tail, catching the downdraft, and he swung to the left, barely avoiding the griffon's attack. He brought up his own talons at the last heartbeat, gouging, grasping the griffon's flesh, coming away with a fistful of feathers.

The griffon screamed, an echo of Mika's earlier cry of rage as he descended upon the stallion. The cry was equally frightening, only now he was the quarry.

Mika would have escaped had he been able. But his griffon persona had no desire to leave and preferred to fight on to the death. Mika's human heart had no wish to perish in these cold mountains, shredded by talon and beak. Yet there was no quarter given. The griffon followed his every move and would seem to be content with nothing less than his death. Mika had no choice, if he were to live, but to fight back.

Talons grappled for flesh, and beaks clashed against each other and then held. Locked in the deadly embrace, talons and claws reached out and found the other's flesh. Blood flowed, dripping from the cold sky, as they tumbled over and over, wings flailing, beating each other as often as the air.

Aided by the additional strength of his demon talon, Mika was able to hold his own, gripping the griffon's throat and squeezing hard in an attempt to cut off its supply of air, much as he had done to the stallion. But the griffon was wilier than the stallion and had lived to attain such great size by intelligence rather than luck. Twisting abruptly, the enemy griffon folded its wings and took them into a steep dive, plummeting toward the cruel peaks below.

Mika, terrified that they would slam into the mountainside, released his hold on the griffon's throat and fought to open his wings, which had been pinned to his body by the rate of their descent. But the griffon had folded its own wings over Mika's, preventing them from opening, and had clung to Mika like a leech.

Hanging upside down beneath his attacker, Mika was presented with a hideous vision of angry gold eyes, and an open beak, which slashed at him, drawing blood at every opportunity. And still the claws and talons were locked in his flesh.

Mika began to panic as their downward speed increased. Suddenly he realized that the griffon had no intention of opening his wings and breaking their speed. It intended to drive them to the ground with Mika pinned beneath, knowing that the impact would kill him.

The ground was rising rapidly; Mika felt hysteria and fear battling within him. He did not want to die, splattered against some rock, and have his flesh picked from his bones by the sharp beak. He did not want to die at all.

Given greater strength by the thought of death, he drove his demon talon up into the slashing beak, between the sharp edges, ignoring the pain as the honed beak sliced through his skin. Extending his own claws, he ripped into the soft flesh that lined the griffon's throat.

He felt the air shiver around him and took it to be a sign of the griffon's distress. Farther and farther he forced his talons, the entire length of his feathered limb engulfed by the inner warmth of the enemy's body. Opening his talons, he reached out and slashed within the narrow confines, cutting, slicing, ripping whatever came within his grasp.

He felt the griffon's body stiffen, and then there was a deluge of hot warmth that saturated his talons, and he knew that he had severed some vital lifesource. The griffon threw back its head, pulling against Mika's arm, trying desperately to free itself. Mika seized the opportunity to lock his own beak onto the griffon's throat, slashing from without as well as within.

Then a sense of dizziness all but overwhelmed him as they plunged oerthward in a tight spin. The bloodlust faded from his mind as he realized his danger. He tried to pull his forelimb from the griffon's throat, tried to open his wings to break their fall. But the griffon had enveloped Mika's body with his own wings, and even though there was no sense of life in the larger body, still they were locked together, and Mika could not free himself from the griffon's deadly embrace.

Down and down they plunged, ever faster. Glimpses of sharp rocky outcroppings flashed by, cruel spears of stone that could pierce flesh and shatter bones. And then there was a greater sense of whirling, of dizziness, and a terrible final impact that brought a bright explosion of pain. Then there was only merciful darkness.

BRADDLE WAS WORRIED. Morning had come and gone, and still there was no sign of Mika. He told Mistress Bonnie that Mika had risen early and was hurrying off to tend to an errand of a personal nature. She had not questioned his explanation.

He paced in his room until well after the midday bells had rung, checking surreptitiously every few moments to see if Mika had returned. By mid-afternoon he was frantic. He could not conceal Mika's absence forever. What was he to do? Unable to think of anything else, or anyone to turn to for advice, he hurried off to the marketplace, hoping against hope that the old wizard would be there.

Braddle was not the only one in an uproar, for it seemed that the entire town was in the grip of a great panic. Merchants, freemen, and servants alike rushed about without any great sense of purpose or accomplishment. Normally Braddle would have found the spectacle amusing and stopped to watch, but now he was too consumed with worries of his own to spare any time or notice for anyone else.

Weapons dealers seemed to be doing a landslide business, as were the food merchants and armorers. The marketplace was a bedlam of screaming sellers and buyers, as each group vied for the attention and services of the other.

The only things that seemed undisturbed by the rumors of war were The Game tenders. Acting much as they always did, the three little men trotted to the meeting board at the center of the market square and posted what Braddle assumed were the newest changes in The Game.

For a brief moment he wondered if the threat of war would disturb the nightly tourney of games at the castle. Surely it would. Then, for an even shorter time, Braddle allowed himself to wonder where The Game tenders came from and how they knew what changes to make in The Game. Who told them, and where did they come from? These were questions he could not answer, and then, all but consumed by his own worries, he hurried on.

Much to his amazement, Braddle found the old man in the same corner where he had seen him last, and for half a heartbeat, it almost seemed as though the oldster had been waiting for him to arrive. But such a thing was unlikely, and Braddle dismissed it from his mind. Once again it seemed as though no one else could see the old man, and Braddle caught the eel seller staring at him with distrust when first he began to talk.

"Strange things are happening, sir," he began in a respectful tone, hoping to conceal his growing sense of alarm. "As you have probably heard from others, there is talk of war, garbled accounts of men and monsters descending on Perrenland." The old man watched Braddle closely, his thin arms folded across his narrow chest, and said nothing.

"Then too, my lord, Mika has disappeared, and I don't know where he has gone or why." He related the mysterious turn of events that had led to his discovery of Mika's absence.

"Describe the items he left behind," said the old man. "Tell me everything that you found." And Braddle did so in great detail.

"Hmm, this necklace . . . you say it is naught but a chunk of worthless quartzite, but the man was never seen without it. Could you bring it to me? I would like to see it," the old man said in a casual tone.

Braddle's senses sent out an alarm. "I do not think that I should remove anything from the room, sir. How would I explain its absence if my lord returns? He would dismiss me instantly, and I would be banished to the kitchens again. What is your interest in this necklace? It is an ugly thing and quite ordinary; surely it cannot be of any value or importance."

"Tut! Do not worry yourself, boy," said the old wizard. "I merely thought . . . well, never you mind. It sounds as though you have enough to think about. Tell me again about the locked door."

Once again Braddle related all there was to tell about the locked room. But even though the old man nodded as Braddle spoke, Braddle could tell that his mind was elsewhere.

"There is no need for you to do anything at all," the old one said at last. "Merely tell the woman that your lord wishes time to himself. Take his meals from her at the kitchen and deliver them to his door. Who is to know if you consume them yourself? It merely means that you will eat better than usual.

"Nor do I think that Mika will be summoned to the castle this night, for the prime minister will have his hands full with decisions and preparations for the coming battle."

"And will there be such a battle, sir?" Braddle asked fearfully. "Will Krestible be attacked? What will become of us?"

"Whatever will be, will be," the wizard said with a shrug. "Nothing you or I say or do will influence the outcome. But as long as you have the magic heart, no great harm will befall you."

"But what about the others?" asked Braddle, thinking of Scylla but seeing the princess's face in his mind's eye, which disturbed him greatly. Who was he to dream of the princess? And why had her face been creeping into his dreams so much of late? She did not even know that he existed.

"The magic heart can protect only those within its immediate vicinity, a distance of no more than ten paces in any direction. And to implement it, you must hold the heart in your hand and say these words. Listen carefully."

Braddle repeated the words after the wizard and muttered them over and over until he had committed them to memory and he felt certain that he would not forget them.

"But my lord, Mika . . ." Braddle continued. "Where has he gone so mysteriously, creeping off in the middle of the night like a thief? What if he doesn't come back? What should I do?"

"You're a clever lad," said the old man. "I'm sure you'll think of something." And then he closed his eyes, leaned back against the sun-warmed bricks, and would say no more.

Braddle turned away and caught the eel seller staring at him suspiciously from under her bushy eyebrows. "Why be you talkin' to yourself in corners?" she asked. "Be you daft?"

"Why, no . . . that is, I don't think so," said Braddle. "I came to see my friend here. You can ask him yourself if you don't believe me." He turned and gestured toward the old man. But there was nothing to be seen except for the corner where two walls met. There was no old man, nor was there any way that he could have slipped past unseen.

Braddle stared at the corner with an open mouth, then turned back to try to explain to the eel seller. But she brandished her basket at him and glowered, and he knew that nothing he could say would allay her suspicions. Lowering his eyes and clutching the magic heart in his fist, he brushed past the hostile woman and hurried back to the inn as fast as his frightened legs would carry him.

Later that afternoon, Braddle slipped into Mika's room by means of the ladder, just in case Mika had somehow returned. Being in the room among Mika's possessions made him feel less alarmed, for, typical of one who had seldom owned more than the clothes on his back, Braddle could not imagine that anyone would choose to leave so much behind.

Mika was still gone; of that there was no doubt. Forgetting himself for the moment, Braddle sat on the edge of Mika's bed and tried to imagine what had happened to him. He picked up the necklace in an absent-minded fashion and stared at it, trying to believe that it was valuable, that it was something other than a worthless trinket in an overlarge setting. But the thing was just too ordinary, too ugly to believe that it was anything other than what it appeared to be.

Still holding the necklace in one hand, he took out the magic heart and held it in the other. At least, he hoped it was a magic heart. Braddle shook his head and sighed. He was a fool, that's what he was. The eel seller was probably right; he was daft. Maybe he had finally taken leave of his senses. Why did he aspire to heights that were not within his reach? Why was he not content to spend the rest of his days in the kitchen like any other normal person? Why did he yearn to be different?

But in spite of his self-deprecations, Braddle could not stop yearning for things to be different than they were. Whatever the reason, he *was* different, and he would go on trying to rise above the kitchen, or die in the attempt.

All of a sudden, all of his years of drudgery seemed to rise up and loom before him as though mocking him, and everything inside him shrank back in protest. "No!" he cried. "I will not do it. I will not return to the kitchens. I wish they would burn to the ground this very day! I *will* be somebody, somebody important. Why, maybe I'll marry the princess and be the king! I could if I wanted to, see if I don't!"

For no reason that he could have given name to, perhaps only the need to make it seem more important, more real to himself, he held the heart more tightly, and the necklace as well, and uttered the words that he had memorized.

No sooner had he spoken the last word than a curious humming seemed to spread from his fingertips, through his hands, down to his elbows, up to his shoulders, and then to radiate through every last crevice of his body, filling him with a warm glow that was like nothing he had ever experienced.

When the last tingle had faded away, Braddle blinked and then moved carefully, as though fearful that something else would happen if he made the slightest move. He was stricken with awe and could not begin to understand what had occurred. He looked down at the magic heart, and for the first time he really dared to believe that it was all that the old man had pronounced it to be.

But the tingle had spread from *both* hands. Was it possible . . . ? Braddle looked at the necklace. But no matter how closely he inspected it, he could see nothing more than a worthless piece of quartzite mounted in a heavy silver setting. No, he was just imagining things again. If anything, it had been the heart.

But something had happened, and if the truth were told, he actually felt different, too. He felt more confident, taller, less worried than he had been before, and somehow he knew that the old man had been right; whatever happened to Krestible, he, Braddle, would be all right.

Perhaps Mika would return; perhaps he would not. That would have to be dealt with when the time came. Now Braddle's efforts had to be aimed at seeing that everything stayed on an even keel, that no one had cause to suspect that Mika was gone. Everything had to appear normal.

His first task was a question of what to send the princess, for Mika had sent her a present daily. An omission would surely be noticed, especially by the princess.

Braddle thought about what he would like if he were a princess. She seemed to lack for nothing, although of late she had begun to look a bit frazzled around the edges, not at all her usual dazzling self. Perhaps, unlikely as it seemed, she was grieving for her father. What she needed was someone who could be a friend, not just a maid who would say "yes, milady" to everything the princess said. Someone real, someone like Scylla. Yes, that was it. If he could do so, he would send Scylla up out of the kitchens and have her be the princess's friend.

Indulging his fit of nonsense still further, Braddle smiled and requested that Scylla be relieved of her kitchen duties and sent forthwith to be the princess's friend. Then he repeated the magic words, wondering if they were anything but a bit of gibberish. Once more the warm tingle spread from his head to his toes, leaving Braddle even more shaken and disturbed than he had been the first time it happened. Dropping the necklace on the bed, he jumped back in alarm, almost afraid to believe the truth, then pocketing the magic heart, he turned and fled from the room.

Later that afternoon, after the fear and bewilderment had worn away, Braddle took himself off to the castle to report that his lordship was suffering from a slight touch of Nomad's Revenge and would not be in any condition to visit the castle that night. But he had no chance to explain, for when he arrived he found the castle engulfed in clouds of heavy smoke and its inhabitants running around the grounds like headless chickens.

"What's happened?" he asked, grabbing a scullery maid who was in the process of filling a bucket of water from the moat.

"Not now, Braddle, there's no time," she snapped, wrenching out of his grasp. "The kitchens be on fire. They be burning to the ground. Lemme go!"

"The kitchen on fire? Burning to the ground?" he whispered to himself, watching dazedly as she hurried back to the castle with her bucket full of murky water. And indeed it appeared to be so; hurrying around the back of the castle, he viewed the damage for himself. Stones had been blackened and cracked by flames, windows had exploded, and the cook sat wheezing on the trampled grass, clutching his favorite, long-handled, copper spoon to his aproned stomach. His whiskers were burned to stubble.

"What happened? Tell me what's happened!" Braddle demanded of an exhausted page who sat on an overturned bucket, his soot-stained hands dragging on the ground.

"I dunno," the lad said, his voice heavy with exhaustion. "It just sprung up out of nowhere. One moment, everything were fine; the next, everything were in flames. We never had no chance of putting it out. It just spread too fast. Water didn't seem to do it no harm. It's gone, the whole kitchen be burned to the ground."

"And Scylla?" Braddle asked. "Is Scylla all right?"

"She be fine," said the page. "No one be hurt. But right afore the fire started, the prime minister sent for Scylla without no warning and told her she was to be first lady in waiting to the princess. He wants them to be friends like. Ain't she the lucky one."

Braddle wasn't even surprised. Somehow, after learning of the fire, he had known that it would be so.

"It were that Womble, if you ask me," said the page, although no had asked him. "Somehow he started the fire, I'll wager. Mark my words, it were him."

But Braddle made no answer. Clutching the magic heart tightly inside his pocket, he wandered away, his mind buzzing with all manner of thoughts. And on his face, he wore a very broad smile.

TRAVAIL WAS NOT LAUGHING, and there was no evidence of a smile, broad or otherwise, on Seldom's whiskered face. Nothing was going right. First Travail had had that irritating thought that refused to go away: Something buzzing around in the back of his brain that whispered softly at first, and then as he did nothing, spoke up loudly, demanding that he cease his vindictive actions against the princess, insisting that he even go so far as to give her a maid. Not just any maid, but one who might actually be her friend.

It was an outrageous thought, and he could not imagine where it had come from. He did his utmost to ignore it. But the voice refused to be ignored, yammering endlessly inside his head, and in the end he gave in to it so that he might get on with the more important business of defending the city.

Travail was very irritated with himself for thinking such soft thoughts and feared that he would lose face by giving in to a mere woman. Perhaps it was a sign that he was growing old, weakening. Now, that was a disturbing thought!

Nor had he any idea where such a person could be found, someone who might actually like the princess and want to be her friend. As he was pondering the problem, wondering which of his minions' wives he could force into service, the midday meal was brought to him by a kitchen wench. She was a handsome girl, with thick ropes of honey-blond hair looped around her head. Bright blue eyes, full of mischief and intelligence, twinkled beneath delicately arched brows, and a tiny, turned-up nose perched atop a wide mouth made for laughter.

Travail stared at the girl, wondering why he had never noticed her before. She was a fine-looking wench, and if he were half, or even a quarter, of the man he used to be, he would be interested in her himself. Travail sat up straighter and rubbed his eyes, wondering where *that* thought had come from. He hadn't thought of a woman in, why, he couldn't even remember the last time! He had given up such thoughts long ago, for they led nowhere except to trouble and took a man's mind off the really important things, like politics and lunch. And besides, women had never really liked him very much, so he had not found them difficult to give up.

"What's your name, girl?" he demanded rudely.

"Scylla," she replied nervously, wondering what she had done to make the prime minister notice her. Her heart sank, and she wondered if there were anything worse than the kitchen, with its long hours and heavy, back-breaking labor.

"How would you like to be the princess's maid? No, forget that. You *will* be the princess's maid from now on. Don't even bother going back to the kitchen. And girl," he said, fixing her with a sharp look, greatly magnified by his thick lenses, "see to it that you like her. You are to be her friend, as well as her maid."

Scylla gave him a startled look and a deep curtsy. As she scurried away, alarm bells began to ring. Travail leaped to his feet, his lunch forgotten for a second time—surely an unprecedented event. A cold fist grabbed at his entrails as he wondered if the invaders had arrived already. But breathless servants soon appeared with word of the kitchen fire, and after sparing a thought for the future of his meals, Travail sat himself down to consume his now-cold lunch and to worry about the advancing army.

"We must know," he commanded Seldom between great, greedy mouthfuls, "what is happening. We must know whether there is an army advancing on us or not, and if so, how many battalions."

"I must guard my strength," said Seldom, tugging on his beard nervously. "Far-seeing requires much energy that might be better used later. Have you sent to Schwartzenbruin for reinforcements?"

"Of course," snapped Travail as he gnawed at the haunch, his thick lips shining with grease. "But energy or no, we must know what we are faced with. Stop complaining and get on with it. What kind of a wizard are you, anyhow?"

"An old and tired one," Seldom replied in a quiet tone. "One who should be resting his old bones in front of a warm fire surrounded by a gaggle of admiring grandchildren whom I shall never have because I have spent all of my days serving you, and to what purpose? None of your schemes have ever paid off, and we are as poor as the day we began together, so many long years ago."

"Poor! You call this poor?" shouted Travail, waving his bone at the rich trappings in the room. His face grew flushed, and his jowls quivered with indignation.

"Wealth has little or nothing to do with the riches I speak of," said Seldom, not the least disturbed by Travail's outburst. "There are things in this world that are far more important than money, old friend. I am only sorry that it has taken me this long to find that out, and it seems that you have not learned the lesson yet. Never mind, it serves no purpose to speak of it now at this late date. I will do your bidding. But if the price falls due at a later time, do not say that I did not warn you."

Travail was more than a little disturbed at his old friend's words. If what Seldom said was true, then it would seem that they had plotted and schemed together their whole lives, only to reach this position of power and wealth and realize that it was but a hollow victory.

The memory of Scylla's smile flashed into his mind, and suddenly Travail felt old and empty inside. The haunch fell from his fingers unnoticed, even though meat still clung to the bone.

"Never mind," he blustered, doing his best to conceal his distress. "Do your stuff, and tell me what we are up against."

"As you wish," said Seldom. Seating himself in a cross-legged position on the floor, he closed his eyes and placed his fingertips against his graying temples.

Travail watched him closely, waiting for the moment when his friend would suddenly appear diminished. There, it was happening; Seldom was still there—his body at least, unmoving on the floor—but something was different. He appeared thinner, somehow, and translucent as well, almost as though he could be seen through if a candle were placed behind his body. The spirit, the soul, whatever one chose to call it, had left its oerthly body.

Travail never ceased to wonder at this feat, and a shiver passed through his enormous frame. He was torn between envy and fear, and he was glad that it was his job to think and command rather than to take leave of his body.

Seldom was wrong. Travail did recognize what a great effort it took, and the risk involved. He wondered that a man would do such a thing at the behest of another. Friendship was a strange thing indeed, and in a rare moment of introspection, Travail wondered if he would be as good a friend to Seldom should the need arise.

Travail shook himself and placed a hand on his brow, wondering if he were feverish. All these strange thoughts: first, feeling sorry for the princess and doing something nice for her when he didn't have to; then looking at the kitchen wench and feeling his manhood stir as it had not done these many years; then wondering at the quality of his friendship. Those were not normal thoughts or actions for him. He would have to guard himself in the future, or men might begin to think him soft.

Seating himself opposite Seldom's silent figure, Travail made himself comfortable and began the long wait for the wizard to emerge from his trance.

The spirit—the invisible, intelligent entity that was Seldom—sped over the plains, seeking out the enemy. It did not reflect on the body it had left behind, nor on the man whom it had left to guard its oerthly dwelling place. What would be, would be. There was danger in being a spirit out of body, but those were the risks one took when one became a wizard. Such decisions had been made long ago, and in fact they no longer worried Seldom. He had told the truth: He was old and tired and empty. If life ceased, he would have little regret in leaving it, and there would be no one other than Travail to mourn his passing.

But there was still important work to be done. He had been charged with the task of searching out the enemy, and many lives depended on his information. He would do the task and do it well, even though he suspected that Travail was somehow to blame for the invasion. How or why he did not know, but Travail's ambition knew no bounds.

Seldom wished to distance himself from Travail's schemes, but now was not the time; knowledge of the size and placement of the army was needed if the citizens of Krestible were to protect themselves. His spirit sped onward, viewing the first of the enemy making camp for the night, still two day's journey from the city. At first, they appeared to be no more than any normal army: men wearing the colors of Tusmit, mules, horses, weapons, doing the things an army did at the end of a long day's march.

There was some evidence of booty, and several oxen were roasting over spits throughout the camp, oxen that Seldom did not doubt had been taken from innocent farmers. But such were the vicissitudes of war. No doubt the farmers were hiding in safety in the hills and would count themselves lucky to lose no more than a few cattle.

Then his eyes were drawn to a second camp, separated from the first by a distance of more than a league. There was something odd about the second camp, although Seldom could not readily distinguish what it was. Seldom's spirit drew closer and then stopped short in absolute horror as it took in the grisly sight below.

They were not men, that second army; they were monsters, as had been reported. The rumors were true. The farmers were not hiding in the hills; they were being consumed by the ravenous horde of monsters gathered below. Limbs had been torn from bodies, heads wrenched from necks, bodies ripped asunder. The flesh of men, women, children, and even tiny babes was being gnashed, ripped, chewed, and gnawed upon by a host of monsters so hideous that the invisible spirit could scarcely bear to watch.

Zombies squabbled with trolls over bits and pieces of corpses. Giant weasels snarled and slavered over their hapless prey. Hawk-headed, lion-bodied hieraco-sphinxes stripped flesh from bones with sharp-edged beaks. Giant rats sat on fat haunches and gnawed on skulls heaped at their feet, while bugbears ripped apart whole bodies and sucked the marrow from the bones. Immense carrion crawlers and tiny rot grubs wriggled among the gathering of monsters, dining on the bloody bits that littered the ground, and stirges, small, pointy-beaked birdthings, clustered on the ground sucking up pools of blood. A pack of displacer beasts, large pantherlike creatures with two jagged-edged tentacles on their backs, gorged on a dismembered mound of flesh. War dogs wearing leather armor and collars studded with metal spikes tolerated each other's company while feasting on human body parts that defied description.

That was not the end of it. Sickened and numbed by all that he had seen, Seldom forced his mind to continue on, viewing the entire desecration.

Ettins, two-headed evil giants more than twice a man's height, each head viewing its neighbors with suspicion, were gobbling down their gruesome rewards. Gnolls and ghouls rubbed shoulders with orcs and hobgoblins, while harpies and winged, taloned hippogriffs squabbled among themselves over the division of the spoils.

Every hideous monster Seldom had ever heard of in his long life was represented in the gruesome gathering, and he could no longer allow himself the luxury of believing that Perrenland could win out, for against such an army there could be no victory.

He could not understand how or why such a thing had come to happen. What had occurred to throw such a disparity of creatures into an alliance with men, and how might it be put asunder? That was the question.

Sickened by all that he had seen, Seldom was about to retreat when he chanced to glimpse a smaller group located halfway between the armies of men and monsters. Curious, he drifted closer.

It was a group of old men, graybeards like himself for the most part, who glanced about them nervously, almost overcome with fear, as any normal being should be in such close proximity to an army of monsters. Only one among them exhibited no fear; he was a younger man, and by his gold armor and his arrogant manner, Seldom identified him as Marcovitti, the young Pasha of Tusmit.

The pasha was standing, his posture both bold and arrogant as he spoke to one who towered above him, more than twice his size. This being was easier to identify despite his lack of national colors or gold armor. Its gray-brown skin and cavernous skull, its long stone club, and the snarling cave bear at its side proclaimed it a stone giant, surely the very largest that Seldom had ever seen. Its eyes were the color of silver, and there was a look of intelligence in their bright glint. Never did it take its eyes off the young pasha, and Seldom drifted closer in order to hear what was being said.

". . . I have kept my word," said the pasha. "Is there not ample feasting for the creatures and more than enough for those night dwellers who follow in our wake? Have I not kept my word?"

"Aye," said the stone giant in a slow and measured tone, like that of two boulders being ground against each other. "And well it is that you have done so, for such as these would not take betrayal lightly."

"Then what is the problem?" the pasha asked, trying hard to hide the irritation in his voice.

"How much longer do you think to continue?" asked the stone giant. "We are two day's journey from the mountains, and the beasts grow restive so far from the safety of their lairs. They are not mine to command; I can but suggest. It is difficult to hold them so far from their lairs. I cannot promise that they will obey. Best it is if we turn back now."

For a heartbeat, hope leaped in Seldom's spirit. Then it was crushed as Marcovitti stamped on the ground with a golden boot and cried, "No! We are still two day's journey from Krestible. If we stop now, nothing will be gained. We must go on. I command you to do so!"

Seldom held his invisible breath, watching as the stone giant regarded the foolish young ruler, obviously toying with the idea of crushing him with one blow of his massive club.

The gaggle of advisors twittered anxiously, like a flock of sparrows under the shadow of a hawk, and tugged at their young ruler's robe, urging him to flee. But he held fast, glaring up at the massive stone man before him, demanding his way in a manner no less stubborn than that of Princess Linea.

The stone giant gazed downward at the petulant pasha, and then it merely shrugged, eyes shining with cold amusement. Without another word, it turned and strode leisurely toward its own lines, the cave bear trailing behind it like a large, tame dog.

Seldom did not pause to hear what would be said between the young ruler and his advisors. It did not matter. The pasha had commanded the stone giant and would not listen to the advice of mere mortals, no matter how sound. The man was a fool. A dangerous fool.

Whispering a reminder to himself to apologize to Travail, whom it seemed he had wronged by his suspicions, Seldom hurried on, anxious to discover what manner of night dwellers followed behind, anxious to learn the whole truth.

His journey took him over ground that was torn and bloodied and burned, mute testimony to the violence that had passed. He saw no signs of life—no human survivors, nor animals either. Not even the smallest cricket chirped in the fields, announcing the advance of night. Even the trees and bushes had been beaten to the ground, crushed beneath the feet of the dual armies.

Then he saw them, the night dwellers: the goblins and the horny-headed kobolds, the orcs with their sneering pig faces, and the wolves and the jackals, hurrying to overtake the front lines and visit death on the hapless countryside beyond.

Steeling himself, Seldom sped on, hoping that he had seen the last of their numbers.

Then he saw them, the man and the griffon lying below him, twisted and tangled together in death. As he recognized the features of the man, hope and fear leaped inside him, and he descended, praying to his gods that he was not too late.

MOVEMENT: PAIN. QUIET: PEACE. Those were his options. Mika did not have a difficult time choosing between them. But something would not allow him to remain in that blissful state of quietude, free of pain. Something kept urging him to open his eyes, to sit up, to live again . . . to suffer. Mika squinched his eyes shut tighter. But it did no good; the thing kept at him, and now he had lost it, that peaceful, dark, quiet place. It had been like floating on a dark sea in silence. Now there was pain, agony everywhere, licking at his body and limbs like fire. He had returned to the land of the living.

Mika opened his eyes, wishing to see who it was who hated him so much that he would drag him back to endure this awful pain. But there was no one and nothing to be seen. He closed his eyes again, hoping that it had been a dream, hoping that he could recapture the dark comfort, the absence of pain.

"Don't do that! You must get up!" the voice cried impatiently. "Get up, I tell you!"

"Go away," said Mika, his eyelids still tightly compressed. "I don't want to get up. I don't think I can, and it hurts too much to try. Go away!"

"Not without you!" replied the voice, which had begun to sound familiar. "You must get up; I need you. All of Krestible needs you if it is to survive. And if you stay here much longer, something will undoubtedly come along and eat you, too."

Mika's eyes blinked open at that thought.

He groaned and tried to rise, but could not. He glanced over and saw that the other griffon had taken the full impact of the fall. It lay on its back, wings akimbo, and piercing up through its chest, narrowly missing his own body, was a spire of black rock still wet with the griffon's blood.

Mika's arm was still imprisoned, wedged in the griffon's jaws as far as the elbow, and the griffon's hindquarters were draped across Mika's midsection. By the gods, the nomad was cold. The wind swept down from the icy peaks above and covered him with a layer of goose bumps.

"I can't get up," he said in a small voice. "I'm trapped."

"You shall have to get up, for I cannot help you," said the invisible voice. "You will have to do it yourself."

"Who are you, and what do you want of me?" asked Mika. "Look at the spot I've gotten myself into. Why do you think I can do anything to help anyone else when I can't even help myself?"

"You must be some sort of magic-user," said the mysterious voice, "and we need every magic-user we can lay our hands on. You didn't get here by taking a leisurely stroll, that's for certain. Nor can you convince me that yon beast decided to kill itself while your hand just happened to be stuffed down its throat. No, you're a magic-user, all right, and we need you.

"You saw all those monsters, didn't you? Well, they've consumed every single man, woman, child, and beast on the western edge of Perrenland, and unless you help, they'll march across Perrenland like a plague of locusts devouring everything in their path. Come on, man, get up and stop wasting time."

Nothing the voice had said convinced Mika that he wanted to face those monsters. In fact, it worked quite the opposite effect. But unless he got up, he could not even flee in the opposite direction. Groaning, he began to push at the carcass. It was heavy, far heavier than one might imagine. Yet now that he had begun, he could scarcely bear being in such close proximity to the awful thing. He relaxed his fist, and his arm slid free from the griffon's throat. At last, using the strength of his demon hand, Mika rolled the dead griffon aside and freed himself from the deadly embrace.

Rising to his feet, Mika was aware of three things: He hurt all over, he was naked, and he was very, very cold. He tried to wrap his arms around his body to protect himself from the cold, but it did little good. His teeth began to chatter.

"What's that?" asked the voice in a curious tone.

Mika looked down and saw nothing unusual other than his hand. "It's a demon hand," he snarled. "That all right with you?"

"Certainly," replied the invisible entity. "Interesting. Might I suggest that you clothe yourself? That's no way to go around in these mountains. It's quite cold at these elevations."

"Can't get dressed, can't do anything," Mika said through chattering teeth. "Don't have my spell book. Need other things to make it happen. Who are you? Can't you help? I was warm until you found me. This is all your fault."

"Scarcely," the voice said mildly. "You got into this mess without my help. You'll have to get out of it by yourself, too. I wouldn't be much help to you anyway. I'm out of my body at the moment, as you can plainly see, and I can't do much of anything except drift around and view things."

"Who are you, anyhow?" demanded Mika. "I recognize the voice, I just can't place the face."

"Seldom, the court magician, although you might also remember me an' my mule, Melba."

"You!" screamed Mika, forgetting the cold and his various injuries as he screamed into the empty air. "You're the reason I'm here in the first place! You sent that cursed succubus to visit me, didn't you?"

"Well, yes," the voice said modestly. "I thought it was rather a nice touch—didn't you?"

"If you call living in endless frustration a 'nice touch,' then sure, it was great. You can't imagine what it feels like, lying there, being ravished by a woman night after night, whether you feel like it or not. You can't even reach out and touch her. There's nothing there, just air!

"And that's not the worst of it. During the day, her face, it's always there in front of me, like a smudge that can't be erased. It's here right now. Look, can't you see it?" He swiped at the air with his demon hand. Then he turned toward the invisible voice with a heaving breast and asked in a thoughtful manner, "Why, why did you do it? I wasn't doing you any harm. Why me?"

"Because we needed a prince," said the voice. "We needed a prince to marry the princess. It was the only way that we could be sure of controlling the country—if we controlled the prince."

"But I'm not a prince," yelled Mika. "I'm nobody, just plain old Mika of the Wolf Nomads! No prince, got that? No king! Not even a courtier!"

"But, but you said that you were a prince . . . " said the voice, faltering for the first time.

"A prince of a fellow, that's me," Mika said sardonically, bowing low despite his many aches, and drawing some small measure of comfort from the voice's distress. "Also, prince of fools!"

"Well, this really is a mess, then," muttered the voice. "Even if we can somehow defeat that army, which is doubtful, we're still stuck without a prince."

"And in the meantime, I'll have frozen to death. What am I supposed to do? How do I get myself out of here?" asked Mika.

"What? . . . oh, uh, I'm afraid I don't know," said the voice, and it seemed to Mika that it had spoken from a greater distance than before.

"Wait! Wait! You're not going, are you?" Mika cried in alarm.

"Well, yes . . . in a manner of speaking," said the voice.

"Wait! Stop! Don't leave me alone like this! I'll be killed!"

"Most likely," said the voice, drifting away still further.

"Wait! Come back! If you help me now, I'll help you do something about those monsters!"

"What? How could *you* do anything?" asked the voice, drifting a little closer.

"I have a magic item that will help me do anything I want," cried Mika, all too aware of the fact that he was revealing his deepest, most closely held secret. "I'll help you if you help me."

"I'm not sure that I can," said the voice. "But it's worth a try; what do you want me to do?"

"Go back to Krestible, go into my room at the inn, and bring back the necklace that you will find on my bed."

"I . . . cannot . . . do . . . anything . . . in . . . this . . . form," the voice repeated slowly, as though Mika were stupid or hard of hearing.

"Then . . . use . . . another . . . form," said Mika. "Your old man with a mule was quite convincing. Just do whatever is necessary and bring me my gem if you want me to help you get rid of that army."

"Swear that you will do it," said the voice in a stern tone. "No tricks if I bring you the necklace?"

"No tricks," said Mika with a deep sigh.

"All right, I'll do it," said the voice after a long pause. "Stay right here so I can find you again."

"Where else would I go?" muttered Mika. And then the invisible entity was gone, and Mika was alone once more.

Slowly, he became aware that he was truly alone. The face was gone. It no longer hovered in the air before him. And it was night, black as black could be. But the succubus did not make her nightly visit, and somehow Mika knew that when he next saw the princess, if ever again, it would be as other men viewed her, fully clothed and acting like a princess rather than a strumpet. Even though he was relieved that she was gone, his relief was tinged with sadness.

He was also freezing cold. Somehow, it had seemed less cold while he had someone to talk to. Now the icy wind swept down from the peaks above, and he could feel his limbs stiffening.

He tried jumping up and down and swinging his arms about, but the ground was rough and sharp and cut the soles of his feet. Nor was it particularly level, and after one such jump he was barely able to keep from tumbling down the slope.

Cold as it was, Mika knew that it would get much colder long before the sun rose again. He did not know how long it would take the old magic-user to return. It seemed quite possible that he would freeze to death before Seldom came back. Fire! He had to make a fire. But there was no firewood! There was nothing but cold, hard stone. And the dead griffon. An idea began to form in his mind. A gruesome idea, but if it saved his life . . .

Mika searched the ground and found a flat stone with a smooth surface. Holding it in his left hand, he used it to sharpen, to file, to shape the longest talon on his demon finger. Normally, he tried to keep the talons filed down, for they tended to cut through the fabric of his gloves, but of late he had forgotten, and they grew devilishly fast.

When the nail had reached the degree of sharpness

that he sought, Mika lifted the dead griffon off the spire of rock, though not without some difficulty, and set to work.

It was easy at first, for the skin beneath the feathers was thin and easy to cut. But then he reached the lower half of the creature, the dense, furry pelt of the lion, and the task grew more difficult. Always, there was the intense cold to spur him on.

At last the grisly job was done. The skin of the griffon was separated from the flesh. Grimacing with distaste, Mika stepped into the furry pelt; feeling his feet settle where paws had once been, he slipped the feathered forelegs over his arms and lowered the feathered headdress onto his head.

The rock had pierced the griffon between its wings and exited along the line of the chest where Mika had cut. There was no way to remove the wings without tearing the fragile skin and making the hole still larger, so Mika allowed them to remain. One small hole was preferable to a large hole. As it was, the cutting line allowed cold air to creep inside the strange garment, and Mika gathered it about him, feeling like a man at a masquerade ball in a too-big costume. Tall as he was in his human state, the griffon had been half again his human height, and the feathered, furry pelt hung from his shoulders in droopy folds.

Mika pushed the headdress back from his face and looked down at himself. He had cut the beak away so that his face was left free, but everywhere else, he was covered with fur and feathers. But without life to animate the body, the wings hung heavily on his back and threw off his balance each time he moved. Then, too, the tail hung limp and straight behind him, dragging along the ground. But he was warmer than he had been. It did not matter if he looked foolish. There was no one to see him, and he was no longer in danger of freezing to death.

Next, Mika turned his attention to altering the garment in some way so that he did not have to hold it up in order to move. Searching the area, he came upon a nest, perhaps that of the griffon itself, for it was very large indeed. Climbing into the nest, he found that it contained lengths of tough vine interspersed with twigs and branches. These he removed from the nest. Using his talon as an awl, he poked holes in the hide on each side of the cut-line, then laced it up and tied it at the throat. Next, he gathered up the excess at his waist and tied it in several places. He stood up and walked about, noting with satisfaction that the hide fit much better and was almost as comfortable as a normal suit of clothes. Feeling safer for having something around him, even if it were only twigs and branches, Mika climbed back into the nest to wait for the wizard's return.

A short time later, he heard the stealthy approach of footsteps, then the sound of crunching, teeth gnashing against flesh and bone. The goosebumps returned in a flash. What could it be? A mountain lion, a cave bear, or one of the horrible night-dwelling creatures following on the heels of the monster army? Whatever it was, Mika did not want to be its dessert.

The smell of blood that clung to the griffon hide would draw the monster like a magnet. There was no way to avoid it. Like it or not, Mika would have to attack first and, with the element of surprise on his side, hope to drive the beast away.

Mika groped around the nest until he found a long, heavy leg bone, all that remained of some hapless animal. It had a good, solid feel to it. Mika gripped it tightly and felt the talons on the demon hand twitch of their own volition in anticipation of the violence to come. Silently, he crept out of the nest and slipped down the slope.

The sound of crunching grew louder, all but covering the sounds of his advance. Now he could see it, the thing. It was a huge, shaggy animal of some sort, a hyena perhaps, or a wolf. He could not be certain, for the moon had not yet risen and the mountain was as dark as could be.

Raising the club above his head, Mika advanced on the creature from the rear. When he was within striking range, he yelled a Wolf Nomad cry of attack and swung the club with all his might, aiming for the creature's head. He was within a hair of his target when it turned to look at him. Tilted eyes stared at him, then the animal stepped to one side as the club descended and crashed harmlessly into the ground.

"Tam!" cried Mika, his jaw dropping and his eyes opening wide with surprise. "Tam, how did you get here?" Dropping the bone club, Mika hurried to the wolf's side and attempted to throw his arms around him.

"Tam! Don't you recognize me? Look, it's me, Mika!" Struggling to undo the knot, he tugged the griffon headdress away from his face. But still the wolf crouched at his feet, teeth barred, growls pouring from between its lips, and for a heartbeat Mika wondered if he were mistaken, if he had gotten the wrong wolf, merely thinking it was Tam. But no, surely not, this wolf was lean and somewhat haggard-looking, but it was Tam. Of that there was no doubt.

"Tam, stop that nonsense. Why are you growling at me? Look, it's me. See, demon hand. Me, Mika, your lifelong pal, remember?"

But the wolf continued to growl, looking up at Mika with slanted eyes that glinted coldly in the dim light.

"All right, so you're mad at me. I can understand that, I got off the track for a while. But you just can't imagine what it was like, that succubus visiting me every night. I felt as though she were draining me of all the blood in my body. I kept seeing her face in front of me all day long. I hated her, but I couldn't do without her. I needed her. I thought that once I had won her, actually had her, the madness would leave.

"Then there was all that business with The Game. I got interested in spite of myself. No wonder the whole country is coming apart. No wonder they can't defend themselves against these monsters. They can't think of anything except that game!

"I'd like to say that I got over it through strength of will, but I didn't. I won't lie to you; it wasn't my doing. It was the court magician. He was responsible for the spell in the first place, and now he's dropped it, saving his strength for what's to come, I suppose. I'm back to normal again. Tam, I know that I was wrong, and I'm sorry that I turned you into a dog. You'll forgive me, won't you?"

The truth of Mika's words must have reached the angry wolf, for he stopped growling and sat upright, regarding the strangely clothed man in a thoughtful manner with his head tilted to one side. Questions and doubts were obvious in his guarded expression.

"I guess you're wondering about the outfit," said Mika, and he began filling in the missing parts of the story, telling Tam all that had gone on in his absence, ending up with why he was wearing the griffon suit. By the end of his story, Tam was curled quietly at his feet, the wolf's muzzle resting on his paws.

"So now I wait here and hope that the wizard comes back with the necklace. I'll be in a fine fix if he decides to keep it for himself. Pray that he needs me enough to bring it back. But what am I to do, Tam? Even with the magic gem, I don't see what I can do to stop that army of horrors. Did you see them? There's every monster ever imagined in those ranks, hundreds and thousands of them. What good is one magic gem against all of them? I'd be a fool to think that I could stop them. They'd tear me apart in two shakes of a hippogriff's tail and eat the gem for lunch. No, our only chance is to get the gem back and then get out of here as fast as we can."

Tam raised his head and looked at Mika. In the rising moonlight, Mika read contempt on the face of his oldest friend.

"Oh, come on, Tam. Don't look at me like that," cried Mika. "Think of all those monsters. What chance would I have against them? Think of how nice it would be to be lying in the sun on Fairwind Isle, the soft sea breezes coming in off the Azure Sea. Why, I can almost taste the berries and hear the native music. And I hear the lady wolves are especially beautiful in that part of the hemisphere."

For a moment, Mika thought he saw a glimmer of

interest in Tam's eyes. But then Tam curled his lip in an obvious sneer of disdain and turned away from Mika, presenting him with a view of his tail and hind-quarters.

"I suppose you'd be happier if we went back there and saved the princess and Mistress Bonnie and Braddle and all the rest of Krestible, even if it means putting ourselves in horrible danger," Mika said slowly. Tam turned around and gazed at Mika, his amber eyes seeing into the heart of his old comrade, seeing more than the outward guise of the buffoon.

"You know, I really hate it when you go all right-eous on me," Mika complained. "Sometimes I don't think you care about me at all." Then Tam moved closer and rested his chin on Mika's foot in an obvi-ous gesture of friendship.

"All right," Mika said glumly. "You win, but I honestly don't know why I'm listening to you. You'll be sorry when we're both dead."

At a loss for further words, Mika began to hum. At first it was a formless tune, having no direction, no words. Then, almost without thought, the hum shaped itself into a tune, a tune that bore distinct overtones of violence and mayhem. Before long, the tune had turned into song, a song of the Wolf Nomads, a war song in celebration of death and honor.

"Onward Wolf Nomads riding into war,
With a flag of honor no one can ignore.
Flee, you yellow cowards; take to your heels and go.
Wolf Nomads can't be beaten; this you surely know.

"Onward valiant nomads, slash and jab and hack.

Villains vanish forthwith, never to come back.
Peace and honor reigneth under nomad rule.
Death and strife are banished. Warfare is our tool.

"Unfurl the nomad banners, wave the wolf tails high.
Heads thrown back for howling, ride across the sky.
Once more right has triumphed, honor truly won;
Nomad comrades, persevere until the job is done."

Wolves had begun to howl soon after Mika began the stirring song. After the first chorus, the hills and peaks around him rang with the howling of wolves and the shrill cries of coyotes, jackals, and hyenas, and the yipping of foxes. They continued their cacophony long after Mika had ceased. A look passed between wolf and man, and unconsciously their posture straightened and their heads were held high.

"You know, Tam," Mika said reflectively, "all this nobility and goodness will be the death of me yet."

Together, man and wolf stared into the night and waited for what was to come.

Chapter 22

MEANWHILE, BACK at the castle, Braddle had grown braver as twilight fell. He sat there in the darkening room holding the magic heart in one hand and the necklace in the other, wondering what would happen if Mika never returned. The magic necklace would be his, and with the magic heart to enhance its power, he might dare to wish for anything; the world would be his. For a heartbeat he dared to think of himself as a free and independent man, belonging to no one other than himself, calling no man master. It was a thought that left him breathless.

He stared down at the fine clothes lying in crumpled mounds all around the room. He fingered the gossamer-fine silks and the brightly colored hose and gloves, the finely woven woolen doublet and knee pants, and wondered what it would be like to dress in something other than rough commonweave.

Almost without thinking, now that the daring thought had actually been imagined, Braddle rose and shed his drab brown commonweave, replacing it with one of Mika's best. The long, silk body stockings were worn all of one piece and fitted to the neck with arms and body as soft as yarpick fluff. This garment was tinted a rich salmon color and caused Braddle's russet hair to glow like a jewel. The jerkin and knee pants were a creamy, buttery color of suede and fitted his long, lean body like a glove. A wide-brimmed slouch hat with a long, curved feather and tall suede knee-boots completed the outfit. Braddle admired himself in the mirror and thought that it would not have looked better on Mika himself.

The two magic items gave him a sense of power, and looking deep into his own eyes in the mirror, Braddle wondered how far he might dare to go. He wanted to show someone, to talk, to think out loud, to share the moment of his independence with someone else. But he could think of no one. His parents were dead, his brothers and sisters gone to serve as apprentices, he knew not where. The only one he could think of who would be the least interested was Scylla, and she was with the princess.

"Well, why not?" he said aloud, still looking at himself in the mirror. "As our old mum used to say, 'In for a pig, in for a pound.' " Slipping the necklace around his throat, he held both items, said, "Take me to Scylla," uttered the magic words, and zip, he was gone.

There was a moment of dizziness and then nausea. Braddle fought to remain upright and waved his arms to dispel the thick cloud of white smoke that enveloped him. Suddenly he became conscious of shrill, high-pitched, feminine cries of alarm. Stepping out of the smoke, he found himself face-to-face with Scylla and the princess, both of whom were coughing and sneezing and rushing about the room, screaming as though they were being attacked by a hive of bees.

"Stop!" he cried. "There's nothing to be afraid of." But Scylla and the princess had been badly frightened, and it would take more than a few words to calm them. Stepping forward, Braddle put out his arms and stepped directly into their path, thinking to catch hold of Scylla. But Scylla stopped to cough, and it was the princess who dashed headlong into his arms. Without thinking, Braddle closed his arms around her. Linea looked up through teary eyes and saw Braddle, his bright brown eyes twinkling down at her, his mouth curved in a tender smile of yearning. She felt his arms around her, and it was as though she had been waiting for him all her life and now he was there.

They stood there for a time, staring at each other, unspeaking. Yet volumes were said; everything that was important was exchanged and in that moment, their souls were joined.

"Scylla, stop, look, it's . . . " said the princess, suddenly at a loss.

"Braddle," he said, smiling down at her.

And Scylla, who had once thought that she and Braddle . . . Scylla saw at a glance what had happened and accepted it with happiness, for she had become fond of the poor, unhappy princess and knew that Braddle would never cause Linea grief.

Meanwhile, one level above them, Seldom had returned to his body. An eyelid twitched, shoulder stretched, toes wiggled. Then, just as he was indulging in a long, pleasant yawn, Travail grabbed his shoulder and shook him back and forth till his head all but fell from his shoulders.

"Well?" he roared. "Did you see them? Did you see the army? Are they really there? How many of them are there? Tell me what you saw!"

"Stop that!" Seldom said sharply. "Stop shaking me, or I won't tell you anything!"

"Tell me! Tell me!" Travail cried, wringing his hands and jiggling from one foot to the other. "It's been agony waiting for you to return."

"What's coming will be even worse," said Seldom. He related all that he had seen, carefully enumerating the numbers of both men and monsters.

"Oh, what shall we do?" wailed Travail. "I never thought it would come to this. Run away, we must all run away! They can't hurt you if they can't find you!"

Seldom looked at his old friend, the person to whom his fate had been bound for so many years, and sighed. Travail had always seemed so strong, destined for high places. They had plotted and schemed together and brought about the downfall of the hetman, ascending to power in his absence. Now it had come to this. Never had he thought that Travail would fall apart in a time of crisis, but it appeared to be so. It wasn't fair, Seldom thought with a sigh. Why couldn't things work out the way they were supposed to?

"All is not lost," he said quietly. "There might be a way to save the day."

"What? What? Tell me!" said Travail, turning to him swiftly.

"I found that fellow, the one we were going to marry off to the princess. I found him halfway through the Yatils stuck on top of a mountain peak."

"Whatever was he doing on a mountain peak, and how did he get there?" asked Travail. "That's an odd place for him to be. He'll never win the princess that way."

"Don't be a fool, Travail," snapped Seldom. "There's no way for him to have gotten there on his own two feet, especially since we just saw him hours earlier."

"Then how . . . ?"

"He's a magic-user," Seldom said with exasperation. "And he's no prince, either. We've been duped."

"Why, I'll have him flogged, thrown in the dungeon, fed to Womble for impersonating a prince!" yelled Travail, his face growing bright red.

"You'll do no such thing," said Seldom, wondering if Travail had lost all of his ability to reason. What had become of the once sharp mind that had planned their takeover of the throne? "We need this man if we are to save the city. You would do well to remember that."

"How so? How can he help us?" asked Travail.

"Magic is the only thing that will save Krestible. We have neither the manpower nor the weaponry to fight Tusmit, much less the monsters. Magic is the only thing that will save us. Therefore, we need every magic-user we can lay our hands on. This fellow is one, so we need him, too."

"Well then, where is he?" demanded Travail. "Have him here at once!"

"He could not return with me," said Seldom, not wishing to explain everything to Travail. "I will do what is necessary, and he will be here in time. In the meantime, you should scour the city and see how many others you can find. Surely, in a city this size there will be others."

"You're a magic-user," said Travail. "Do you know of any others in the city?"

"No," Seldom replied sadly. "I have let it be known that magic-users are not welcome in Krestible. But wizards are an obstinate lot, and surely there are those who have ignored my warning. I hope. It is up to you to find them."

"Where are you going?" asked Travail, beads of moisture appearing on his forehead as Seldom rose wearily and made for the doorway.

"To bring back the magic-user," replied Seldom. "Please do your mission with zeal, or we will not have a city on the morrow."

Seldom took the steps two at a time, trying to ignore the flurry of cries that followed his exit. Surely Travail would pull himself together.

Mika's room was easy enough to find. But Seldom had no better luck than Braddle at opening the door, for Mika had sealed it with his own personal lock spell, and it would undo for no one other than he. Eventually, Seldom came to the same conclusion that Braddle had reached and hurried out of the building in search of a ladder. His blood ran cold when he discovered a ladder already leaning against the side of the building. Hoping that he was mistaken, Seldom scurried up the ladder and entered Mika's room, only to find his worst fears come true. The necklace was gone.

Once more he hurried back inside the building and sought out Mistress Bonnie, whom he found taking a taste from a large cauldron of broth. Wasting no time for niceties, he grabbed the woman by her arm and flung her around to face him. "Where is it?" he screamed. "What have you done with the necklace?"

For a brief heartbeat, Mistress Bonnie just stared down at him in amazement. Then, noticing the spill of broth on the front of her best yellow silk gown, an expression of anger settled on her normally good-natured features, and with one sweep of her enor mous hand, she grabbed Seldom by the front of his weskit and raised him to face-level. "What did you say, little man?" she asked in an ominously quiet tone that even a foolish man would have taken heed of.

But Seldom was too outraged over the loss of the necklace to give thought to his words. He kicked and squirmed in Mistress Bonnie's grasp, adding injury to insult, and he shrieked aloud, "The necklace, the one that belongs to Mika. I demand that you give it to me now!"

Mistress Bonnie looked at him much as she would have regarded a worm who dared to appear in the center of a fruit she was eating.

"Be you saying that I have stolen something from a lodger?" she asked softly.

"It's gone! Who else could have taken it? Give it back!" cried Seldom. Angry, upset, and tired of being held by the large woman, he took leave of his senses and struck Mistress Bonnie full on the chin with his closed fist.

Unfortunately, this was the wrong thing to do. Accusing Mistress Bonnie of theft was bad enough. But striking her was the ultimate mistake. Mistress Bonnie did not hesitate. Turning Seldom over, she deposited him in the soup caldron, head-first.

Seldom emerged several heartbeats later, noodles and vegetables streaming from his nose and mouth, spluttering and cursing Mistress Bonnie as he reached blindly for the edge of the pot. Mistress Bonnie watched impassively, and just before he touched the edge, she jabbed his head with her long wooden spoon and shoved him under again.

Three times he rose, and three times she dunked him. Then, when all the fight seemed to have left him, and his skin had turned a brilliant shade of red, she fished him out of the cauldron and set him, dripping, at the edge of the hearth.

"Now, then," she said pleasantly, "speak up if you have something to say, or something you wish to ask, but mind you, 'tis a lady you are speaking to, so do so with respect."

Seldom was too exhausted to do otherwise. He had tried to level a spell against the woman, but it was difficult to do so when one was drowning in chicken soup.

"The necklace that belongs to your boarder, one Mika by name, the Wolf Nomad. The necklace is missing, and the door is locked. There is a ladder leaning against the window of the room. I assumed that you had taken the necklace. I must find it. It is very important. The safety of the entire city may well rest on our finding it. Indeed, our very lives may hang in the balance. If you know where the necklace is, you must tell me."

Mistress Bonnie regarded Seldom silently, a small, sad smile on her face, shaking her head over the stupidity of men. "Look you, mister smartie, mister important court personage," she said indulgently. "Do it be looking as though I spend my leisure time crawling up and down skinny ladders?"

Viewing her generous proportions, Seldom had to admit that the ladder outside the window would scarcely bear her weight without breaking under the first step. "No," he said in a small voice.

"Nor do I enter rooms without the lodger's permission," added Mistress Bonnie. "I have not seen yon gentleman for several days past, nor entered his room for even longer. I know nothing of a necklace. If, as you say, it is so truly important, the one who can tell you more is young Braddle. If anyone knows anything, it is he. Now go away, little man, and don't come back until you've learned how to speak to a lady proper-like."

As Seldom squished away, licking soup from his lips and noodles from his mustache, he wondered why he had not thought of young Braddle in the first place.

He did not stop to change, time being of the essence, but he paused to consider where Braddle might have gone. Seldom realized that he knew nothing of the lad, nothing about his friends, his habits, his life. Perhaps the boy had merely stolen the necklace and left town. Perhaps he would never be found!

Panic began to rise in Seldom's scrawny chest. But, remembering the terrible mistake he had made with Mistress Bonnie, he forced himself to remain calm and think. The kitchen. That was where Braddle had come from. Perhaps that was where he had gone, or maybe someone there would know what had become of him.

Trying to contain his anxiety, brushing the worst of the clinging noodles and vegetables from his clothes, Seldom hurried through the castle gates, glaring at the started guards, daring them to question him. He trotted around the edge of the castle to the charred ground where the kitchen had once stood.

There he found the chief cook morosely supervising the roasting of an ox and the simmering of vegetables over open fires. The utensils were blackened and dented, and most of the helpers wore garments that bore the mark of the fire—scorched fabric and singed holes. The chief cook's eyebrows, mustache, and beard had vanished as well; they had shriveled in the intense heat when he attempted to rescue several of his favorite pots. Seldom's strange appearance scarcely merited a second glance among those who had suffered more than he.

"I am looking for one named Braddle who was one of you until recently," he announced to the gathering as a whole. But typical of survivors of some dread event, none of the kitchen folk paid him any attention. They continued on with their own activities. Seldom moved to the center of the grassy area that was serving as a make-do kitchen and repeated his question in a somewhat louder tone of voice.

Finally, a small girl, just a tiny slip of a thing with a halo of white-blonde hair, looked up and said shyly, "He be with the princess. I sawed him there when I taked her the midday meal. He be dressed very grand-like, but it were our Braddle, I be sure of that."

Seldom thanked the child and gave her a silver grushnik for her answer before hurrying off to climb the stairs to the tower.

Braddle and the princess and Scylla were sitting on a pile of pillows spread out on a gaily colored quilt, laughing and talking easily while sharing a simple meal, when Seldom threw open the door and burst into the room.

The three of them stopped in mid-munch and stared at the strange apparition, dressed in wet clothes that clung to his skinny frame, with what appeared to be noodles and carrots dotting his sodden locks. He gasped and held a hand to his chest, exhausted after the long climb. His eyes were wild as they darted around the room taking in the scene.

Suddenly, it was all too much to bear. Seldom had been rushing around like a fool, looking for the magic necklace, the item that was their sole hope for saving the canton, getting himself dunked upside down in a pot of chicken soup and mauled by a crazy woman, while Braddle, a lowly page, was up in the princess's room lolling around on silk pillows, dressed in fancy clothes, having a picnic! It was the final straw; the back of the hieraco-sphinx had been broken! Enraged, Seldom charged across the room and flung himself at Braddle, grabbing the necklace and trying to rip it off while all but strangling Braddle in the process.

"URKKK!" gargled Braddle as he attempted to fight off the crazed magician. "Stop!" cried the princess and Scylla as they pummeled Seldom's scrawny back and pulled at his dripping clothes. Finally, the efforts of all three proved greater than Seldom's flagging strength, and he fell back on the quilt with an exhausted moan and lay there gasping for breath.

"What is the meaning of this?" cried the princess, her eyes flashing dangerously. "Sit up and explain yourself!" So used to obeying her orders was he that Seldom did just that.

". . . and so, we've got to get him back here if we are to save the canton," Seldom concluded at last.

"Oh, that poor man," said the princess, her eyes brimming over with tears. "To think that he fought with a griffon and is lying there all bruised and cold just so he could save us. Braddle, you've got to do something. We have to help that poor man."

Looking into her eyes, Braddle was lost. She could have commanded him to leap from the tower window, and he would have done so. Seldom regarded the pair with a twisted grimace and thought to himself that true love was surely as powerful as the strongest magic.

Braddle straightened under the princess's gaze. Holding the necklace in one hand and the magic heart in the other, he said, "I'll bring him back, my love, never worry." Even as he wondered whether Mika's presence would cause the princess to forget him, he said, "Bring my lord Mika back to us here and now." Then he said the magic words under his breath so that none might hear him.

There was a tremendous billow of white smoke. Coughing and hacking, fanning it away with waving hands, they beheld Mika, still dressed in his griffon suit, with TamTur standing at his side.

"Well, sir wizard, you did not tell me that this was your intent," said Mika. "I did not know that you intended to *use* the stone. I will thank you to hand it over, now that I am here."

"Whatever are you wearing?" asked the princess, staring at Mika as though he were something she had dreamed after a bad meal.

"But sir, I did not bring you here," replied Seldom, ignoring the princess, as did Mika. "That was not my intent. My own powers are not that great. I would have had to don the guise of a bird and bring the necklace to you so that you might make use of it yourself," he explained, hoping to avoid the wrath of the magic-user.

"Then who . . . " said Mika, taking another step into the room.

"It was I, sir," said Braddle as he held out his palm, showing everyone the small, brown object that nestled there, knowing that it would be taken from him, knowing that his time of freedom, his time of hope, was over.

"Ughhh!" said the princess. "Throw it away; it's disgusting."

"Yuck!" added Scylla.

"I think that you have some explaining to do, young man," Mika said sternly. "You'd best take it from the beginning.

". . . and so I came here and met the princess. And I don't care if I get sent back to the kitchens," Braddle said with a look of defiance on his face. Then, turning to look at the princess with lovesick eyes, he added,

"Being here with you for even this short time was worth being banished to the kitchens forever."

"Well, that's all very lovely," said Mika as he took the necklace from Braddle's hands and slipped it over his feathered headdress. "But if we don't come up with some sort of plan, you'll be lucky if you have any sort of days left at all. Those monsters and that army aren't the least bit interested in your love life; they're more interested in what you and your precious princess taste like. So unless you care to see the lady skewered on the end of a pike staff, I suggest we come up with a plan. Now, about this wizard of yours . . . "

THE WORD HAD GONE out, and all of those persons living outside the walls of the city had brought themselves and all the food and firewood that they could carry inside the walls, driving their livestock before them. They had left behind not one thing that was edible, save the crops in the field, which would be of little interest to men or monsters with their minds fixed on death and destruction.

The city was filled to capacity. Men crouched in corners, sharpening seldom-used weapons with awkward, calloused fingers more accustomed to handling heavy plows and sacks of feed. They milled about anxiously, talking loudly to hide their fear and bolster their courage, and they peered over the walls wondering when the enemy would appear.

The women and children did their best to tend to the animals and make a place for themselves with town-bred relatives or in out-of-the-way corners wherever accommodations might be found. They built their fires and cooked their meals and swept the dust from their tiny bit of ground in a brave pretense, knowing full well that even that tiny bit of dust would no longer be a concern if their menfolk did not succeed in driving the attackers from the gates.

The city was filled with talk of the invaders, from the lips of those few who had actually seen them up close and who had lived to tell the tale. Others, with active imaginations, also told tales, imagining it all too vividly.

The castle and the small armed city guard had been mobilized. It was still hoped that the reinforcements from Schwartzenbruin would arrive in time. Weapons had been dispersed among the men, small groups of whom were being coached in the rudiments of warfare by the elderly and somewhat paunchy captain of the guards. Still others, gingerly holding their new weapons before them like lightning bolts, were parading back and forth under the hot sun in meaningless formations.

Children, too young to believe in death and still convinced of their own immortality, viewed the occasion with excited eyes. Freed from the drudgery and endless chores of farm life, they raced around the town in large gangs, yelling and screaming exuberantly, having the time of their young lives.

Mika, Braddle, and Seldom, realizing full well the seriousness of the occasion, knowing that it could put an end to all life in Krestible and most probably many lives in the lands beyond, went about their business more grimly.

Travail had locked himself in his rooms and would not come out. Giving him up as a lost cause, they had left the castle in the hands of the princess and Scylla, who appeared surprisingly capable. No one dared to ignore an order when it was the princess who issued it.

The three men headed for the marketplace with TamTur trotting beside them, in search of the mysterious wizard who had sold Braddle the magic items. None of them knew what to expect and could only hope that he would still be there.

Despite the nearness of the approaching army, the market was not abandoned; rather, it was packed with sellers and buyers. A festive air prevailed, as though a carnival were about to occur instead of war.

They forced their way through the throng of people toward the sun-drenched corner where the old man was usually to be found. Much to their surprise, Braddle began to talk, exclaiming excitedly even before they reached their destination as though he could see someone, while they saw nothing but the joining of two walls. Then Tam's hackles raised, and he lowered his head, beginning to growl.

Mika, alert to Tam's reactions, knowing that the wolf's instincts were more finely honed than his own, squinted his eyes and looked at the brick walls. Only then did he notice a peculiar wavering in the air as though there were a rising of heated currents. Gripping Seldom's shoulder, he pointed at the disturbance, and Seldom nodded silently.

"Please, sire. Your services are needed," Braddle was saying earnestly. "The city is in great danger. As you can see, I have brought my lords Seldom and Mika to meet you. If you can help us, I beg you to do so."

There was a heartbeat of silence, and then the wavering currents seemed to still themselves. Mika grew alarmed that the invisible magic-user might simply drift away and be lost to them forever.

"Wait, you sir!" he cried aloud. "Do not leave until you hear what has happened and know that your abilities might save many from death!" Quickly he told the story of the advancing men and monsters.

"And why should I concern myself with the lives of those who mean nothing to me," said a voice much like the sound of wind through a tunnel, a voice that seemed older than time itself. "And those who care nothing for anyone other than themselves and their own blind ambition." Now there was the sound of bitterness in the voice.

"Because you are a magic-user, and that is a noble profession," said Mika. "This is not a skill that can be learned by any lad fresh from the farm; it is a gift that is given to the precious few, a gift that must be nurtured with honor and respect by its practitioners.

"There are only two types of magic, as you well know: that which is used for good and that which is used for evil. The boy, Braddle, has told us about you and showed me the magic heart. It is apparent that you have sought to aid him and that the heart contains no evil. Therefore, you are on the side of good. And therefore, it follows that in the face of the evil that is advancing on us rapidly, you can do no other than to join forces with us. For if you are not evil, then you must be good and therefore aligned on our side."

Much to his surprise, Mika discovered that he believed everything that he had said. "I ask you to show yourself now and join us in defeating the enemy," he said quietly.

The air currents seemed to become still, and then, as though a morning mist had risen, the air began to solidify, taking shape before their eyes. Tam growled, falling silent only when Mika sliced the air with his demon hand. Then he was there in the corner formed by the joining of the two buildings, a little man, smaller even than Seldom, with straggly white hair drifting about his shoulders, his face withered and wrinkled by more than a hundred seasons. He stared at them defiantly through blue eyes as clear and bright and wide as those of a child.

"Why, why . . . I know you," said Seldom, falling to his knees. "My lord," he said, with his head bowed in deference.

"Kadis is the name," said the old one, nodding with satisfaction toward Seldom's bowed figure. Then, turning back to Mika and the very confused Braddle, he drew himself up proudly and said, "Kadis, chief magician to the old king, Dorbin, Hettman of Krestible, before yon fellow and his cohort, that overstuffed pincushion, fashioned his downfall."

"We wondered what had become of you," whispered Seldom. "We thought you had gone with the hettman. We wondered why you did nothing. We . . . we expected some reprisal, some form of retaliation from you. But nothing happened. We did not know what to think. Travail said that you were dead."

"Dead? No, not yet," said the old man. "I did not choose to go with Hettman Dorbin. He had become too weak, too easily led astray, as evidenced by his passion with your evil game. That game has laid ruin and havoc to a kingdom that I spent my entire lifetime protecting.

"I had no wish to remain and watch you continue to destroy everything that is good about this place. And yet I could not rest easy or die until I saw you and your master lose all you had obtained, until you had suffered as much as those whom you had so wrongly stripped of the works of their lifetime. I could not go until I had found one whose heart was pure, yet who was strong enough to love my precious princess.

"Now you dare to come sniveling to me when the kingdom is taken by surprise, the army decimated, the people unprepared, the country undone, and all because of you and your meddling, you and your deadly game."

"But The Game is not ours," said Seldom, unable to disclaim anything but that small fact. "We did not devise it; we merely used it to our advantage."

"Do not jest with me, sir; I am in no mood for jokes," said the old man. "I would just as soon snuff out your life here and now than wait for this army of monsters to do it for me." He lifted a wrinkled, liver-spotted hand, as though to do just that.

"I do not jest with you, sir," Seldom replied steadfastly, rising to his feet and standing as tall as his small stature would allow, not even attempting to shield himself from whatever dread thing the magician might chose to do. "I tell you that The Game was already in place before we came to power, and I know nothing of its origins."

"These game wizards who scurry back and forth each day, posting new rules and addenda *ad nauseum*, they are not your minions?" asked Kadis, peering intently into Seldom's eyes.

"I swear it," said Seldom, and there was no mistaking the truth in his voice. "It is not our game, and we have had nothing to do with its workings other than to take advantage of those who risked everything and lost."

The old wizard studied Seldom for a long time, searching out the truth of his words, while Braddle looked on open-mouthed, attempting to sort out what was happening and how it related to him. Mika held his silence, much relieved that the old man was someone of power rather than a charlatan, for while the magic gem was powerful indeed, it could not defeat an entire army of men and monsters by itself. Now it appeared that they had a chance.

"Why did you choose Braddle?" asked Mika, breaking into the old man's thoughts. "How does he figure into this?"

"Could you not tell?" asked Kadis, turning to Mika in surprise. "He is a natural. There is an aura about him that even the most ignorant should be able to see. He is destined for great things. Also, I thought it a great joke that one from such a lowly position should be the instrument of the downfall of the great." Then, noticing Braddle's crestfallen expression, he added in softer tones, "There is also the fact that he is a gentle man, pure of heart and sweet of nature. I knew that I could give Linea into his keeping and that they would grow and learn from each other. They would love and be happy."

"Why, sir, it is so!" Braddle exclaimed in amazement. "It was your doing that brought us together. I thought, I . . . I . . . "

"It does not matter, young Braddle," Kadis said softly, taking the young man's hands between his own. "She is a good girl, headstrong and spoiled, tempestuous of nature, and quite a handful altogether. But she is precious and will make a good ruler, as well as a good wife, with the right man at her side. You are that man; I charge you not to fail her."

"I will not," replied Braddle, and the light shining in his eyes gave testament to his simple words.

Embarrassed by the display of naked emotion and anxious to steer the conversation back toward more pertinent ground, Mika cleared his throat and said, "The aura, of course, I noticed it immediately." The fact was that he had noticed nothing at all unusual about Braddle other than his bright red hair and the inordinate number of freckles. "The aura was why I chose him in the first place."

TamTur sat back on his haunches just out of Mika's reach and scratched vigorously at his ear, uttering noises that sounded suspiciously like laughter.

"He has no skills as yet, but he can be used to channel certain effects, using his natural power to increase them. He will serve your purposes nicely," said the old wizard.

"Will it hurt?" croaked Braddle, somewhat alarmed at the thought of being used as a channel, whatever that might mean.

"No, lad," Kadis said kindly, laying his wrinkled hand on Braddle's arm. "You might even learn to like it. Come now, back to the castle. There is much to be done if we are to save the city. We can't have Linea living in a cave, now, can we?" Echoing his dry chuckle, the others fell into step behind him.

Upon entering the castle, they encountered a group of young pages carrying armloads of weapons. After a single startled glance, they immediately dropped to one knee and lowered their heads in deference.

"Up, up, up!" Kadis commanded casually, but Mika could see that he was pleased by his reception. Time and again it happened as they met members of the staff in the corridors. Then, turning a corner, they came face-to-face with the Princess Linea and Scylla, who were directing a large gathering of women as they carefully ripped the castle linen into rolls of bandages.

The princess was transformed. Dressed casually in an old skirt and blouse with a mere half-dozen petticoats peeping out beneath the hem, her hair tied up with ribbons to keep it out of her face, which was prettily flushed with effort, she could scarcely be recongized as the pampered darling. But as soon as she saw the old wizard, she burst into tears and flung herself at him, nearly bowling him over with the strength of her greeting.

"Oh, Kadis-sahn," she cried, hugging him tightly and raining kisses down on his balding crown. "Where have you been? Never did I think to see you again. I have been so lonely and so afraid. Where is papa—is he coming, too?" She looked behind him with large eyes, as though perhaps she had overlooked the figure of her father.

"Child, child, forgive me. I did not stop to think of your sorrow and fears. I was too wrapped up in my own," Kadis said softly as he smoothed back the curls that had escaped her ribbons and sprung up around her face. "I am sorry to say that your father is not with me. I could not leave. Krestible has been my home for too long, and I am far too old to seek another at this late date. But your father could not stay. His shame was too great for him to endure the company of others, their pitying glances and knowing eyes. He needed to be alone. Even I was wrapped in bitterness and thought to remove myself from all that I had known.

"But you, my dear, how have you fared? If appearances are any guide, you are doing well, for never have I seen you look more beautiful. Come, tell me, what has brought the blush to your cheeks and the brightness to your eyes? It cannot be all for the sake of this old man?" he teased, knowing full-well the reason for her happiness, which he had caused to come about.

Linea blushed bright crimson from the edges of her hairline down to her bosom, which heaved prettily. Turning aside, she caught Braddle's admiring glance and stood riveted, captivated by his gaze.

"Oh ho, so that's how it is, aye? Well then, good, I say. It seems we have both chosen wisely, my dear, for I have chosen yon fellow to inherit my mantle after I am gone."

"Gone!" cried the princess, wrenching her gaze away from Braddle and turning once again to face the old man. "You would not leave me again, now that I have found you! Say that you will not go, Kadissahn!"

"We must all leave this good Oerth, when it is our time," the old wizard said softly, stroking the princess's downy cheek with his fingertips. "But I do not think that I will be so eager to go just yet. I have things to live for now. Rest easy, little one. I am back!"

"But not for long if we do not get on with the business at hand," said Mika, all too aware that the army was advancing on them rapidly and that they had little time to spare for niceties. "Hello and goodbye to you, Princess. We shall see you later if the gods will it," said Mika summarily. Taking the old wizard by the elbow, he steered him around the gathering of women and on down the corridor.

The meeting with the princess seemed to have done the old man a world of good, for his step was stronger and his back straighter. Climbing the staircase to the tower, they chanced to pass the door to Travail's chambers, those that had once belonged to the hettman. Travail's chubby face appeared in the opening, and as he glimpsed the old wizard he let out a terrified shriek and slammed the door shut with a resounding bang. They heard the sound of a bar being shoved into place. Kadis never broke stride, but Mika could have sworn that he heard him chuckle.

Reaching the very top of the staircase, they were faced with a blank brick wall. Kadis waved his hand in the air and muttered beneath his breath, and a wooden door appeared before them, swinging open on silent hinges. Kadis marched inside without looking to see if they followed. Looking to each other for reassurance, Mika, Braddle, and Seldom entered as well. TamTur was the last, slinking low with his belly and tail all but touching the floor. No sooner had the tip of his tail cleared the threshold than the door disappeared again, leaving nothing but blank brick wall. Tam snarled with fright and huddled at Mika's feet.

Mika stared around him, dumbstruck. From outside the castle, it had appeared that there were only three levels to the tower, yet this room comprised a fourth, and altogether invisible, level. From inside, it appeared as real as any other room Mika had ever been in, possessing walls, floor, and ceiling, as well as enormous windows which looked out over the countryside in all directions.

The center of the room was taken up with a very large work bench fitted out with a variety of crystal beakers, decanters, tubes, and jars. Most were filled with dried mixtures, but some were liquid in still and bubbling states, while others held glittering crystals. Strings of dried bats hung from the rafters. Mika peered into a murky container, and hundreds of disembodied eyes stared back at him.

Seldom had ventured close to a large, half-round object situated on top of a stone pedestal in front of a window. He was putting out a finger as though to touch it when the wizard's voice cracked out authoritatively, "Don't touch that, it's very sensitive!" Seldom's fingers retreated like those of a small boy caught with his hand in the cookie jar.

"Sorry, didn't mean to yell," said the wizard in a more conciliatory tone. "It's just that the thing is so temperamental—gets out of whack if you even look at it wrong."

"What is it?" asked Braddle. "Looks sort of like a large egg shell broken in half."

"So it does," chuckled the wizard. "It's a little device I invented for far-seeing. When you get as old as I am, it's dangerous to take leave of your body. Sometimes I think it might not stay alive if I leave it alone too long."

"How does it work?" asked Mika. He was always interested in learning a new trick that was safer and more dependable than hands-on magic, which had been known to backfire on him more than once, leaving him in strange and uncomfortable circumstances.

"Well, you just look into the bowl and conjure up the scene you want to see most," said Kadis. "Here, you try it."

"Me?" said Braddle. "I don't know how!"

"Well, then you're not the lad I took you to be," replied Kadis. "Go on, give it a try."

Braddle stood before the device and concentrated so hard that his forehead wrinkled, his eyes squeezed shut, and the tip of his nose turned red. And then everyone began to laugh. Braddle's eyes flew open, and his face turned bright red, all but obliterating his freckles. Pictured in the center of the bowl was the princess, looking quite fetching with curls dangling over her rosy cheeks. Braddle gave a gargle of distress and turned as if to go, but Mika grabbed the lad's shoulder with his demon hand and brought him to a standstill.

"Never mind, lad," Mika said. "It's only natural that you would be more interested in love than war. Can't say as I don't agree with you myself."

"Aye, but there are more serious things to consider, or none of us shall love again, not on this green Oerth," Kadis said solemnly. "Let us deal with the situation at hand first, then you shall have your time, youngster." Placing his hands on each side of the bowl, he stared into its murky depths and concentrated.

Watching closely from his position behind the old wizard, Mika saw the mists in the bowl curl about the edges and weave themselves into a design. Slowly, slowly, they took shape, sinuously writhing about, taking on color and definition, and then, there before him, he saw the army advancing, seeming almost to march out of the mists at the edge of the bowl before unraveling and disappearing.

Wave after wave of armed men passed. Then came the monsters, more horrible than Mika had remembered. It seemed that there were more of them than there had been before, and still they came in a never-ending flow of horror. Finally it was done, the last vile creature slinking out of the mists and fading from view, but the sight of them was still vivid in their mind's eye.

"I did not know that it would be this bad," Seldom said at length, breaking the silence that held them all in thrall. "We are outnumbered more than ten times over. We cannot hope to win; all that we can do is to flee and hope to save ourselves."

Braddle looked to the old wizard, waiting for him to say something, but Kadis seemed to have shrunken in on himself, overwhelmed by the sight of the unholy alliance of men and monsters. Even in the magic bowl, it had been possible to see the blood that coated the spears and pikestaffs and mouths and fur of the monsters, gory evidence of the death they had brought upon the innocent and defenseless inhabitants of the countryside.

Mika, who had seriously entertained the thought of disappearing, removing himself and Tam from a fight in which they had no stake, was stricken to a depth that he did not know he possessed. No matter how hard he tried to shake the vision from his mind, he could not help but picture Gemmy and Hilda and their shy, well-mannered brood, now just so much meat in the bellies of the ravening horde. The indignity and uselessness of their deaths rose up in his throat like bile, and before he knew what he was doing, he heard himself say, "We'll make them pay for what they've done. We are not lost yet. Let us put our heads together and fashion a welcome that they will not forget—those few who live."

MIKA BURIED HIS FACE in his demon hand and groaned inwardly. What had he done? Committed himself to the worst folly of his entire lifetime. Here he was, surrounded by two old wizards who had probably forgotten more than they had ever known, and a young boy who knew nothing, least of all his own abilities. And all of them were looking to him to come up with the solution to their problems.

It was a simple problem, really. All he had to do was defeat an army of two thousand well-armed and well-trained men as well as a rampaging tailgate of twice as many monsters, all of whom would be upon them in less than a day's time.

Still worse, much as he wanted to leave, he couldn't. It wasn't the way the trio of wizards, old and new, looked at him; nor was it the way the woman treated him, fussing over him and commenting on his bravery. It was something even more horrible. It was something inside himself that refused to let him leave, to flee the scene of danger as he had so many times before, leaving better men to face the danger and, if need be, the death. Running away had never bothered him before. But it bothered him now.

Thinking back on it, he realized that he had been changing for some time. Little by little, he had felt the change coming over him as he did things that were good and noble, things that were totally out of character.

Was he not a man who looked to his own safety first and foremost? A man whose pleasure was more important than intangibles such as ideals and values? Those were the things that caused a man to suffer and, frequently, to die.

Mika has always preferred the fast and easy life, and his women the same way, but of late those things had begun to pale. He had no less interest in remaining alive, nor did he object to pleasure. But somehow, in a way that eluded close introspection, it was becoming more difficult to sacrifice principles and other people's lives so that he might better enjoy himself.

It was a new way of thinking, and for a long time he did his best to ignore it or to attribute it to some passing illness. But now there was no avoiding the truth, sickening as it was. He, Mika, was becoming good. Even worse than good, he was becoming, ugh, noble and ugh, ugh, righteous. He knew that his father and mother, both long-dead, as well as the rest of the Wolf Nomads, would be proud of him. And in a flash of rare insight, Mika realized that in spite of himself and all efforts to the contrary, he was growing up, becoming all that a Wolf Nomad was supposed to be in spirit, as well as in name.

He looked down at his chest, at the gem that gleamed dully in its heavy silver setting, and he wondered, not for the first time, whether it had had some part in his transformation. Perhaps it was so, for it was a powerful gem indeed.

For a heartbeat or two, Mika considered getting rid of the gem and returning to his old and much safer way of life. But just as quickly, he abandoned the idea, knowing that such a thing was not possible. His responsibility to the gem could not be set aside, even if the gem did endanger his life. It was too valuable. Aside from making spell-casting easy, it enabled him to do much good, and by possessing it, he was charged with the duty of acting in a responsible manner.

Mika moaned, unable to think of a solution to the dilemma. He would have to avoid getting himself killed and then, after the danger was past, think of some way to discharge his responsibility to the gem. Perhaps Braddle would like it! TamTur whined and laid his head across the bridge of Mika's foot, perhaps sympathizing with him for once.

Groaning, Mika tried to force his aching head to think of a plan that would save them. Perhaps it was the danger to his own skin, or maybe it really was concern for the innocents in the town below, but whatever the reason, by nightfall he had come up with the rudiments of a plan.

Sighing deeply and hoping for the best, he called the others to his side.

Morning rose, dim and misty, the shadowy half-light revealing the ranks of the enemy camped just out of bow range. Tiny fires winked in the gloom like forgotten stars, heating huge cauldrons of tar and oil, the tips of arrows and other deadly missiles.

Inside the walls, all was calm. The small Perrenlandian army and every available male, young as well as old, were huddled behind the walls, gripping swords, pikes, maces, morning stars, bows and arrows, pitchforks, and even clubs, as they waited for the melee to begin.

The women were inside the sturdiest of buildings, rolling bandages and heating still more cauldrons filled with thick brews of soup and stew to satisfy the hunger that would eventually overrule the nervous stomachs and fearful hearts. The children were all hidden inside the castle itself. Scylla and the princess, as well as her bevy of former maids, were there to comfort them as best they were able.

Taking time only to change out of the griffon suit, which had attracted many a strange look, Mika had assumed his position on top of the tower where he could see all that was happening and issue orders directing the attack. Tam stood bravely at his side. This position took him out of the most direct confrontation, yet seemed to satisfy his inner urge for nobility or suicide; under the circumstances, they seemed interchangeable. He felt sick to his stomach, and the sense of fear was overwhelming, but it was too late to do anything but procede and pray for the best.

Mika felt somewhat reassured, knowing that Kadis was manning the bowl of vision with young Braddle and Seldom at his side. The plan was a good one. He could but hope that it would be good enough to win the day.

In the distance, he heard a trumpet blow, the mellow tones floating over the fields, strangely pleasing to the ear. His stomach clenched into a hard knot, knowing that the signal had been given and the battle had begun.

Mika waited until he could see the glint of the morning sun lighting the armor of the leading flank before he pointed the magic gem with one hand and, holding his book of spells in the other, recited a magic formula. There was no explosion, no burst of colors, no outcry. But heartbeats later, the first row of Tusmitians crashed headlong into an invisible barrier that stopped them as effectively as a stone wall. Row after row of soldiers piled into those in front of them, unable to stop because of the mass of men following on their heels in tight formation. Chaos errupted, spears jangled, swords clashed, and casualties were suffered as men, wound too tightly from the excitement of battle, panicked and lashed out, striking down their own companions.

Mika concentrated on the spell, holding the invisible shield, strengthening it, willing it to last. Below him, he could hear Kadis and Seldom reciting the words of a second spell and knew that they would use Braddle to channel the magic, using his unformed power and the strength of his youth to boost their spell and give it additional power. They reached the end of the formula, and Mika felt the whiplash, the recoil of the spell as it sped toward the unsuspecting Tusmitian Army.

Suddenly it was as though some dread horror had exploded in the midst of the enemy ranks. Men turned upon each other with a look of terror, as each in his own mind's eye saw that which he most dreaded. In some instances, the men struck out, striking their own comrades with weapons meant for the enemy. Those struck fought back, seeing not their own mates, but the horror inside their own heads.

Some chose not to fight at all but laid down their weapons and fled the field, bringing further chaos to all those they encountered, as they screamed out warnings of giant cockroaches, banshees, ghosts, and impending doom.

Their terror was contagious and affected all they came in contact with. Men and monsters joined in the rout, turning the battlefield into a hopeless jangle of men running in all directions, slashing out at their former comrades, and holding their heads in a futile attempt to shut out the demons that possessed them and struck fear in their hearts.

Mika did not let down his concentration for a heartbeat, but allowed himself a wide grin as he viewed the havoc they had caused. But the grin faltered and fell from his face as he began to notice those in the farthest ranks continuing on toward the invisible barrier, seemingly unaffected by the magic. Then he saw several old men—civilians—marching alongside the soldiers, reading out of books, and gesturing toward the walls of the city.

Just as he was wondering who they were and what they were doing in the middle of a battle, a terrible howling pain, like a tornado magnified ten times over, went whirling through his head.

Mika clutched his head and fell to his knees, stunned, knowing now that the old men were Tusmitian magicians fighting back, protecting their soldiers as best they were able. Tam yipped in pain and snapped at the air, trying to dislodge the hurtful sounds that reverberated inside his sensitive ears. Cries of pain floated to the rooftop from the level below, and Mika knew that Braddle and the others had been affected as well.

Staggering to his feet, Mika repeated the words to a spell, a spell so simple that he did not even need the magic gem or his spell book to aid him. Instantly, the sound ceased as Mika sealed himself inside a cone of personal protection that took in only the small area where he stood. Shuffling forward, careful to keep the cone around him, he enveloped TamTur in the safe area, sparing him further anguish. A cessation of sound from below him told him that Kadis or Seldom had invoked a similar spell, protecting themselves as well.

Now Mika was angry. He really disliked pain. Next to death, pain was the thing he hated most. Glancing quickly at the advancing army, he could see that the invisible barrier was down, although the confusion spell still seemed to be in effect on the forward ranks.

Mika summoned up fireballs, one of his very favorite spells. Standing on his tiptoes, he hurled the spell at the oncoming army. Heartbeats later, he watched in satisfaction as the flaming orbs of fire crashed into their ranks like a shower of meteors, bringing death to all who were unlucky enough to be in their path.

The fireballs continued to rain down out of the clear morning sky, and Mika was heartened to see that Kadis and Seldom had added pryotechnics of their own. Huge explosions in midair showered the enemy with drops of fire that could not be extinguished, even when the men flung themselves down and rolled on the ground. Those affected dropped their weapons, ripped off their burning armor, and fled the field.

Then Mika became alarmed, for several of the fireballs rose up from the battlefield and hurled themselves upward in the path of their original trajectory, which would eventually cause them to descend upon Mika.

Mika raised his hand to do something. But before he could summon words to prevent the return of the fireballs, they faltered in midair and then dropped like lead, setting aflame still more of the enemy beneath their fiery mantle. Mika and Tam howled their happiness into the air.

"AOOOOOWWW!" cheered Mika. "Did you see that, Tam? Their magicians aren't strong enough. They're doing our work for us!"

The Tusmitians had a superior army, of that there was no doubt. But their magicians were inferior to those in the castle, and Mika rejoiced, for it was clear that if the battle were to be won, it would be won by magic rather than strength.

Holding the magic gem aloft and flipping through his spell book, Mika called down one plague of horrors after another upon the unfortunate army. Sheets of fire toasted them inside their heavy metal armor; torrents of water cooled them, so that plummeting temperatures sheathed them in layers of ice and they were toppling where they stood, frozen in position until they were crushed underfoot.

Wild laughter burst out of the windowed room below. Glancing down, Mika saw a lightning bolt zap forth, streak over the walls, and fry an entire contingent of gnolls. TamTur, unable to control himself, burst out of the confining shield and ran back and forth behind the battlement, howling hysterically, adding his voice to that of the unending rain of magic.

Returning to his spell of confusion, Mika shouted out the words and laughed with glee as an ogre glared down at a pack of orcs marching at his side and, gathering them by the necks in two massive fists, banged their heads together before they realized what was happening. A hippogriff turned on a covey of harpies in midair, and they plunged to the ground, ripping and tearing at each other, blood streaming from countless wounds and soaking into the thirsty oerth as they fought to the death, locked in the grip of insanity.

Mika could see the fragile old ones, white hair and whiskers flying as they tried to make their way out onto the battlefield, holding up their withered old hands, attempting to stem the tide of confusion, trying to direct the attention of men and monsters against the city rather than each other.

Below him, Braddle stood between Kadis and Seldom, his mind clear, focusing on the enemy as they had instructed him. Laying their hands on Braddle, the two old magicians called up their own spell of confusion, adding a dose of undying hatred for good measure, and channeled it through Braddle, speeding it on its way, watching as it exploded in the enemy's midst.

Monster turned against monster, man against man, monster against man, man against monster, all of them fighting for a reason that they could not have explained, yet fighting to the death with a black hatred that drove them on till they were coated with blood and could not lift their arms to strike another blow.

Then, and only then, did the Perrenlandian army emerge from the gates, armed to the teeth and ready to do their best to finish the conflict. They worked their way inward, slashing, hacking, slicing, stabbing, plunging, piercing, ripping, and chopping as they went, taking advantage of the confusion that had all but destroyed the enemy. Although the spell was lifted as the Perrenlandians entered the battlefield, the enemy was unable to rally in any large numbers, debilitated by the combined effects of the double spell. Here and there, small pockets of resistance arose, but these were dealt with swiftly.

Then, it was over, almost before it began, the field strewn with the dead, all of whom were Tusmitians and monsters.

High on a hill beyond the battlefield, a large gray monolith of a stone giant stood looking down on the carnage. Beside him stood young Pasha Marcovitti, staring down at the battlefield with disbelieving eyes. His few advisors, those who had not been killed outright, stood apart from their young charge and moved backward on spindly shanks, putting even more space between themselves and the young ruler, unwilling in the final reckoning to take the blame for his mistake.

The stone giant turned slowly and looked behind him at the horde of monsters that had not yet advanced onto the field, and he signaled them to retreat, shaking his head solemnly.

"No!" screamed Marcovitti, losing what remaining reason he possessed and daring to pound his fists on the stone giant's massive thigh. "You must send them in. Do not call them off. We could win now, we could beat them, they would not expect it, and . . . "

The stone giant looked down at the small man with cold, hard eyes and twitched a muscle, flinging the man backward. "We had a bargain," he rumbled. "You said they would be easy. You said they did not have a chance. You said we would win. You asked for an army, and I gave you one. But they were not easy, nor did we have a chance. We did not win."

"But it wasn't my fault!" wailed the Pasha of Tusmit. "It wasn't supposed to happen like this! It's not my fault. Surely you don't mean to hold me to the bargain?"

"The hills will be empty tonight," the stone giant said stolidly. "Burrows and lairs and caves and dens have lost their men, those that fathered their children, those that hunted for them and kept them safe. You have caused those deaths, and you will be the cause of many more as little ones starve in their burrows, and humans enter the hills and hunt them down. You made the bargain. It was not kept. Now you will pay the price."

Beckoning with a single finger as long as the pasha's arm, he urged the remaining monsters forward. They advanced on the young pasha as his ancient advisors took to their heels and ran. Their young charge was seized in the deadly serrated-toothed jaws of the dreaded land shark. And then the monsters, those who remained, swarmed around him and made their way toward the dead, those who but recently had been comrades and littermates, and settled down to feed.

It was ugly, but it was war, and their old mums had taught them that there was no sense in wasting good meat.

Chapter 25

IT WAS ALL OVER but the shouting, and there was plenty of that, as wild huzzahs and exuberant yells rang out from the rooftops and echoed off the sides of buildings. Strangers hugged each other, and more than a few women were kissed by men who were not their mates. Under the circumstances, it seemed the thing to do.

Thus, no one was very surprised, or even very shocked, when the princess, her hair billowing about in an untamed cloud of curls, burst into the room and threw her arms around Braddle, all but knocking him off his feet. Her kiss caused him to turn as brilliant a shade of red as his hair, and his freckles faded into obscurity as he folded his arms around the princess and kissed her in return.

Kadis, and then Seldom, looked on in a proprietary manner, beaming as though it had been their doing which had brought the two youngsters together, as indeed it had been. Mika, entering the room in time to see the end of the embrace, grinned broadly as he noted the dewy look in their eyes, eyes that saw no one other than each other. Freed at last from the spell of the succubus, Mika was able to enjoy the look of love that passed between the two young people.

But there were still many matters left undone, matters that had to be resolved before the kingdom could be considered safe.

For one thing, there was the matter of The Game. Already, only a number of heartbeats after the cessation of war, sounds could be heard coming from the Great Hall below, indicating that The Game had begun again.

The Game had been responsible for nearly all the mayhem that had occurred in Perrenland. It had caused havoc from the highest ruler in the land to the lowest peasant, uprooting and ruining lives as though they were no more than so many broken cups to be discarded once they had served their purpose.

Mika had crossed the room, intending to share his concerns with the two old magicians who had their heads together and were immersed in deep conversation.

All of a sudden the air was filled with a blaring of trumpets. Everyone in the room looked up with alarm and ran for the window, one thing uppermost in their minds: Had the enemy changed its mind and decided to attack once more?

"Hooray!" cried the princess, who reached the window first. Then she turned and raced for the door, dragging Braddle behind her. Puzzled, Mika, Seldom, and Kadis hurried the last few steps and gazed out of the window over the city walls and beheld an oncoming force of men. The hettman had returned!

"My lord!" croaked Kadis, and he too turned and ran toward the door as swiftly as his scrawny legs could carry him, a look of joy animating his old, wrinkled face.

Even Tam barked and woofed with excitement and ran in circles chasing his tail even though he was totally unaffected by the hettman's return. Only Seldom remained uncheered. In fact, his face was set in the saddest of expressions.

Mika, being no dummy, could easily ascertain the reason for the man's discomfort.

"How much of this was your doing?" he asked.

"None," replied Seldom, "although I did not disagree when Travail offered me the opportunity to ride on his coattails. I was tired of being overlooked. The hettman allowed no other counsel other than Kadis. I had no opportunity for advancement, my life was going nowhere, and I am no longer a young man. I was flattered that Travail wished my help, and I listened to his blandishments and allowed myself to be persuaded. And now I will pay the price, I suppose. A public beheading in the square, or banishment if I am lucky."

"Tell me truthfully," said Mika. "Is Travail behind this game?"

"No," said Seldom, shaking his head wearily. "The Game has always been a part of Perrenland, but it was harmless. Only recently did the changes begin, the changes that turned it into the chaotic, disruptive menance that almost destroyed us. But we did not create it. Travail did naught but take advantage of the way it worked on men's natural greed. He had nothing to do with its formation."

"Then who are these people, those three little men who come and go, rushing about like beetles, posting new rules and addenda?"

"I don't know," said Seldom. "I never really thought about it."

"Well, now is the time to do just that," said Mika. "I think we might find some badly needed answers at the bottom of that puzzle. Shall we?"

Holding out his arm to the old man, the two of them and Tam made their way down the stairs.

Entering the Great Hall, they were momentarily thunderstruck to see that the hettman and a full contingent of men had entered on horseback and were busily overturning table after table. The Game's pieces, falling on the floor, were crushed beneath the horses' hooves.

Distraught players rushed about, uttering cries of distress like those of sparrows fleeing a rapidly descending hawk. But it was of no use. The soldiers swung their maces, and the gaming tables shattered under the impact of the spiked metal balls, the brightly colored pawns turning into so many useless splinters.

Mika and Tam stood at the foot of the staircase with Seldom cowering behind them, trying to avoid being noticed. The Hettman Dorbin was enjoying himself greatly, riding about on an enormous warhorse and roaring with glee as gaming tables became little more than dust underfoot.

Only when the last table was destroyed did he appear to notice Mika and TamTur. Spurring his steed to within a hand's breadth of the nomad, he glared down at him over a huge curling mustache and roared, "And who be you, another of those cursed monsters? Speak up, or I'll slit your gullet!"

"I am Mika of the Wolf Nomads, no monster, sire, only a friendly magic-user who has, along with this brave fellow, helped to save your kingdom while you were riding for reinforcements." So saying, Mika drew Seldom out from behind his back and held him for the hettman's inspection.

"Um, Sometimes, isn't it?" said the hettman, squinting down at the wriggling wizard.

"Seldom, my lord," squeaked the magician, certain that his head soon would be separated from his body.

"Right," said the hettman. "Didn't I hear some rumor that you and Travail, that fat ne'er-do-well, had taken over the kingdom and were being mean to my baby?" His hand tightened on the hilt of his sword.

"I think you'll find, my lord Hettman," said Mika, before Seldom could speak, "that your kingdom is quite intact. And from the looks of it, Princess Linea is extremely happy."

The hettman forgot his sword and leaned back in his saddle to stare toward the princess and Braddle as they gazed at each other in dreamy-eyed fascination, totally oblivious to the occurrences around them. "I suppose I'll have to make the fellow a prince and let her marry him. Never could say no to her, muttered the hettman, "What about him? Is he worth a damn?"

"I think you'll find that he's worth several damns," said Mika with a grin, remembering Braddle's incredible daring. "He's also a promising young magician. Put him in Seldom and Kadis's care, and when they retire, he'll stand you in good stead."

"Might as well keep it all in the family, I suppose," grunted the hettman. "Now, what are we to do about this cursed game? Can't let it continue, that's for sure."

"Follow it to its source, sire," said Mika

"And chop its head off!" exclaimed the hettman, swinging his sword through the air to make his point. "But how do we find it . . . the head?"

"Those little men who bring the rules, that's a good place to start," suggested Mika as he ducked to avoid the passage of the sword.

"Right! String them up by their heels, put their heads on spikes!" roared the hettman.

"Leave them alone and follow them to their source," suggested Mika.

"Right!" roared the hettman, his face growing bright red. Spurring his horse into a full rear, he bellowed, "Onward, men! Follow me!" and clattered out of the palace.

"I don't think he knows where he's going," said Seldom. "He never paid much attention to the rules, which is why he lost."

"All the better," said Mika. "Come on, before that occurs to him." Gathering up Kadis and Braddle, promising the princess to return him to her quickly, they made their way out of the castle, over the moat, and into the crowded town.

It was easy to see which way the hettman had gone, for there were ample signs of horse manure and not a few people still flattened against the walls for safety. Fortunately, the path they had taken was the opposite direction from the marketplace, where the gamekeepers were generally to be found.

Nor did it prove difficult to find the gamekeepers, for just as they arrived, one of the old men, a small fellow sporting a slick pompador atop his strangely youthful face, hurried up to the bulletin board, ripped down the other rules posted there, dropping them in crumpled balls to the ground, and began tacking up several new sheets of parchment.

The gamekeeper was not even aware of their presence until Mika reached out with his demon hand and ripped the sheets off the board.

"See here, you can't do that!" said the fellow, turning around and fixing Mika with an angry glare.

"But I have done that," said Mika, crumpling the sheets in his fist and reaching over to grab the man by the joining of his neck and shoulder, pinching the nerve and causing him exquisite agony.

"Who are you?" Mika asked pleasantly.

"Nevin," whispered the man in a breathless gasp. "Game wizard extraordinaire."

"And where do you come from, Nevin?" Mika asked pleasantly, as though they were but two strangers passing the time of day over a mug of ale.

"Tusmit," replied the game wizard, looking not the least bit extraordinaire.

"Oho," said Seldom. "I begin to understand."

"Tell me, Nevin, are there more of you?" asked Mika, exerting a little more pressure on the man's neck.

"Two more!" squeaked Nevin, all but paralyzed by Mika's grip. "Lary and Ryion—we're all game wizards."

"And all from Tusmit," mused Mika. "Then this game was a Tusmitian plot to overthrow the government and make it easy for an invasion."

"I don't know," whispered Nevin. "I'm only a game wizard. I was only following orders."

"Whose orders?" asked Braddle.

"The pasha's," whimpered Nevin as Mika squeezed harder. "He ordered us to come here and alter The Game. We only did as he told us."

"And now The Game is over," Mika said pleasantly. "Braddle, conduct our friend here to his quarters. Find his associates, Lary and Ryion, and escort them to the outskirts of town. The western edge should do quite nicely. And see to it that they don't return."

"Yes, sire," said Braddle with a wide grin. Replacing Mika's grip with one of his own, he led the protesting Nevin away.

"But you can't do that!" Nevin cried, looking back at Mika with large, stricken eyes. "There are monsters out there. They'll eat us. We'll never get back alive."

"I'm really sorry about that," said Mika, looking not the least contrite. "But I really can't do anything about it. It's not my fault, you see. The hettman has decreed that The Game is over, and I, well, I'm just following orders."

Kadis wore a large grin on his face. Looking up at Mika, he said, "You know, the canton could use a fellow like you. What are your plans after this is all resolved?"

"To leave as soon as possible," Mika said promptly. "Tam and I do better outside of towns. A fellow could get himself killed in a place like this." Then, glancing after Braddle, he added, "Or married. And what about you, sir? What are your plans?"

"Oh, I expect I shall have to take young Braddle under my wing," replied the old magic-user. "And Seldom here, he is quite good. My laboratory can use some new young blood," he continued, overlooking the fact that Seldom could not be too many years younger than he himself.

"And then there is the matter of Travail. I shall have to think of something to do with bread and water, and lots of exercise I think." Roaring with laughter, Kadis and Seldom threw their arms around each other's shoulders and began their leisurely return to the castle.

Strolling back through the crowded town, Mika caught a glimpse of a familiar face, or rather, a familiar head, tow-headed with big, blue, innocent eyes. For an anguished heartbeat, Mika was filled with hope, but even as he hurried after the child, he told himself that it could not be, that it was not possible, that it could only be a mistake. Laying a hand on the child's shoulder, he spun him around and looked into the clear blue eyes of Gemmy and Hilda's youngest.

"How? Where? When?" he croaked, all but overwhelmed with sweet relief. "How came you to be here? The others . . . ?"

"They be here, too," said the child with its high, piping voice, pointing down the crowded street.

"But the monsters . . . ?" said Mika. "I saw what was left of your farm."

"We comed on the horses," said the child. "I rode

all by myself. We comed fast!"

"The horses? But I told your father to sell them!" said Mika.

"He din't," said the child. "He keeped 'um. Pa said they would help with plowin'. An' now that we be here, he aims to sell 'um and make lots o' money!"

Mika smiled and shook his head, thinking of the huge warhorses, so unsuitable for plowing but quite adequate for outrunning a slow-moving land army and carrying the family to safety on their broad backs.

Patting the child on his shiny blond head, Mika watched him run off until his pale tresses could no longer be seen in the crowds of people. Only then did the Wolf Nomad continue on his way, feeling the last of the gloom lift from his heart.

Returning to the castle briefly before gathering his possessions from Mistress Bonnie and taking his leave, Mika was surprised to see the hettman standing on the steps where all could see him, with a crestfallen Travail standing by his side.

"The Game is over," cried the hettman. "Too many lives have been cast into ruin because of it. Beginning tomorrow, everything will return to the way it was before The Game came to Perrenland. And to make certain that it is done right, Prime Minister Travail has agreed to preside over the transactions. Right, Travail?"

The prime minister nodded sorrowfully in agreement, his plump form seeming to shrink before Mika's eyes.

Chuckling to himself, Mika shook hands with Seldom, Braddle, and Kadis, and received a warm hug from the princess and Scylia, knowing that they would be all right, and took himself off to the inn to pack his belongings.

The inn was deserted, but Mika knew that it would not be so for long, for with the threat of war abated and the deadly game over, it seemed likely that there would be much celebrating in Perrenland that night.

Curiously, Mika had no desire to remain among the celebrants, even though the wine and women would both be plentiful. There were other voices in his head, those that were more urgent. Home was near, the cold, brisk, pine-scented ancestral forests of the Wolf Nomads. It was there he wanted to be. He did not understand it, this mysterious longing, for long it had been his intent to seek out new lands and new adventures.

Halfway up the long, dark, narrow stairway that led to his room, he heard Tam growl behind him. Looking up, he scarcely had time to see more than a dark blur before he was struck full in the chest by a great weight. He fought to keep his balance, to reach for his sword, to stave off the attack. Overbalanced, he plunged backward, somersaulting over and over, head over heels, caught up in a huge ball with Tam and his attacker, arms and legs waving wildly as they crashed down the staircase to land on the floor at the bottom with a great thump.

Mika raised his head groggily and blinked to clear his vision, to see what had attacked him in such an unexpected manner. But all he saw was a golden blur. There was a hard pull around his neck, a snapping sound. And then whatever it was, was gone.

Mika crawled to his feet, sorting himself out from Tam, who had had no opportunity to protect either of them from the unknown assailant. "What was that?" asked Mika and, unconsciously, his hand went to his chest to stroke the magic gem as he did a hundred times a day. But his hand faltered in midair, for there was nothing there. The gem was gone!

Remembering the pull against his neck and the snap that now reverberated loudly in his ears, Mika fell upon the floor and began searching in desperation. Time and again he quartered the floor and climbed the stairs, but no matter how many times he looked, it soon became apparent that the magic gem was gone.

Safe in his den at the edge of the moat, Womble mumbled to himself, displeased that he had not succeeded in killing the fellow who had turned the princess away from him. He nibbled on the heavy silver links of the chain and cursed the wolf whose growl had distracted him, causing him to misgauge his leap so that he had missed the man's neck and struck his chest instead.

Even though the heavy silver links of the chain were more tasty than blood, Womble was still unhappy. The princess had given her love to another, never again would he matter to her in quite the same way, and this was a grief that no amount of silver links would cure. With this sadness in mind, he finished the last of the links and began to nibble on the silver setting of the magic gem itself.

Realizing that the princess was probably lost to him for good, Womble turned to his inward vision, his unutterable longing toward his long-lost home. With that image firm-fixed in his mind, he swallowed the magic gem whole, and in the blink of an eye, he and the gem vanished and then reappeared half the Oerth away, in the den that in his heart had always been home.

Astride his horse, with TamTur trotting by his side, Mika exited the eastern gate of Krestible and lifted his head, sniffing the air. It seemed to him that he could almost smell the pine trees, the vast conifer forest that stretched across half the continent, the domain of the Wolf Nomads.

The gem was gone, never to return, but strangely enough, after the initial shock of its loss, Mika felt relieved, as though a great weight had been lifted from his shoulders. Now, he was only himself, Mika of the Wolf Nomads, and he and Tam were almost home.

ABOUT THE AUTHOR

ROSE ESTES has lived in Chicago, Houston, Mexico, and Canada, in a driftwood house on an island, a log cabin in the mountains, and a broken Volkswagon van under a viaduct.

At present she is sharing her life with an eccentric game designer/cartoonist, three children, one slightly demented dog, and a pride of occasionally domestic cats.

Other books written by Ms. Estes include nine of TSR, Inc.'s ENDLESS QUEST® series of books, as well as *Children of the Dragon* and *The Turkish Tattoo* published by Random House, and *Blood of the Tiger* from Bantam.

She began her GREYHAWK™ trilogy of Mika-oba, Shaman of the Wolf Nomads, with the best-selling *Master Wolf,* and continued with *Price of Power* and *The Demon Hand,* all from TSR, Inc.

DRAGONLANCE TALES, VOL. I: THE MAGIC OF KRYNN

First in the series of short-story collections set in the popular world of the DRAGONLANCE® saga, as edited by Margaret Weis and Tracy Hickman. Seven weeks on The New York Times' list of paperback best-sellers, this volume boasts sea monsters, dark elves, ice bears, hideous, hydra-headed serpents, loathsome draconian troops, and all the familiar companions. The acclaimed new novella by Weis and Hickman gazes into the future of Caramon and his mage-son, and into the dark nether-past of Raistlin.

Available now!

DRAGONLANCE TALES, VOL. II: KENDER, GULLY DWARVES, AND GNOMES

Second in the series of short-story collections, as edited by Margaret Weis and Tracy Hickman, spotlights the fascinating other-worldly creatures of Krynn—with untold tales about the irrepressible kender, gully dwarves, gnomes, and other minor races. Includes short story contributions by some of America's finest young fantasy writers and a fascinating new novella by Weis and Hickman chronicling the new generation of heroes!

Available now!

DRAGONLANCE TALES, VOL. III: LOVE AND WAR

Third in the series of short story collections, as edited by Margaret Weis and Tracy Hickman, recounting DRAGONLANCE® tales of heroism and romance, of noble sacrifice and doomed friendship, of conquest and endearment. This volume of fresh Krynn lore by a group of TSR writers will be capped by "Raistlin's Daughter," a powerful new novella that will open yet another chapter in the life of the series' most complex and extraordinary character, Raistlin, the sickly mage-scholar.

Available now!

Explore the FORGOTTEN REALMS™ Fantasy Campaign Setting!

From the fog-enshrouded moors of Moonshae to the pristine peaks overlooking Bloodstone Pass; from Waterdeep, City of Splendors to Thay; from the Pirates of the Inner Sea to the kingdoms of Calimshan in the South—these are the lands of the Forgotten Realms.

The FORGOTTEN REALMS Fantasy Campaign Setting is the most elaborate and detailed presented by TSR, Inc. to date. An entire new line of novels, AD&D® adventure modules and sourcebooks, and other exciting accessories have been created for gamers adventurous enough to explore the ultimate adventure game setting.

The FORGOTTEN REALMS Boxed Campaign Setting
Ed Greenwood and Jeff Grubb

The cornerstone for AD&D adventures set in the Forgotten Realms, and the basis for all novels and sourcebooks in the series, this set includes four-color maps of the world and almost 200 pages of vital information, both on the Forgotten Realms themselves and on setting up AD&D campaigns in this fabulous land.

AD&D® Sourcebooks:

WATERDEEP AND THE NORTH
Ed Greenwood

Waterdeep, the largest city of the northern realms, home to half a million humans, dwarves, elves, and halflings, is a city of power and evil, intrigue and wealth, ruled by unseen and mysterious lords. FORGOTTEN REALMS creator Ed Greenwood takes you on a grand tour of this, the mightiest city of the Realms.

MOONSHAE
Doug Niles

Exploring in depth the islands off the Sword Coast, home to *Darkwalker on Moonshae,* this sourcebook provides further detailed information on the Realms and adapts adventures found within this novel to an AD&D game campaign.

EMPIRES OF THE SANDS
Scott Haring

The arid, inhospitable countries on the southeastern corner of the continent of Faerun are the subject of *Empires of the Sands,* a 64-page sourcebook. Players wanting to explore this section of the Realms campaign setting can decide whether they prefer to seek their fortunes in the mercenary, Machiavellian country of Amn; the merchant state of Calimshan; or the anarchic land of Tethyr.

THE MAGISTER
Ed Greenwood and Steve Perrin

The Magister is the first word on magic in the FORGOTTEN REALMS campaign setting. It provides thorough coverage of new spells and magical items and instructions for generating new magical items.

AD&D® Adventure Modules:

UNDER ILLEFARN
Steve Perrin

An introductory campaign base for new players of the AD&D game or for experienced players starting a new campaign in the Forgotten Realms. An earthquake rattles the small town of Daggerford, south of Waterdeep. Can your characters handle what the earth brings forth?

DESERT OF DESOLATION
Tracy and Laura Hickman,
Phil Meyers, Peter Rice, and John Wheeler

This epic trilogy outlining the power and mystery of tremendous magical forces is set in the great dust desert of Raurin. For characters of intermediate level.

THE BLOODSTONE PASS SERIES
Michael Dobson and Doug Niles

Only the powerful need apply. A great danger is growing in the North, in the ice-blasted desolation that is Vaasa, and threatening to engulf the shattered nation of Damara. Can your characters stem the tide in this epic four-volume series?

SWORDS OF THE IRON LEGION

An evil power is training armies in a lonely stretch of the Forgotten Realms, and a band of tough-guy player characters—namely the Iron Legion—is the only thing that can keep the power from taking over. *Swords of the Iron Legion* is a series of short adventurers, each by a different author, and each incorporating BATTLESYSTEM™ rules.

New From the Creators of the DRAGONLANCE® Saga in 1988

Wondrous TSR® Books!

STARSONG
by Dan Parkinson

First in TSR's new fiction line, Dan Parkinson's elegiac novel tells the tale of elves who return to Earth after a voluntary exile of hundreds of thousands of years, and band together with the humans to defeat the Darkness plaguing the land.

On sale in July!

ST. JOHN THE PURSUER: VAMPIRE IN MOSCOW
by Richard Henrick

For centuries, the men of a forgotten monastic order have dedicated their lives to the pursuit of unspeakable fiends. A vampire is now walking the streets of Moscow, and the Communist ruling order is doing is best to deny the existence of a creature that leaves the drained bodies of victims in its wake. St. John the Pursuer is summoned . . .

On sale in September!

HELLFLOWER
by eluki bes shahar

A wild and funny, imaginative "new wave space opera" in which an Amazonian space pirate digs herself deeper and deeper into dangerous capers and skullduggery, as she races from galaxy to galaxy.

On sale in November!